Jake put his hands on her shoulders, gently pulling her close, brushing his lips against her

Brianna felt the shock to her toes. Heat filled her, breathing grew difficult. Slowly she opened her eyes and looked into his. She was used to reading people. With Jake, she hadn't a clue.

"What are you doing?" Was that her voice? So husky and breathless?

"Figured we needed to get that out of the way. Babies don't just grow on trees."

Her heart beat heavily in her chest. Unable to look away, she tried to think of something clever to say. But her mind remained blank while her body moved closer.

"So we'll do it? For better or worse?" he asked.

"Yes." Her blood pulsed through her, hot and quick. She'd just committed to marry this stranger!

"It's either the start of a great adventure or the biggest mistake of our lives...."

Dear Reader,

We all think we have plenty of time to meet our goals and seek our heart's desire. But sometimes life has a way of making us realize time can run short. Then hard choices have to be made. That's what happens to Brianna Dawson. When illness brings her face-to-face with her own mortality, she has to make those hard choices. She has long thought one day she'll find Mr. Right, marry and start a family of her own. But she might not have time to do that—especially when her current Mr. Right turns out to be Mr. Wrong.

Taking a risk to seek what she wants most in life, she contacts an old acquaintance who is looking for a wife. Whoever heard of mail-order brides in the twenty-first century? Still, if this gives her a chance to have the family she's always wanted, she'll marry him.

I had the same illness as Brianna when I was working in a high-profile position. I had lots of decisions to make, or risk further problems. For me, the other choice was to be what I wanted most—a writer. I quit my stressful job, moved to a very small town in the mountains and have embarked on the most fun I've ever had—writing romance novels.

I hope you enjoy Brianna's story. Write and let me know: www.barbaramcmahon.com, or snail mail at P.O. Box 977, Pioneer, CA 95666. Happy reading!

All the best,

Barbara

The Rancher's Bride

Barbara McMahon

HARLEQUIN®

TORONTO • NEW YORK • LONDON
AMSTERDAM • PARIS • SYDNEY • HAMBURG
STOCKHOLM • ATHENS • TOKYO • MILAN • MADRID
PRAGUE • WARSAW • BUDAPEST • AUCKLAND

ISBN 0-373-71179-4

THE RANCHER'S BRIDE

Copyright © 2004 by Barbara McMahon.

This edition published by arrangement with Harlequin Books S.A.

® and TM are trademarks of the publisher. Trademarks indicated with ® are registered in the United States Patent and Trademark Office, the Canadian Trade Marks Office and in other countries.

Visit us at www.eHarlequin.com

Printed in U.S.A.

To the Hillsdale Lunch Bunch—
Barbara, Candice, Carol, Lynn, Kate and Sheila.
Thanks for the laughter, sharing and all the support!
Y'all are the best!

he thought would be his, and romance with Lisa

PROLOGUE

JAKE MARSHALL crested the hill and reined in his horse. He was bone-tired, cold and hungry. The gelding blew hard in the frigid air, his flanks heaving as he caught his breath. They didn't have far to go now. They'd beaten the night home. Jake scanned the horizon, noting with quiet satisfaction that everything was as it should be. He focused on the house in the distance. The late-afternoon sun gleamed against several windows, and it looked as if lamps shone in every room. The distance and the waning light hid the disrepair. For an instant he saw the house as it had been twenty years ago. Structurally it was still sound. With some repairs, cosmetic work, a new coat of paint, it could become a showplace again.

Only, who had the time or the money?

"Damn the old bitch!" he muttered. For what had to be the millionth time, he cursed the old woman who still manipulated people from beyond the grave. This land was his by blood and heritage, but not in the eyes of the law. She'd seen to that.

He'd never forget his shock after his father died, when he'd learned that the title to the ranch, a ranch he'd thought would be his, had remained with Elsa

Marshall—his father's mother. And she'd wanted nothing to do with her grandson. The bitterness had festered over the years. He'd returned to Texas immediately after his father's funeral and sworn he wouldn't return to Wyoming. He'd meant it at the time, but life had intervened.

He hadn't moved back, however, until he heard of Elsa's death—and the terms of her will.

"Damn her," he said again, anger flaring at the thought of Elsa and her conditions. For months he'd insisted he would not be dictated to, would not follow her directive. But working the range his father's family had first settled five generations ago, he'd gradually felt his bond with the land strengthen. Now the longing for continuity was strong. He wanted to reverse the decay and return the spread to its former glory.

And he had to admit that he'd love to thumb his nose at Elsa's dire predictions once he achieved his goal.

What vindictiveness had made the old woman ignore the ranch for the dozen years since his father's death? Revenge against her son's one act of defiance years before? Hell, his father had died trying to do what she'd wanted.

Now Jake and Shell and the two hired hands worked from sunup to sundown. For more than eleven months they'd fought a hard battle. Slowly things were turning around. If no catastrophic losses occurred during the winter, he'd have a fighting chance come spring to pull out of the morass.

Had he waited too long, though? Stubborn pride in

refusing to knuckle down to Elsa's outlandish codicil was one thing, but holding on to some righteous principle just to be ornery was foolish.

He calculated the time remaining as he urged his mount forward. He knew he'd cut it close. He had delayed until he had just over a year remaining of the original two in which to marry and produce a child.

Jake walked the horse down the slope and toward the barn. The sun slipped behind the mountain peaks and the landscape quickly faded into indiscriminate gray. A string of lights came on in the barn. Shell, probably. The boy worked hard.

Jake sighed. Another insurmountable problem. He didn't know what to do about the kid. The man. He had a difficult time remembering sometimes that his son was grown, especially since he'd only learned of his existence six years ago when Shell had turned fifteen.

Was the resentfulness with which he was so familiar a family curse? Shell resented Jake almost as much as Jake resented Elsa. When Shelly Bluefeather had died unexpectedly of appendicitis, Jake had been stunned to discover they'd created a child together before he'd left Sweetwater the first time, immediately after his high-school graduation. She'd never told him. At the end, however, she'd told their boy his father's name. When Jake showed up at her funeral, he'd been met by his angry son.

Shell had gone with Jake back to Texas to the Bar-XT ranch, which Jake was managing, and then had taken a job on the Rocking M when Jake had moved back last fall.

Jake was aware that part of Shell's hostility stemmed from the terms of his great-grandmother's will. Elsa Harrington Marshall had refused to acknowledge the illegitimate offspring of her only grandson. *Join the club, kid,* he thought. She'd barely acknowledged her grandson when she'd been alive.

He wished he knew how to heal the breach. The kid had a way with cattle. And he could calm a rambunctious horse like no one Jake had ever seen.

What would happen if they lost the ranch? Would their tenuous tie be severed? Jake could always get a job back in Texas, but would Shell go back with him?

Jake rode in to the barn. The sweet smell of hay filled the air. A light in the tack room indicated his son's location. Jake checked his watch. There was a half hour left before supper. He'd brush his horse and feed him, then squeeze in a quick shower.

After dinner, he'd tackle the books again, chipping away at accounts until he couldn't stand it any longer. Never his favorite pastime, he had to keep it up, needing to know at all times where they stood. The bank held the title in escrow and had refused any more loans. Credit was stretched wire-thin. No one wanted to spring for more until it was certain he'd inherit the place and could turn a profit.

He regretted not having the office staff he'd had at the Bar-XT and the computer programs that made things so easy to track. But money was too tight, and there were more pressing needs.

"Fence okay?" Shell came to the door of the tack room, a rag in one hand. His hat was pulled low over his forehead, shading his eyes.

"Two sections were pulled loose. I fixed one. We need more wire for the other. It's about a mile down from where the creek bends."

Jake dismounted. He felt stiff. Another sign of growing old, that and the regrets for decisions made in the unchangeable past.

He thought back to his rodeo days—riding, roping, throwing steers and partying well into the night, raring to go again the next morning. Now he was glad to get off the horse at the end of ten or twelve hours and sit in a comfortable chair.

"I'll get Nolan to repair it tomorrow," he said, hitching the gelding to a rail. "Did Hank take care of the tally?"

"Yeah, all accounted for," Shell replied. "If we don't lose many head this winter, we should have a good count of calves come spring. Loni said dinner will be ready at seven-thirty tonight. She's running late. She went into town today to see the doctor again." His voice remained neutral.

Jake nodded, wondering if the kid would ever warm up. "Everything okay with her?"

Shell shrugged. "She wouldn't tell me if it wasn't."

Jake paused and looked at Shell. He wished he could change the course of the world, could do something to make things come right for his boy.

Loni Peterson was eight months pregnant with Shell's baby, but refused to marry him. Shell was crazy about the young woman, but she insisted she was too young to be tied down. Accepting the job as cook at the ranch had been as close as she'd come to accepting any support from Shell. And that had been necessary only because her own folks had kicked her out after discovering she was pregnant by a Native-American—a half-breed, they called him. Some prejudices died hard, even in Wyoming.

Jake turned back to the horse, picked up the brush and began the familiar grooming tasks. Nothing he could do about anything right now. He couldn't seem to get his own life under control, so how could he help his son?

"She got the mail in town," Shell said a few moments later. He leaned against the wall, crossing his arms over his chest, idly watching his father tend to the horse.

"More bills, I'm sure."

Jake led the horse to its stall, checking to see that the manger was full. He slapped the gelding's rump as the horse headed for the feed trough.

He was closing the stall door when Shell added, "Yeah. And there was a postcard from that woman who plans to marry you. She'll be here tomorrow."

CHAPTER ONE

"WHOEVER HEARD of a mail-order bride in the twenty-first century?" Brianna Dawson asked as she pulled to a stop on the deserted two-lane highway to reread her quickly jotted directions.

The notion conjured up the Old West with covered wagons and homesteaders.

Instead, she was driving a brand new SUV down a paved highway. Not a wagon in sight.

The gravel road heading off to the left had to be the ranch road she was looking for. Couldn't they have sprung for a sign? She thought ranches had big gates with their brand clearly displayed. Even a mailbox with a name would have been helpful. After checking for nonexistent traffic, she made the turn and left the highway behind. She'd been traveling for more than a week. She hoped the postcard she'd sent telling them to expect her today had arrived.

Should she have taken time when passing through town to call?

Again Brianna pulled over and stopped. She looked around, acknowledging to herself she was stalling.

The huge dome of blue sky beckoned. She turned off the ignition and climbed out, then leaned against the door, enjoying the solitude. The stress that had been so much a part of her life for so long had disappeared bit by bit as she'd driven closer to her destination, leaving New York far behind.

She couldn't believe the difference. For the first time in years she felt young, carefree, alive! And in perfect health. There were no more impossible demands, no hurried deadlines. Instead, when she'd checked in to a motel, she slept straight through the night.

She gazed around. The landscape was comparable with what a mail-order bride of the 1800s would probably have seen. Except for the graveled road and the barbed-wire fencing, the land was all empty rolling hills and scattered trees.

From that first summer she'd stayed on a ranch near Jackson Hole with her uncle, she'd had a love affair with Wyoming. Eagerly she searched the hills now seeking familiarity, that sense of homecoming.

"I'm moving here!" she said softly, the warmth of the late-afternoon sun on her cheeks contrasting with the hint of winter in the breeze. If she said the words often enough, maybe she'd believe them. She'd left one life behind her. Now the future called.

"You're procrastinating," she muttered as her eyes feasted on the golden grassland, the rim of distant mountains already dusted with snow.

What she needed to do was take the final plunge. She had told Jake Marshall she was coming, but now reality was catching up. She was nine-tenths of the way committed to marrying a virtual stranger.

It didn't matter that she'd known him briefly, years ago. She'd been a teenager with a crush on a brash young cowboy. He'd thought her a pest. Was that any kind of basis for marriage?

Her nerves danced as she considered the next step. She had never done anything so crazy in her life. Nor so awkward. She rubbed her palms against her jeans. What would they talk about? Would they have any interests in common? Could she remember what she'd learned those three precious summers spent with Uncle Buck?

How would they handle the lights-out part?

That worry had niggled her off and on for the entire drive from Manhattan.

Time enough to deal with that if they chose to pursue the marriage, she thought, still reluctant to get back into the car. They could wait a while, see how things went before doing anything irreversible. Heat engulfed her at the thought of sharing a bed with a man she hardly knew, one, moreover, she'd never even kissed.

Once they grew comfortable with each other, they could decide if this would work. And if they did, maybe they would try for a baby after a while. She'd have a child—maybe children—to lavish her love on. A rough-and-tumble little boy to follow in his father's footsteps. Or maybe a daughter who would learn to cook the old family recipes her mother had treasured and Brianna still had.

Brianna would start her own traditions with her children. Didn't ranches support huge families? Maybe she could have half-a-dozen babies!

But reality might not be as rosy as she hoped. What if Jake Marshall chewed tobacco and had a beer belly? What if he was bald and had lost half his teeth and looked nothing like the sexy, daring cowboy she remembered?

No time like the present to find out. Determined to see it through, she climbed back into the car, switched on the ignition and started down the lonely road.

Questions and doubts rose as they had whenever she thought about the new direction she'd chosen. She wished she knew more about Jake, what he'd been doing these past dozen years. But the few brief telephone conversations they'd had focused on the possibility of marriage. Or on the mechanics of her driving to Wyoming, directions, dates. His voice had been clipped, abrupt, as if talking was something he didn't do often.

His letters had been equally terse. They'd revealed nothing of the man himself, his likes and dislikes, his feelings about his past, his future...

Keeping her options open, she studied what might become her new home. Cattle dotted the hills, where the dry, golden grass undulated in the afternoon breeze, like waves in a saffron sea.

She had a moment's panic about this plunge into the unknown. She'd left everything familiar—her apartment, the deli at the corner, friends and colleagues, the career as an ad executive she'd taken pains to build so carefully. Even Steven. Though in truth, she had to admit, he'd left her first.

"You'll be fine," she said aloud to herself as she kept her foot firmly on the accelerator. For generations women had gone into arranged marriages. She was just one more in a long line. Everyone who knew her would admit she always achieved her goals. This was just another one.

As she drove around a bend in the road, she crested a small hill. She stopped once more to look at the scene spread before her. This was her first glimpse of her new home.

The house stood on a knoll about two hundred yards away. Despite the distance, she could see that a shutter was missing from one of the second-story windows, and the porch railing was missing several slats. No garden at all, just dirt, and no trees. In fact, the house seemed abandoned.

Her heart sank.

What had she done? This was nothing like what she'd imagined. Nothing like the ranches she'd seen on her previous visits to the state. Had she left Manhattan for *this?*

She'd expected at least a bustling prosperous ranch. This looked more like a nightmare. Was this the reason Jake Marshall hadn't been able to find a wife before? The reason he'd advertised in *Western Ranchers?* She should have known the solution to her own situation had been too good to be true.

It wasn't too late to change her mind. She could back up until she found a spot in the road wide enough to turn around. Leave without ever seeing anyone. She could call from town and tell Jake she'd changed her mind.

Or head for California and never contact the man at all.

Panic flared. But she tried to reassure herself. She wasn't committed to anything. He couldn't force her to marry him.

On the other hand, maybe this particular rancher desperately needed a helpmate. Maybe ranching was too much for one person and he didn't have time for the homey things that women liked. The bizarre events that had led her to read his personal ad, remembering him from her youth and the letter he'd sent to her mother after Uncle Buck died—all had seemed serendipitous.

Optimistically, she'd begun to picture the place painted a pristine white, with kelly-green shutters on every window. She'd envisioned mounds of colorful flowers flanking the front porch. The mingling of fragrant scents would greet Jake and her as they sat outside in the evenings after working hard all day. A lush tree or two would provide shade against the hot summer sun.

Brianna began to drive the final distance to her future. As she drew closer, she took note of the barn and corrals several hundred yards behind the house.

The barn was bare, weathered wood. A rusting tractor was parked to the left. Rolls of barbed wire in the midst of weeds leaned against the outside wall. Three horses stood in the corral.

It was definitely a working cattle ranch. The scents of cattle, hay and dust were at once familiar and foreign. A feeling of nostalgia settled on her.

She followed the driveway around the house and stopped near the rear. The back door opened and a young blond woman peered out, pulling on a sweater to combat the cool air. Two men appeared simultaneously at the entrance to the barn. Cowboys from their look—dark felt hats, worn jeans, scuffed leather boots.

Brianna had dealt with presidents and CEOs of major corporations, with irate marketing managers and prima-donna sales executives in her position as an account executive for a Manhattan advertising firm. She'd convinced herself she could handle one down-in-the-heels rancher who owed her family a favor.

And offered her the chance to change her life.

She turned off the SUV's engine, opened the door and stepped out, trying to still the butterflies in her stomach. She could do this. She *had* to do this.

The taller of the two men walked toward her.

"Brianna Dawson?" he asked, studying her from head to toe.

She nodded, reciprocating with a look of her own. He hadn't grown any taller since she'd known him, but he'd sure filled out! His hat was pulled low on his forehead, obscuring his hair and shading his eyes, eyes that had once danced in amusement when he teased her.

She longed to see them now, hoping they'd convince her she hadn't been insane to consider this plan.

She swallowed hard, her heart beginning to beat heavily. From what she could see, he was a walking heartthrob destined to rob most women of their good sense. He definitely wasn't fat, hairy or old; to the contrary, he was hot sex in boots and a Stetson. The years had been good to this brash and provocative cowboy.

Brianna held out her hand. "Jake Marshall. It's been a long time."

"You've changed a bit, but I'd have recognized you anywhere," he said. "You made good time."

Calluses from years of ranch work pressed her smooth skin. Her hand looked lost in his. The flutters in her stomach increased.

Unable to form a coherent thought, she could only stare. He was just the way she'd remembered, only more. Broader, older, with lines bracketing his mouth. He'd gone through a lot, she'd bet.

Once again she wondered why this man had needed to ask a stranger to marry him. It seemed to Brianna that women would line up for a shot at matrimony with Jake Marshall. What was she not seeing?

The seconds ticked by. She began to feel self-conscious under his steady regard.

"I drove straight through," she said, tugging her hand from his. "Maybe I should have called from town."

He released her, tucking his fingers into the pockets of his jeans. Brianna speculated about where he found the room. She raised her gaze, conscious of where she'd been looking.

"I'm glad you came. We got your card yesterday so we were expecting you."

Jake turned to the other cowboy, an obviously younger man, who'd ambled over to join them. "This is Shell Bluefeather, my son," he said with some pride.

Shell was almost as tall as his father, but not as broad in the shoulders and chest. He reminded her of the Jake she'd known in the past.

Jake had told her little about the others on the ranch, but she had been surprised when he'd told her he had a grown son.

Shell's hand was almost as callused as Jake's, his grip firm.

"Ma'am." There was no warmth in his voice or dark, guarded eyes.

"Don't keep her out there in the cold, Jake," the blonde called from the doorway. "Come in the house."

He nodded. "Good idea," he said to Brianna, "if we don't want to freeze. Once the sun sets these days, the temperature drops."

Jake gestured for Brianna to lead the way.

The blonde greeted her at the door with a friendly "Hi, I'm Loni Peterson." She offered her hand and Brianna took it, trying to avoid staring at her swollen belly.

"I'm Brianna Dawson. It's nice to meet you."

Brianna stepped inside and looked around the old-fashioned kitchen. What was Loni's place here? Jake hadn't mentioned her. His daughter? Shell's wife?

"I've been waiting forever for you to get here. It seems like a year since Jake said you were coming. It'll be so nice to have another woman around. I get so tired of nothing but dumb old cowboys all the time." Loni flashed a grin at the men, who'd followed Brianna inside. She moved to the stove and said, "I have coffee going, want a cup? I can't believe you left New York City for Wyoming. Tell me all about it. I plan to go there someday. Isn't it the most exciting place on earth? I want to see Times Square and all the museums, visit every art gallery there, walk down Broadway and take in all the latest shows. Then shop till I drop."

Brianna tried to keep up with Loni's chatter as she assessed her surroundings. The stove looked like an antique. How anyone could cook on it boggled the mind. The refrigerator was small and ancient, reminding her of one she and her mother had had in an apartment ages ago—the kind that needed constant defrosting.

Still feeling nervous, Brianna moved to the table. Before she could pull out a chair, Shell was there doing it for her. She smiled at him.

He'd removed his hat and she was able to see his face. His eyes were almost black, and his skin was a shade or two darker than his father's.

Brianna glanced over her shoulder at Jake Marshall. He'd taken off his hat, as well, tossing it on a rack by the door. His brown hair was thick, a little ragged around the edges. Not stylishly cut like Steven's. His jeans and wrinkled shirt were far different from the Armani suits and silk shirts she was used to.

He appeared older than she'd expected. The laughter she remembered was missing. He looked serious, hard and a bit intimidating.

His spurs clinked as he crossed to the table and pulled out a chair. Reversing it, he straddled the seat and rested his hands on the back.

His eyes met hers, and she felt, suddenly, mesmerized by them, as if they could hold hers fast while they looked clear to her soul. She'd had such a crush on him that last summer. Had he ever suspected?

"Good trip?" he asked.

She nodded, still holding his gaze, hoping he couldn't read minds. For she'd just realized that eventually going to bed with Jake would probably not be the problem she'd anticipated.

His touch had made her acutely aware of herself as a female creature, one suddenly and strongly attracted to a male of the species. Good heavens, she'd never felt like this around Steven Forrest, and they'd been lovers for two years!

"Here's your coffee. We have milk but no cream. No one here uses it, but if you want it, we can get some next time we go into town." Loni placed the mug before Brianna and sat in the chair Shell held for her. She ignored him, gazing, instead, at Brianna, her expression curious.

"I can't believe anyone would deliberately choose to move here. There's nothing to do. We're miles from Sweetwater, which is a dump, anyway."

"Loni," Jake warned.

"What's wrong with living here?" Brianna asked, taken aback by Loni's outburst.

"She may as well hear it all, Jake." Loni would not be stopped. "Everything's wrong. We're at the back of beyond. Sweetwater doesn't even have a movie theater. If you stay, Brianna, you'll die of boredom within six months—if the work doesn't kill you first. Or the winter weather."

"You've lived here all your life and haven't died yet," Shell said casually. He leaned against the counter, keeping himself apart from the others, as if the scene unfolding before him held little interest. Yet his gaze never left Loni.

"That's because I have a goal—to get out," she said quickly.

Brianna noticed the tension between the two of them. What was going on?

"Let Brianna make her own decisions." Jake's voice was strong, husky, with a hint of a drawl. As she swung back to him, Brianna wondered what it would be like to hear that voice in the darkness of a bedroom. He would speak softly and for her alone. Hearing him now, she hardly recognized the abrupt voice from the phone. The slow drawl was intoxicating, rather like—

Brianna pushed such thoughts to the back of her mind and sipped her coffee.

"Did you live right in Manhattan?" Loni asked brightly. "What did you do there? Were you born and raised in New York?"

"There'll be time enough for Brianna to fill you in on her entire life, if she stays," Jake said.

Loni looked at him in surprise. "I thought it was all settled. You said she was coming to marry you. She drove all this way." She looked at Brianna. "Aren't you staying?"

Jake got up and pushed his chair into the table. "Maybe we better speak in private, Brianna. The office is just down the hall. We can talk there." He waited while she picked up her cup and started for the door he'd indicated.

Was there a problem? Had she come all this way only to be jilted? Brianna almost smiled at the old-fashioned term. But that was what being a mail-order bride did for a woman, filled her mind with old-fashioned ideas. But it was no smiling matter if he really had changed his mind.

CHAPTER TWO

WHY HADN'T Jake answered Loni's question? It seemed straightforward to her—yes, we're getting married. Or no, it'll never happen.

While just minutes before arriving she'd hesitated at the thought of marrying this stranger, now she almost panicked at the thought he would reject her.

When she paused in the dim doorway, Jake reached around her and flicked on a light. Brianna stepped inside, and he closed the door behind them. The office had probably been a parlor when the house was first built, Brianna thought, as she crossed to the worn leather couch along one wall and sat. The windows were tall and uncovered, allowing in the last weak vestiges of afternoon light. The wooden desk held haphazard piles of papers and magazines. The fireplace looked as if it hadn't been used in decades.

Jake pulled the chair from the desk over until he sat opposite Brianna.

"Who is Loni?" she asked.

"Shell's girlfriend, or she was. She doesn't want anything to do with him now. She blames him for the baby."

Brianna wasn't sure why the girl was staying at the

ranch if that was the case, but she had more pressing matters to resolve. "She seems to think I'm here for good. So do I. Is there a problem?"

"No problem. You got here fast."

"Is that good or bad?" she asked, twisting the cup in her hand. He kept saying that. Wasn't she supposed to show up? During one of their brief phone calls, they'd discussed how long it would take her.

The warmth of the coffee cup eased part of the chill from her fingers. She wished she felt more comfortable. How were mail-order brides supposed to feel? Maybe she should have looked up the subject on the Internet before packing her laptop.

"Didn't you explain to the others what we're doing?" she asked.

"Nothing's set in stone," he said evasively, looking awkward.

Brianna said nothing. Just being in the same room with the man made her have trouble concentrating. She hadn't a clue what he was thinking. Had he expected someone different? Now that he'd met her, was he reconsidering?

"As you already know, I'm thirty-four, never married and I want a family," Brianna offered, wondering if she was making things worse by blurting out the truth. But the silence was making her more nervous.

"And there wasn't a man in New York you'd consider tying the knot with, so you chose a total stranger in Wyoming?" Jake asked, settling back in his chair, his long legs stretched out in front of him.

She cleared her throat, swirling the cooling coffee

around in her cup. "Well, hardly a total stranger. I remember you from the summers at the Garretson ranch." Brianna wished she could think of a way to stave off questions about former relationships, but her mind was blank. She could only tell the truth. As far as she was willing. At this point, full disclosure could prove detrimental.

"Actually, there was someone I was involved with. But…it didn't work out. He didn't want to get married or have children. And I very much want both," she said candidly. She hoped he wouldn't push the issue. Even now the pain from Steven's defection was almost more than she could bear.

"That's honest."

"I needed, uh, *wanted* to make a big change in my lifestyle. I told you that when I first wrote in answer to your ad. I've wanted a family to belong to, a place to call home ever since I spent those summers with Uncle Buck. I've been on my own since my mother died when I was eighteen. I'm not getting any younger. It's not like I'm plunging into something without any idea of how it will be. I'd be an asset to you. I have experience from the Garretson ranch."

She was babbling and promptly shut up. She knew she should tell why she'd left her old life, but she couldn't bring herself to discuss it. Steven had turned from her so fast she was still reeling. What if Jake did the same?

A few months earlier an emergency-room physician had diagnosed her with a TIA, a transient ischemic attack. Something like a mini-stroke, but a TIA left no permanent damage. However, TIAs could presage strokes, hence the need for preventing their recurrence by taking steps to eliminate the cause—in her case changing her stressful lifestyle. Counting on her doctor's being right, here she was, embarking on that change.

She *would* tell Jake, just not yet.

The way she saw things, Jake needed her as much as she needed him, or he wouldn't have made this outlandish proposal. And while she hoped he wouldn't desert her as Steven had, she couldn't take the risk. Not yet. Everything would be fine. She was betting her future on it.

Once Jake had realized who she was, he'd proposed on the phone. He'd mentioned a debt he owed her uncle. Even though the man had died eighteen years ago, Jake wished to honor that debt.

Crazy reasons for marriage—a necessary change of lifestyle and the discharge of a debt.

Life didn't come with any guarantees, she knew that. But at one time she had so hoped for love before marriage. Ironically, she had that. Just not in the usual way—she'd loved Steven, and now would be marrying Jake.

Jake stared at her for a long moment, and Brianna took another sip of coffee, forcing herself to swallow it. Caffeine was something else she was supposed to give up. But a sip or two wouldn't hurt.

"I wonder why you're really here," he said slowly.

She stared at him. There was no way he could possibly know. She tried to smile. "I just told you."

"Seeing the ranch must have been a disappointment. I know it looks as if it's on its last legs."

She was surprised he'd brought that up. What could she say? It did look in bad shape, but a little work could change that. Or was that just her habit of viewing the world through rose-colored glasses?

"I remember what this place looked like twenty years ago," Jake said. "The fencing was sound, the house freshly painted, flowers everywhere. The barn weather-tight, fat, healthy cattle roaming every acre. Now it's fallen into such disrepair that sometimes I'm not sure it's worth trying to hold on to." His face changed. "But I will! The land's been in my family for five generations. I don't plan to be the one to let it go."

She nodded. The passion in his voice spoke to her. He sounded as if he loved the ranch and wanted to keep it as much as she wanted somewhere to belong.

For a moment she wondered why he'd been working at the Garretson ranch near Jackson Hole if he loved this place so much. True, it had been years ago, and he'd just been a kid about Shell's age. Had he been getting experience? Did ranchers do that? Work different spreads to get new or different ideas on how to run things?

"If we fix it up, it'll be beautiful," she said enthusiastically. "Some paint and a new porch railing would work a miracle on the house. I thought maybe flowers and some trees in front, too." She would love to have a hand in the restoration, put something of herself into the place. A new stove and refrigerator, maybe some new furniture. She had yet to see the rest of the house, but a quick glance around the office showed there were challenges everywhere.

"Let me give you a few facts about the situation," Jake said. "First, the woman who owned the ranch until last year let it fall to ruin, not just the house. Fences are down, which allows cattle to wander off. Water holes need cleaning. The herd is old and in need of good young stock. There was no money left to fix anything. We're barely making ends meet. Even if I had some capital, which I don't, the last thing I'd spend it on is cosmetic work on the house. The roof was repaired last spring—it doesn't leak. All our money is plowed back into the stock and supplies and the equipment needed to run the spread. We need to repair the barn, buy hay for winter, get a new bull..." He shook his head, took a deep breath. "There's so much to do—the house itself is far down on the list."

"A woman owned it?" she repeated, surprised at the venom in his tone.

"Elsa Marshall—my grandmother."

Brianna stared, too surprised at his tone to speak. His grandmother must have hated seeing the place deteriorate. Had money been so scarce?

"It's too bad your grandmother couldn't keep it up," she said softly, sympathetically. She wondered how long Jake had been struggling on the ranch.

He gave a harsh laugh. "Save your sympathy. It wasn't a case of couldn't, but wouldn't. The old witch had a fortune when she died. And every dime went to various charities or artist groups in Wyoming. Not a plug nickel to the ranch.''

"I don't understand. She left you the ranch, but no money?"

Jake frowned. "She didn't precisely leave the ranch to me. That's why you're here. According to her will, I have to marry and produce a child before the deadline she set, or the ranch—every board, steer and blade of grass—goes to some damn artists' colony. Why else would I consider tying myself to a woman I haven't seen in almost two decades and don't know at all? Time is short and I have to move fast to keep this place. In order to inherit, I need a baby within the year.''

Brianna was stunned. She'd received one surprise after another since seeing that personal ad in the issue of *Western Ranchers* her roommate, Connie, had given her as a joke several months ago.

He needed a baby? Within the year? That had *not* been in the ad.

"What's wrong with Shell? Isn't he your son and heir?" she asked. Why hadn't he explained all this before? Afraid she wouldn't come?

"My son, but born out of wedlock. Elsa had no use for him. Nor for me, when she was alive. The provision in her will was her last attack. I'm sure she thought I'd thumb my nose at her terms. But I plan to prove her wrong. I want this ranch, and I mean to have it.''

"I see.'' Brianna didn't understand the background

at all, but she understood the ringing determination in his voice.

Unexpectedly her heart went out to Shell. Brianna's parents had never married, either. When her father had learned of her mother's pregnancy, he'd taken off like a rocket.

Old anger rose in her, and Brianna wasn't sure whether to direct it to her absent father or to Jake for treating his son in a similar manner. Why hadn't he married Shell's mother?

"So do you stay or do you go?" he asked.

"Just like that I'm supposed to decide? For heaven's sake, I just got here and you hit me with this? I'm not sure I can make a decision that quickly. I know I want children, but you never said there was such an immediate deadline."

"Time is a luxury I don't have. There's less than a year remaining before I have to have a legitimate heir. If you aren't going to do your part, I need to find someone else."

"So all you want is a body to produce a child? You don't care about the woman you'd be marrying?" she asked, in growing irritation. He was being so cold-blooded.

Yet what had she expected? Wasn't that her primary reason for coming this far—to have a family? A chance at having a baby of her own?

So the timetable got pushed up a bit. She could deal with it.

"I will take care of the mother of my child," Jake replied. "But I'm not looking for some fairy-tale marriage where everyone loves everyone else. Life doesn't work that way. You said you wanted to leave New York. I haven't pushed to find out why, though I suspect something more than a desire to get married and have kids. You're not on the run, are you?''

She shook her head, not wanting to pursue that topic today.

''I figure I owed your uncle. This is the best I can offer. But it's a two-way street. I need your compliance in this, too.''

She studied the man sitting opposite her. He was masculine and sexy and knew what he wanted. Was that enough to start with? Could they build some kind of life together? Maybe not the one she'd originally dreamed of, but a comfortable one? One in which she'd at least find contentment?

At last she spoke. ''I still have the letter you wrote to my mother when Uncle Buck died. You said he'd done you a favor and you felt obliged, and if we ever needed anything, to contact you.''

He nodded.

''My mom and I…we never knew what that favor was.''

He hesitated a moment, then shrugged. ''I was a green kid on the rodeo circuit. Your uncle stood up for me when I was accused of something I didn't do. He risked his own standing and chances. It was a matter of honor, he said when my accuser—a rodeo producer—backed down. He hardly knew me. But he did what he thought was right. I owed him.''

Now that her uncle was dead, she realized that

Jake's own code of honor demanded he extend the
debt to her uncle's family.

She placed her cup on the flat arm of the sofa, got
to her feet and crossed to the window. She stared out
for a minute, not really seeing the view. Slowly she
turned to look at Jake.

"So that was the reason for your offer of marriage—to repay a debt?"

He shook his head. "Actually, when you answered
the ad, I remembered you from those summers on the
Garretson Ranch."

He stopped. Brianna waited for several beats. Then,
"And?"

He shrugged. "I figured we could make a go of it.
At least I knew who I was getting. I knew your family."

She turned and looked back out the window in frustration. So much for cockeyed optimism. She thought
she could visit for a while, see if she wanted to marry
the man. Then, if they did marry, decide over time if
they wanted more. Make sure they got along before
bringing any kids into the world.

Instead, he wanted a baby right away.

A baby. A precious child of her own. She could
have one within the year if she agreed to this prepos-
terous plan.

"This is crazy," she murmured.

"Yeah, well, so was my grandmother." Jake stood
up and contemplated her, folding his arms across his
chest.

"I can't decide this today," Brianna said quickly.

"I'm running out of time."

"A few more days won't hurt, will it? And if there's someone else waiting in the wings, have at it," she snapped.

"There's no one else. I can give you until the end of the week, I suppose."

"I *suppose* I can decide by then. Would you limit our number of offspring to one?" She faced him squarely.

He tilted his head. "You want more than one?"

"I might like to have five or six," she stated boldly.

His expression softened. "I think I could handle that if the ranch starts to pay."

"I have some money—"

He interrupted her. "I'm not taking anyone's money. This place will be mine alone once I fulfill all the terms of the will. I won't risk that ownership by commingling my assets with a stranger's."

"What are you talking about? I'm not a stranger and if we go through with this, I'll be your wife. Try *not* commingling things."

"If we get a divorce, I don't want to have to give up any part of the ranch. That price would be too high."

"I wasn't planning on a divorce," she said through gritted teeth. "Is that your plan, have the baby and then dump me?"

"Hell, I'm no good at this." He ran his fingers through his hair, then dropped his hand. "I'm not starting out with this *planning* to get a divorce. But there is a bit of truth in what Loni had to say a few minutes ago. You're used to life in the big city, where there are theaters, cafés, fancy stores and nightclubs.''

He gestured vaguely with his hand. "We don't have that here, Brianna. The local catalog store is the best shopping you're going to get unless we go to Laramie or Cheyenne. In winter we sometimes get snow window-deep. Our nearest neighbor lives seven miles away, and Dexter and I don't see eye to eye on most things, so we aren't exactly close friends. There'll be a lot of work necessary to bring this ranch up to scratch. Hard work. I wouldn't blame you for taking off once you've been here a while.''

"If I go through with this, I plan to stay." She tilted her chin with determination. Granted, she'd never lived through a Wyoming winter, but she'd sure loved the summers. Not to mention the land itself, its wide-open spaces. And hard work didn't scare her. Hadn't she worked hard at the ad agency?

Besides there was no going back to her old life.

"You didn't stay in New York," he argued.

"I lived there for fifteen years. Anyway, that's not the point. I have no intention of ever abandoning a child of mine. If you're not looking for forever, let's call it quits now.''

Jake hesitated, then nodded. "If you still feel that way by the end of the week, we can go into town and have a lawyer draw up a prenuptial agreement to protect us both. Once signed, we can get married next week.''

"I won't sign anything that would ever take my babies away from me," Brianna warned. Was she really going to have a baby with this man? Sexy was well and good for climbing into bed, but she wasn't sure she liked his thoughts about the future. She'd come here in good faith; he needed to demonstrate the same.

When she inhaled, she smelled leather, hay and a hint of his unique scent. If she was serious about this marriage, she'd better start getting used to him and what marriage would entail.

She cleared her throat and added, "I know your time is tight, but we also need to make sure you want to be married to me."

"I'm not worried about that. In the prenup we'll state that if things don't work out, or if there is no baby in time, we'll agree to divorce—each keeping what we brought to the marriage."

Jake crossed to her and put his hands on her shoulders. He gently pulled her closer and kissed her on the mouth. His lips were warm and soft, surprising given the tight control he demonstrated. The kiss lasted long enough for her to respond. Long enough for her to want more.

Brianna felt the shock to her toes. Slowly she opened her eyes and looked into his. She was used to reading people, but with Jake she hadn't a clue.

"What are you doing?" Was that her voice? So husky and breathless?

"Figured we needed to get that out of the way. Babies don't just grow on trees."

"It's hard to think about that when we don't know each other at all," she said.

Jake's narrowed gaze met hers. He stepped back but did not release her shoulders.

"I know a lot about you. I remember how stubborn you used to be once you set your mind on something. How you'd plug away at a task until you mastered it. You have a spirit of adventure, or you wouldn't have come to Wyoming—then or now. You're confident and assured—it shows in the way you carry yourself— and stand up for yourself. You wouldn't turn your back on a child and will work to be the best mother you can be. And you have definite ideas about what you want in life. And I liked the kiss, so did you, I believe, and so that aspect should not be a problem. Did I miss anything?"

Surprised, Brianna shook her head. "You got all that from seeing me today?"

"Some of it from those summers when you visited your uncle." He shrugged. "Care to give it a try with me?"

She swallowed. It was hard to think straight. She wanted to touch his face, run her fingers through his hair, test the strength of his muscles.

Despite her racing heart and the light-headed sensations being near him brought, she tried to formulate some semblance of analysis. She tried to forget the crush she'd once had on a wild young cowboy and see him as he was today.

"You're a stubborn man," she began, "because you refuse to give in to your grandmother, but will find a way to get this ranch. You have a strong sense of honor, or you wouldn't have contacted my mother when Uncle Buck died. I don't know why you didn't marry Shell's mother, but you must be doing something right as a father. He lives with you and seems like a nice young man. You have a vision—to make this ranch a success. And you also have a streak of adventure, or you wouldn't take a chance on marrying an unknown woman.''

He nodded. "Anything else you need to know?"

"A million things." But it was increasingly hard to think, distracted as she was by the sensations coursing through her from the feel of his palms on her shoulders.

"I don't smoke, rarely drink," he said. "I'd never raise my hand to a woman. For the most part, I pick up after myself. There would always be food on the table and a roof over your head as long as I draw breath. What else?"

Her heart beat heavily in her chest. His words echoed in her mind. Unable to look away she tried to think of something clever to say. But her mind remained blank while her body inched closer.

"Nothing. I guess I'll learn the rest over the years ahead."

"So we'll do it?" he asked. "For better or worse?"

"Yes." Her blood pulsed through her, hot and thick. The familiar longing for children changed into a different kind of longing. Bravely she brushed his jaw, then his cheek, with her fingertips, touching him as if they were already lovers.

She'd just committed to marry this stranger!

"It's either the start of a great adventure or the biggest mistake of our lives," Jake said sardonically.

"We are going to wait a week...," she said, nervousness sweeping through her. Marriage was a huge step, one that, despite her words, she still wasn't sure was wise. She'd thought once the decision was made, she'd feel good about it. Assured.

She felt scared silly.

"Okay. Tell me by Friday if you change your mind and want to back out. Otherwise, welcome to the Rocking M ranch, Brianna Dawson. Or should I practice and say Brianna Marshall?"

"Dinner!" Loni called from the kitchen.

"Her timing's good."

Jake dropped his hands from Brianna's shoulders and turned for the door. He opened it and waited for Brianna to pass. Apparently he liked calling the shots. If they continued together, he'd find out soon enough she also liked her own way. If nothing else, this marriage should prove to be an interesting merger.

CHAPTER THREE

THE TWO HIRED HANDS were already in the kitchen when Jake and Brianna entered. Jake introduced her to Hank and Nolan. He could use three more, but that would have to wait until spring.

If they lasted until spring. And if he could afford to pay them.

Hank had a thick thatch of gray hair, was lean to the point of emaciation and nodded calmly when they were introduced. Nolan was younger, about Jake's age. His smile was friendly.

Shell looked at Jake, then Brianna. "You staying?"

She nodded.

"Brianna and I will be married next week," Jake said as he pulled out the chair at the foot of the long table for Brianna. No one else had sat in it since Jake had returned to the ranch. Might as well get in the habit.

Jake took his seat at the other end and looked down the table at Brianna. Her blond hair was shining, and soft color rode high in her cheeks. A man could get used to seeing her opposite him at every meal, he thought, not feeling the constraint he expected. The question was, could she get used to the ranch?

She looked young and sophisticated and as out of place in his kitchen as he would have been in one of her trendy Manhattan restaurants. Would she go through with the marriage? Seemed to him, he'd be getting the better end of the bargain.

She was almost too thin, though he couldn't fault her femininity. She carried herself with pride and self-assurance. How much had she changed from that enthusiastic teenager who loved to visit her uncle?

But Loni had a point. Would she last? A few weeks' visit during summer didn't make her a rancher. After years in one of the world's most exciting cities, Wyoming would seem deadly dull in comparison.

Loni poured into the mugs at each place, then set a huge platter of roast beef in the center of the table, next to bowls of mashed potatoes, green beans, creamed onions and fluffy biscuits.

As she returned to the stove for the gravy, Jake thought how, from the back, no one would know she was pregnant. Her jeans hugged a trim bottom, and her long blond hair was pulled back into a ponytail that swayed with each step. But when she turned around, her pregnancy was instantly obvious. The baby would be big, he judged.

He saw Shell watching Loni with hungry eyes as she moved around the kitchen. Whenever she turned to face Shell, he looked elsewhere. Jake wished again he could do something to help his son.

Jake shifted his eyes to Brianna. He knew she was in her early thirties, but her optimism was like that of a twenty-year-old. Would the reality of the ranch crush that optimism?

He found it hard to believe she'd forsake everything to live here. Yet he dared not question her too closely. He needed an heir and soon. He needed Brianna—to hell with her reasons. Did it matter as long as she stayed?

IT SEEMED to be every man for himself at the table, and as soon as the first bowl was handed to her, Brianna took a helping. She wanted to fit in, yet what could she talk about that would be of interest to these cowboys and yet wouldn't reveal her ignorance about ranching?

She needn't have worried. Conversation was non-existent as the men fell to eating, which made her realize how much of an outsider she was. Everything was foreign to a career woman from Manhattan. She knew very little about cattle or horses or ranching. Three summers as a visitor hadn't taught her much.

She tried to imagine herself feeling included in this group. Could she make a place for herself? She and Jake needed to discuss that. What was he expecting—besides a baby?

Suddenly she missed home. She missed the bustle and energy of the city. Missed her familiar routine, her friends, even her hectic job. She especially missed feeling as if she belonged. Even the thought of having a baby didn't help her envision a future on the ranch. Had she fooled herself—and Jake?

She glanced at the others, settling on Shell. Jake's

son favored him. She moved her gaze to Jake again. In nine months she could have a son or daughter. Would that child favor Jake in appearance, or her? What about its personality? Like Jake's—brooding, watchful, stubborn? Or would it have some traits from her, such as her unfailing optimism?

"Heard you worked on a ranch before," Nolan said to her when his plate was almost empty. "Here-abouts?"

"Why, yes," Brianna said, grateful for a chance to escape her thoughts. "In Wyoming, anyway. The Garretson ranch near Jackson Hole. Ever hear of it?"

"Sure, know a few fellas who worked it. What did you do?"

"I spent summers there when I was a teenager. I rode the fence line, did some mustering and mucked out a million stalls," she said, wrinkling her nose.

Everyone laughed.

"Haven't we all," Nolan said.

"Do you still ride?" Jake asked.

Brianna shrugged. "Mmm," she murmured. Now was not the time to tell him she hadn't been on a horse in years. She was sure she'd remember once she got back on.

"You're not thinking that living on a ranch is romantic, are you?" Loni asked.

"You mean it ain't?" Nolan said, eyes twinkling.

Hank chuckled. "It's so-o-o romantic dealing with calving in the worst blizzard of the season."

"Yeah, and how about the sweet romantic smell of branding?"

"How about the joys of dipping?"

"Or all the flies in the middle of summer, which makes working in the hot sun such a pleasure?"

Loni giggled. "Shut up, you guys. Brianna, they're joking, even if what they're saying is true. The flies are awful in summer if the wind dies down. And the winters are terrible. I'd rather hear more about New York. How could you bear to leave? Are you planning to go back? Maybe you and Jake could take your honeymoon there."

"I think you're a damn fool, Jake, to marry to please that old woman," Shell said with a snarl. He hadn't joined in the fun, and his comment put an instant damper on the others. He glared at Jake.

"It's that or lose the place," Jake answered calmly. "I think the best revenge would be to keep the ranch in the family and make it a huge success."

Brianna studied Shell, struck by the thought he probably resented her. Did he see her pushing him aside while a child of hers took his place as heir? Were there restrictions on who Jake's heir was to be, as well?

Shell shoved back his chair and tossed his napkin on the table. "I'm done," he said, and stalked out of the kitchen to the hallway. The sound of his steps soon faded.

Loni fiddled with her glass, turning it around and around. She glanced at Brianna and smiled.

Brianna returned the smile and said, "Maybe you and I can get together later and I'll answer all your questions. I don't think the men are interested in hearing about New York. I need to learn more about Wyoming. We can exchange information, okay?''

''Well, I can definitely give you an unbiased view of the wonders of living on this place,'' Loni said. But before Brianna could say anything else, she jumped to her feet, snatched up a jacket and slammed out of the kitchen, the back door reverberating behind her.

''What did I say?'' Brianna asked, looking at Jake.

''Nothing,'' Jake said. ''She's pregnant—her hormones are crazy. She'll get over her snit soon enough and be back when the cold drives her inside.'' He got to his feet and then stood there, looking almost uncertain. ''I have work to do with the accounts. I'll bring in your bags and show you to a bedroom. You can unpack and get an early night. We get up at dawn.''

''Shall I do the dishes or something?'' she asked.

''If you want. It's Loni's job, but she might appreciate the help.''

''Yeah, or get bent out of shape because someone's encroaching on her territory,'' Nolan said. ''Glad the cows aren't as temperamental when calving.''

''I'll chance it,'' Brianna said, glad for something to do. Maybe she'd feel she was contributing.

Jake went to get her bags after Brianna gave him the keys to her car, and Nolan and Hank departed for the bunkhouse, bidding her good-night.

''Obviously women's lib hasn't made its way here,'' she murmured, clearing the plates and utensils from the table. ''It wouldn't hurt them to carry their plates to the sink on their way out. Doesn't it occur to them to help out a pregnant woman?''

''Did you say something?'' Jake asked as he entered carrying two of her cases.

Brianna glanced at him in embarrassment. ''No. Sorry. I talk to myself a lot. My roommate, Connie, was always telling me she felt she was eavesdropping on my conversations with myself!''

He stared at her for a long moment, then nodded, his eyes gleaming in the light. ''I'll try not to eavesdrop.''

Brianna smiled, pleased to see Jake had a sense of humor. They might need it in the months to come.

She efficiently cleaned up the kitchen, trying to make sense of everything that had happened since she arrived. But all she could focus on was that she might have a child of her own this time next year.

She dried her hands and hung up the towel. Heading out into the hall, she climbed the stairs to the second floor. Jake hadn't said where she'd sleep, but she could find where he'd put her suitcases on her own. And maybe peek into some of the other rooms to get to know her new home.

Not at all tired, despite the long drive, she was glad to have the evening to herself. Meeting the inhabitants of the ranch had been stressful. No one could expect to instantly fit in. And until she felt more comfortable, she needed some time on her own. She also wanted to call Connie and Nancy, another close friend, before it was too late. They would be waiting to hear she'd arrived safely; they'd also want to hear her impressions of Jake.

As she passed a closed door, she heard country music coming from the other side. Was that Shell's room? The door to the next room was also shut. So much for learning more about the house. Across the hall a bathroom door stood open.

Brianna saw her suitcases in a room at the end of the hall. The room directly across was dark, but she peeked inside. From the large bed and the masculine attire draped on a chair, she suspected it was Jake's room. She studied the bed. In only a few days, that would be where she slept.

JAKE PACED the office floor. He didn't feel like doing accounts. He was restless, edgy. So why was he holed up here? He should be out there talking with Brianna, learning more about her, telling her more about the ranch and what he hoped to accomplish once the place was his.

Faintly he heard the music coming from Shell's room. He moved to the window and looked out into the black night. Once again he wished the past had been different. Or that he knew how to change the present. Futile thoughts, but ones that plagued him.

Shelly Bluefeather had been his saving grace. She'd made a play for him their senior year in school. True, if he hadn't taken up with Shelly, he'd have quit school and run away long before he turned eighteen. But even her love wasn't strong enough to keep him in Sweetwater when he graduated. He'd been gone the next day.

Yeah, he thought, rubbing a hand over his face. *Gone before she could tell me I was going to be a father. Gone so far no one tracked me down for more than five years.*

And then only because he'd started making a name for himself on the rodeo circuit. By that time Shelly had decided he didn't need to know about his only son. And she made sure no one else learned Shell's daddy's name except Shell on her deathbed. It had come out for the rest of the world after she died, though gossip had been right on the money.

He went over and sat behind the desk, staring blindly at the papers covering it, thoughts still churning. Jake had missed his son's growing up. He hadn't known a thing about him until Shelly's funeral.

Jake could almost hear the resentment in his son's mind some days. He hadn't married Shelly, had had nothing to do with them—but to keep the ranch he'd marry some stranger and father another child.

Maybe he should just thumb his nose at the terms of the will, live on the place until the deadline and then move on. It wasn't as if he couldn't find a job on another ranch. His position at the Bar-XT had been filled, but there were other spreads looking for someone to ramrod their operations.

Jake rocked back in the old chair, remembering when he and his father had first moved back to the ranch. His parents had never lived here. His father had married against Elsa's wishes, and she'd ordered him off her property.

Jake couldn't recall much about his mother—Annie had died when he was four. Would his life have been different had she lived? It was likely he would have had brothers or sisters. Would that have helped when things fell apart?

With his mother's death, the light had gone out of his father's eyes. With his son, he'd struggled for years, moving from ranch to ranch. Every time Jake thought they'd settle in, his father would go off on a bender and get fired. So they'd pack up and move again.

Until finally his old man had decided to eat crow and return home.

His old man had spent hours at this same desk every evening, grumbling about all the paperwork connected with the spread. His real love had been riding the range, dealing with the varied challenges of raising cattle. He liked the outdoors, no matter what the weather. He'd hated being confined inside.

Had he always been like that? Or was it a result of his Annie's dying?

As long as Jake's father did as Elsa directed, he could run the ranch as he saw fit.

Unfortunately the old woman had not extended that largesse to the son of the woman she despised. Jake was a constant reminder of her son's rebellion—he'd married Annie Colter when she'd become pregnant, instead of following his mother's orders.

Just as Jake would have married Shelly if he'd

known. If only she'd told him. Instead, he'd brought shame and dishonor to one of the few people who had genuinely cared about him.

Even now he ached with the pain she must have endured. When he thought of all the rude and ribald remarks cowboys must have made to her over the years, he clenched his fists in futile anger. His grandmother must have known. She should have contacted him. Another wrong to lay at her feet.

If he and Brianna had a baby, he'd do things differently. He'd start with spending a lot of time with the child. He wanted to teach him…

Jake realized he could just as easily have a daughter. A sweet little girl with blond curls who would look at him with adoring eyes. Or would the child have his darker coloring? A baby was hard to imagine.

Almost as difficult as imagining himself married. He'd never even lived with a woman. What would it be like to share a bed with Brianna—to wake up beside her every morning? To touch her, kiss her, try for a baby? He felt himself grow hard just thinking about the sophisticated blonde he'd said he'd marry.

He heard the shower and knew it was probably Brianna. In his mind's eye, he could see her beneath the spray. She was a bit thin and not very tall, but trim and curved in all the right places. Jake closed his eyes, imagining those curves in his palms, imaging the softness of her skin, the heat they'd generate together.

Damn! At the rate he was going, the blasted accounts would never get done.

He disciplined his thoughts and pulled the ledger

closer. There was plenty to keep his mind occupied. And nothing cooled a man's desire faster than a stack of bills he couldn't pay.

LONI HUGGED herself in an effect to ward off the chill of the late-October night. She'd been hot with anger when she'd slammed from the kitchen. Shell made her furious. And Jake wasn't much better. How could Jake even think of marrying someone just to save his stupid ranch? And why in the world had Brianna Dawson come here? She was so sophisticated, so pretty, so elegant. She'd lived in New York City! Why forsake that to come to this crummy ranch?

She frowned, kicked a dirt clod. She couldn't wait to leave. Once her baby was born, she was out of here. Nineteen was too young to be tied down with a baby. She had plans and dreams that were too big to ignore. And Shell had wrecked them all when he got her pregnant. She'd already be on her own if it hadn't been for that.

It wasn't fair. They'd been so careful. They'd used a condom every time. Maybe she should sue the manufacturer for damaged goods. One time, one lousy time, and she was stuck.

Only she wasn't going to be stuck in Sweetwater the rest of her life. She had talent, promise. Elsa had told her that. And she wanted so much more than the life her mother or her aunts had, wanted more than to be at the beck and call of men all the time, cooking, cleaning, helping at roundup.

She was determined to see the world. Visit places

that offered more than this one-horse town a million miles from anywhere. She wanted to live somewhere exciting.

If she could just resist Shell.

She stared across the range. The stars were low in the sky tonight. When she'd been little, she'd thought that once she grew up, she'd be tall enough to reach up and touch them. She'd been stupid. But she wouldn't stay stupid.

Elsa Harrington Marshall had been renowned for her paintings. If she said Loni had talent, Loni believed her.

The baby kicked, stretched and moved. Rolling over, Loni thought. She patted her swollen stomach, then snatched her hand away. She would not grow attached to this child, not when she was thinking of giving it up for adoption.

She hadn't told Shell. He'd be angry. But it was too much to expect her to give up her life for a mistake.

Not that loving Shell was a mistake. It just wasn't something she could afford right now. She had a greater destiny. Slowly she walked toward the studio, a small building on the far side of the barn.

It wasn't easy being destined for greatness. She'd miss him. These last few months she'd tried hard to keep her distance, but the truth was, she ached for him to hold her, ached for the feel of his hard body.

But she knew she had to hold firm or she'd cave in, and the next thing she knew she'd agree to marriage and settle down on the ranch and never get away. Just like her mother. Loni did not want to be like her mother.

She pushed open the door to the studio and switched on the light. The familiar smells of turpentine, paints and fresh canvas filled the room. She loved it. Every day she painted. As soon as the baby was born, she was heading for Denver, or maybe Dallas. Some city where she could establish herself as an artist of some renown. And when she was famous, she'd move to New York and have a loft apartment in SoHo and really live. Or maybe even Paris.

Shell had offered her the use of the studio when she'd first moved to the ranch. He'd told her she could paint here forever if she'd marry him. But it wasn't enough.

She refused to be dependent on a man. Shell wanted her to lean on him. But she had to be free.

When she was a monumentally successful artist, she'd eat in fancy restaurants every night, buy expensive gowns and jewelry. And she'd have a cook and a maid so she never had to prepare another meal or scrub another bathroom.

And she'd never marry.

As she slowly walked around the huge room, Loni studied the canvases propped against the walls. The good pieces she'd take with her, the rest she'd leave behind. When she became famous, she'd tell Shell of her sacrifice, how much she loved him, but how she'd had to follow a higher calling.

He'd be sad she couldn't stay with him. But he'd

have to understand. Maybe he'd visit her. Maybe they could make love again.

Tears filled her eyes as she thought of the bittersweet love she had for the man. But even at nineteen, she knew if she didn't escape Wyoming soon, she'd never be able to leave.

And staying wasn't an option.

CHAPTER FOUR

DESPITE SETTING her alarm for five, Brianna was the last one up the next morning. She stumbled into the kitchen, willing to kill for a cup of coffee, but knowing she shouldn't have any—she had to watch the caffeine. Did they have any herbal tea?

The men looked up from the table where they were eating. Loni turned from the stove and grinned at her.

"Good morning. I'll have a stack of hotcakes ready for you in a moment. Help yourself to coffee. Do you want sausage or bacon, or both?"

"Do you have tea?" Brianna asked, conscious she wasn't making the best impression showing up so late, but too tired to care. She hadn't slept well, tossing and turning most of the night. To have to get up after only a few hours' sleep made her cranky.

Loni shook her head. Shrugging, Brianna poured herself half a cup of coffee and took a sip. It was too hot to gulp the way she wanted, but hopefully it was strong enough that the first few sips would give her a jump-start.

How did Loni do it? She looked bright and fresh, and had obviously been up long enough to prepare the enormous breakfast the men were devouring.

"Sleep well?" Jake asked when she went to the table.

"As well as anyone in a new place, I guess." Brianna didn't want him to know she'd been too busy worrying to sleep.

The men ate quickly and without wasted motion. Brianna marveled at the huge stack of hotcakes they devoured, not to mention the sausages and bacon and side of scrambled eggs. Then, almost as one, they got up and headed outdoors.

"We'll be back for supper, Brianna," Jake said. "Loni will show you around, help you get settled. Ask her for anything you want."

"You won't be in for lunch?" she asked. There was so much to discuss, and he was leaving before she'd asked a single question.

"Not today. We'll be too far from the house to make it worth the trip." Jake looked at Loni. "Take care of her."

Loni nodded, already clearing the dishes.

"I can take care of myself," Brianna said, amused Jake thought the younger woman needed to watch out for her. Shouldn't she be watching out for Loni? She had at least a dozen years on the younger woman.

As soon as Jake left, Brianna turned to Loni.

"I can help you clean up as soon as I'm finished eating," Brianna said, taking another bite of the heavenly pancakes. No wonder Jake liked having Lori around—she was a wonderful cook.

"I don't mind. There's not much to do. I'm going into town today to grocery-shop. Want to come with me? See some of the town. Not that it can begin to compare with New York. I want you to tell me all about it."

"Yes, I'd like to come. In the future, I'll take on the shopping, if you like. I mean, being pregnant and all has to be tiring."

Loni looked at Brianna suspiciously.

"I do get tired. Normally I take a nap in the afternoon. Unless I have to go into town for a doctor's appointment."

"When's the baby due?"

"In another month. I can't wait!"

"I can imagine. I'm hoping to have a baby of my own soon," Brianna confided, the thought making her almost smile. What had been such a nebulous dream for so long now looked as if it would come true.

Loni shook her head. "I can't wait to be unpregnant again. I'm so tired of being huge. I have things to do, places to go."

"Oh," Brianna murmured, surprised by the vehemence in the girl's tone. "Where? I thought you lived here."

"This is only temporary. I'm going to Dallas or at least Denver."

"With a new baby?"

Loni shrugged. "I haven't decided yet what to do about the baby," she said defiantly.

Brianna sipped her coffee, at a loss as to what to say. Was Loni planning to give her baby up for adoption? How could any mother not love her child and want to be with it? Her own mother had told her over and over that she was worth any price. And her mother had paid a big one.

"Well, I'm sure you'll do what's best," Brianna said inadequately, fearing she was treading on dangerous ground.

Loni looked at her cautiously. "I usually clean up the kitchen after the men leave. Then do a quick and dirty swing through the rest of the rooms tidying up, then go to my studio."

"Studio? Are you an artist?" Steven owned a gallery, and Brianna had attended many showings at his place, wishing often that she had some talent for art.

"I paint," she said dramatically.

"I'd love to see some of your work," Brianna said.

"Come over to the studio, and I'll show you. Elsa said I have great promise."

"Jake's grandmother?" Hadn't he called her Elsa last night?

"She was a great artist, Elsa Harrington."

"Elsa Harrington was Jake's grandmother?" Brianna was stunned. No wonder he was angry about the state of the ranch. She'd been one of America's foremost artists, and her paintings commanded huge sums. Brianna remembered Steven talking about her death last year. Her paintings had jumped dramatically in value upon her death, and he'd been bemoaning the fact that he didn't have any.

So Elsa Harrington had left nothing to her grandson but this ramshackle old ranch. Why?

"Yes. She said I'd waste my life staying here. So I'm leaving as soon as the baby's born."

"Why?"

"It was fine for Elsa to live here—she'd already made her mark. But I need new experiences to broaden my scope. I can't stay in this backwater. I need to escape."

Brianna blinked. Was Loni trying to convince her or herself?

How odd life was. She needed to escape the frenetic pace of city life for the quiet of this "backwater" at the same time Loni was champing at the bit to leave. Would either of them find happiness with change?

"Is that why you want to go to Dallas?" Brianna asked.

"Yes, but now I wonder if I should consider New York. That's why I want you to tell me all about it, so I'll know stuff when I get there. I don't want to look like some dumb country hick."

"The Mecca of the young," Brianna murmured. "If you're serious, I can give you names of some friends who'll look out for you." Maybe Brianna could even put her in contact with Steven. She was sure he'd be willing to examine paintings from someone Elsa Harrington pronounced promising. Brianna would have to warn Loni, however, not to take to heart too much of what Steven said. She knew how quickly he could change his mind.

"You would? That's wonderful. Thank you! I can't wait. I wish the baby would come today!" Loni's face lit with an excited smile.

"Not just yet, please. I need to get a feel for things

so I can take over running the house when you leave,'' Brianna protested.

"It's a piece of cake,'' Loni declared.

"We'll see. I haven't done much around a house before. The small apartment I shared in New York didn't take much to keep clean. As for cooking, I have a feeling that cooking for four men is a lot different from cooking for one or two girlfriends!''

They quickly finished the dishes. Loni then led the way to the studio, proudly showing off her work. Brianna liked several of the paintings. The style was pleasing, though there wasn't a lot of variety. They were all either local landscapes or still-life studies. Nonetheless she bet there would be a market for the paintings.

IT WAS MIDMORNING by the time they left for town. The sheer size of the grocery list was amazing. Brianna was glad she'd offered her SUV. They'd need every bit of room to cart the groceries home. Normally, Loni told her, she drove one of the ranch pickup trucks, but couldn't shop if it rained.

When they had two carts full and still more to buy, Brianna asked Loni how she managed on her own.

"I pick up the nonperishables first, leave the carts near the checkout and go back for another. The clerks know the ranchers around here, and they're used to it. When I have everything, I start lining them up. The bag boys usually load the truck for me. Especially lately. But there's no one to unload at home but me! It can take forever to unload one bag at a time.''

A middle-aged woman came around the aisle and stopped in obvious surprise.

"Hello, Mama," Loni said quietly.

Brianna turned and smiled. But the woman merely nodded, backed away and headed for another aisle.

"What was that about?" Brianna asked, startled by the rude behavior of the woman, who was apparently Loni's mother.

Loni took a deep breath. "My folks kicked me out when I got pregnant. I guess they haven't softened any."

"Oh, Loni, I'm so sorry." Brianna touched her lightly on the shoulder. She knew what Loni was going through—hadn't the same thing happened to her own mother?

"It's okay. As soon as the baby comes, I'm outta here."

Despite the oft-repeated mantra, Brianna could see the hurt lingering in Loni's eyes, but she wisely changed the subject. By the time they were ready to check out, Brianna saw Loni's mother hurrying out the door. Family should rally around in a time of need, not desert. Even though her mother's parents had not stood by her when Brianna's father had taken off without marrying their only daughter, her mother had always talked of an ideal family whose members supported one another in times of difficulty. Thank heavens for Uncle Buck, the only member of Brianna's family who had helped.

Which was why Brianna had accepted that Steven

wasn't for her. Hadn't he fled at the first sign of trouble?

She wanted someone to count on, someone to be there for her always, even if honor, not love, kept him there.

By the time they returned to the ranch and put away the food, it was well past noon. After a hasty sandwich, Loni went to lie down, leaving Brianna with the afternoon to herself.

She finished unpacking her suitcases. Except for a few favorite outfits suitable for an evening at home or going to dinner, the clothes she'd brought were new—jeans and flannel shirts for the most part, sturdy sportswear suitable for a ranch. There was one new dress, a beautiful cream-colored concoction that Brianna had optimistically bought for her wedding.

When she finished, she wondered what to do next. She was used to having every moment full of activity and now she felt at loose ends. She headed for the main floor. Wandering around, she studied the rooms. They were furnished with sturdy pieces, all dreary and old. Functional, she supposed, but depressing. Knowing that bright flowers and sunshine had been a trademark of Elsa Harrington paintings, she wondered how the woman had stood the rooms. Why hadn't she redecorate while she lived here?

Brianna went to open the front door and was enchanted with the old-fashioned lock and key. Obviously crime wasn't very likely out here—a ten-year-old could pick this lock. She had to laugh, though, when the door stuck—maybe that was why no one had done anything about the lock.

She wrestled open the door and stepped out into the porch. The afternoon sun was behind the house, so the porch was in shadow. The view was terrific, an endless vista of rolling hills beneath a cloudless blue sky.

A pair of dusty rocking chairs sat to the left of the door. To the right were the remnants of an old porch swing, slats broken, the chains rusty.

Brianna continued down the three wooden steps to the dirt. Flanking the steps were small areas that appeared to have once been flower beds. It was too late in the year to plant anything new, but come spring, she could have flower beds. And in the meantime, maybe she'd pick up a couple of pots of bright-colored mums to place on the steps.

She wandered around the yard, planning where to plant shrubs and trees. If Jake didn't like her spending her money, he could reimburse her when the ranch began to pay. She understood his hesitancy in jeopardizing full ownership. She might feel the same way if she had something that had been in her family for generations. But she wasn't after his ranch.

She headed to the barn to explore more of her new home and was startled to find Shell there grooming a horse.

"Back already?" she asked, stepping into the dimness of the huge structure. "I thought you'd be gone all day."

"One of us tries to stay closer in case Loni needs anything," he said, brushing his horse in long even strokes. "I finished up and came in early. There's plenty to do around here."

"Well, I'm here, too, so I can help if needed."

"I guess." He continued to work, ignoring her.

She watched for a while, wondering what she could do to make friends with her future husband's son. From his attitude, she doubted he made friends easily.

"Have you worked on a ranch your whole life?" she asked at last.

"Since I was sixteen."

"Oh. Here?"

He gave a short laugh. "Not until last year when we moved back here. My great-grandmother liked to pretend I didn't exist."

"She didn't seem to care for your father, either," Brianna returned.

He unhitched the horse and turned him out into the corral. Gathering his saddle and bridle, he slung them over one shoulder and headed for the tack room. Brianna followed, still racking her brain for some safe topic of conversation. Nothing came to mind except what was at the forefront.

"I'm not planning to take your father away from you," she said.

He looked at her in surprise. "I didn't think you were."

"He won't love any baby we have any more than you," she continued almost desperately. She wanted to make sure Shell knew he wouldn't be replaced in his father's eyes.

"He might."

"No!"

He looked amused at her adamant denial. Setting the saddle on a stand, he began wiping down the reins.

"I know you don't believe in this marriage, but I'll do my best to be a good wife," she said.

"I don't care what Jake does. It just bugs me that he's kowtowing to that old witch. If it were me, I'd thumb my nose at her and her damn will."

"And lose the family ranch?"

He shrugged. "It doesn't mean anything to me."

She suspected that wasn't true, but wasn't going to challenge him at this juncture. "It means something to your father. And in time it could mean a lot to you."

"If I stay, maybe."

"Are you thinking of leaving?"

Again he shrugged. Shell Bluefeather was a man of few words.

"Loni's talking about leaving," Brianna said. Did Shell already know that?

"Yeah, well, if she goes, there's nothing really holding me, is there?" he responded.

"So why don't you marry her and settle down to raise that baby?" Brianna's sense of outrage grew as the injustice of it all hit her. Like father like son? she wondered. What was she getting herself into?

"You think I haven't asked her? I do at least once a week, if she lets me get close enough. I asked her daily when I first found out she was pregnant. But she doesn't want to marry some dumb old half-breed. She wants the bright lights of Dallas or Denver, not the back of beyond in this falling-down-around-our-ears ranch! Elsa filled her head with nonsense that she could be the next great American painter, and Loni sees nothing else but that!''

Brianna didn't know what to say. Why didn't the girl marry Shell? She could still paint. He was steady, had a good job and prospects for the future if she and Jake were able to fulfill the stipulations of the will. She shied away from that thought. She needed to focus on the current situation.

Jake was going to be a grandfather soon. Brianna blinked. If she married him, she was going to be a grandmother! She wasn't even a mother yet.

''Maybe you better rethink joining this family before it's too late,'' Shell said before heading outside. Brianna turned to follow, already coming up with another bunch of questions for Jake.

Did Loni really not want to marry Shell because he was part Native? She doubted that; the girl wouldn't have gotten involved with him to begin with. It sounded more as if Loni just wanted to go to the big city. And Brianna could not picture Shell living anywhere but here.

Later, at dinner, Brianna watched the pair, curious about the relationship.

When her eyes met Jake's, he raised an eyebrow in silent question.

''Maybe you and I could sit out front after dinner,'' Brianna said brightly. ''I cleaned the rocking chairs and swept the porch.''

''Rocking chairs?'' Nolan laughed. ''Hee-hee, she's

got you pegged for the rockers already, Jake! And you ain't a grandpa yet!''

''I would have suggested the swing, but it's not all there,'' Brianna said with some asperity. Then she smiled. ''If we're going to be grandparents, maybe we should get some practice in. What's more fun than rocking a baby?''

The silence around the table was complete. Everyone stared at Brianna.

''What? Are you going to tell me you all didn't think about vying for times to rock the baby? I'd have thought you'd have to schedule everyone weeks in advance.''

Jake cleared his throat. ''We're not sure where Loni and the baby will be.''

''Not here, that's for sure,'' Loni said pushing back her chair and standing. ''I'm going to paint.'' She grabbed her jacket and slammed out of the kitchen.

Shell glared at Brianna.

Nolan and Hank looked at their plates, pushing around the little food that remained. Jake's eyes were still on Brianna.

''If she and the baby stay, then I get first turn to rock him or her,'' he said.

''After Shell,'' Brianna said.

The young man stood and left the table much as he had the night before.

''Gee, can I clear a room or what,'' Brianna said wryly. ''Or is this their normal exit every night?''

''Pert near,'' Hank said. ''One or the other most always gets into a snit. Love, ain't it grand?''

Nolan laughed, and grabbed another biscuit. "Come on, I'll beat you at poker again."

"In your dreams, old son."

The cowhands got up, bid Jake and Brianna good-night and left.

The two of them met each other's gazes across the table.

"Shell says he wants to marry her, but she refuses," Brianna said.

"Yeah. Hell of a thing. He's crazy about her and she won't give him the time of day now that she's pregnant. They were close as could be before. She sees him as holding her back."

"I wonder if she has any chance at success."

"I don't know," he said. "Her pictures are pretty, but whether commercially strong, I haven't a clue. Apparently Elsa told her once they were. But knowing Elsa, it could have just been to throw a sop to an admirer. Loni has stars in her eyes."

"She wants to be a famous artist somewhere that's not here."

"That's her current goal."

"And if she goes, will Shell stay?"

Jake looked startled. "Why wouldn't he? This is his home. If we get to keep the ranch, it'll be part his one day."

"I thought he couldn't inherit."

"Interestingly enough, the will merely says that for *me* to inherit I have to have a legitimate heir within two years of the reading of the will. But there's no restriction saying I have to leave the ranch to the le-

gitimate heir if I gain title. I've had more lawyers than
fleas on a dog look at the thing. If I could have broken
it in court, I would have.''

Brianna rose and began to stack the dishes.

''You still want to sit outside?'' Jake asked. ''It's a
lot colder now that the sun's gone down.'' He tilted
back in his chair, watching her.

''Yes. It'll give us some privacy.''

''Ah, that sounds promising,'' Jake drawled. He
brought the chair level again and reached out to stack
the dishes near him. When he carried them to the sink,
Brianna glanced his way.

''Stay and talk to me while I do the dishes.''

''Loni can do them later.''

''I can do them now. Stay,'' Brianna said, running
hot water into the sink.

He leaned against the counter next to the sink,
crossing his arms over his chest, and studied her. ''If
this is where you rope me into helping, come right out
and say so.''

''Helping how? By drying and putting away?'' she
said, throwing him a teasing look.

''I might be talked into it. For the right price.''

''Hmm, didn't you say last night you didn't want
my money?''

He inched closer, his arms still crossed. ''There are
other things besides money.''

He was flirting with her. How long had it been since
anyone had played such games with her?

''Okay, I'll bite, what's the price?''

He leaned even closer. ''Where will you bite?''

Brianna laughed softly and leaned toward him until she could feel his breath on her face.

"Oh, cowboy, I can bite where you've never been bit before."

"I do believe you could." His mouth came down on hers.

Brianna savored the feelings that rushed through her. His lips were warm and firm, moving gently as if seeking more. She leaned closer, conscious that her hands were wet and soapy. She longed to throw them around his neck and hold on for the ride.

Jake took his time, as if he, too, was exploring her and the feelings she evoked.

When eventually he pulled back, she stared into his eyes, trying to divine his thoughts.

"Just getting it out of the way again?" she asked.

"No, seeing if it's worth putting away the dishes."

She splashed him with water.

The banter they exchanged as they proceeded to do the dishes made Brianna feel better about her choices. If they could go day to day as friends, life would be fine.

"So are you planning on this every night?" Jake asked as he put the last pot away in the cupboard beneath the counter.

"Only until the kids are old enough to take over."

He paused a moment, then nodded. "So we'll do the dishes for a few years, have a twenty-year or so hiatus, then back to you and me?"

"Sounds like a plan." Twenty years into the future.

Who thought that far ahead? Yet Jake seem to accept it naturally.

"So we're still a go to talk to the attorney on Friday?"

"Nothing's happened to change my mind," she said. "How about you?"

"No."

"I tried to talk to Shell earlier. He says he doesn't feel the tie to the ranch you do," Brianna said.

"I can't change things for Shell, much as I'd like to. The only thing I think will help is getting the ranch, and I need you for that."

CHAPTER FIVE

MONDAY WAS Brianna's wedding day. Big puffy white clouds dotted the blue sky. The air was crisp and the sun shone. She'd talked to Connie and Nancy for hours the previous night. After fretting about whether she was making the right choice, now that the day arrived, she felt calm and confident. At least, she told herself she did.

Dressing slowly, she stood before the dresser-top mirror and gazed pensively at her reflection. In less than an hour she was meeting Jake at the courthouse. They were being married in the judge's chambers. She sighed faintly at the lack of a formal church wedding, with lots of attendants and family. All young women dream of that, but she had no friends in Wyoming. No family—until she was married. Then Jake and Shell would become her family.

Six months ago if anyone had told her she'd be getting married today, she'd have assumed it would be to Steven. Steven, the man she'd thought she'd loved for two years. They'd seemed a perfect pair. Both dedicated to their jobs, yet able to squeeze in time for each other. They'd enjoyed the same activities—nightclubs, museum visits on rainy Sunday af-

ternoons, off-Broadway shows. She'd loved mingling
with the artists at his gallery during first-night showings. And their two brief vacations had been to a ski
resort in Vermont and a white-sand beach in Jamaica.

She blinked and glanced around. A far cry from
New York and the bustling life she'd led.

Turning, she picked up the small hat that comple-
mented her dress and put it on. She hoped she looked
like a bride. It was the least she could do for Jake.
And for herself.

A knock on the door interrupted her thoughts.

"Come in," she called.

Loni peeped in, then opened the door and entered.
She was wearing a pretty lavender maternity dress. In
her hand she had a bride's bouquet.

"I had Jake get these for you," she said, holding
them out for Brianna. "You know guys, they'd never
think of it on their own."

"Thank you, Loni!" Brianna took the bouquet of
white roses and baby's breath. The long, cream-
colored satin ribbon matched her dress perfectly.

She smiled at the younger girl, struck again by the
romantic streak she displayed from time to time. Loni
had brought her breakfast in bed that morning and
insisted she not see Jake before the ceremony. He had
already left for the courthouse, and she and Loni were
going into town together. Shell and Loni would stand
up with them, then when Brianna and Jake rode back
in his truck, Shell would drive Loni back in Brianna's SUV.

"Are you sure about this?" Loni asked, tilting her head slightly. "No doubts."

"Oh, Loni, I have a boatload of doubts. But I'm as sure as I'm ever gonna be. It's lonely being on my own all the time. And I'm not getting any younger. If I don't start a family soon, I might miss out." Brianna looked into the mirror one more time, as if to assure herself she could do this.

Pushing away all memories of Steven, their last confrontation and the might-have-beens, she raised her chin and said, "Okay, I'm ready to go."

Brianna kept her mind on the moment as she drove into Sweetwater. Loni continued to ask endless questions about New York. Brianna had never known anyone with such a insatiable need for information. She was repeating herself now, but Loni didn't seem to mind. She remained starry-eyed and hopeful. Brianna wondered if she herself had ever been so young and idealistic.

When they reached the courthouse, Shell was standing on the steps. He walked to the car when they parked and opened the door for Brianna. Dressed in a charcoal-gray suit, his boots polished, he looked devastatingly handsome. Brianna glanced at Loni, but the younger woman was getting out of the car on her own, avoiding Shell.

The breeze tugged at her hat, and she clasped it firmly to her head. "Windy," she said.

"Fixing to storm later, I think. Jake's inside with the judge. Said he'd wait for you there." Shell's voice was gruff.

Brianna looked at him. "I hope you're all right with this, Shell. I'm going to be the best wife I can be to him."

"It's not like I can change either of your minds. I just hope you two know what you're doing."

Brianna felt nervous, made more so by the curious glances she was receiving from passersby. She nodded once at an openly staring woman, and then turned toward the courthouse steps.

Stepping inside the judge's chambers a few moments later, she felt almost light-headed. This was it. Last chance to change her mind. She saw a silver-haired man she didn't know, undoubtably the judge. Nolan and Hank were standing by dressed in their Sunday best, their grins welcoming.

Jake stood near the window. He turned when she entered, and his familiar features sent a shiver of awareness through her. In only minutes this man would bind his life to hers. Mentally bidding Steven a final goodbye, she stepped up to meet her future husband.

The judge's words were familiar, yet seemed filled with more meaning since they applied to them personally. When he pronounced them husband and wife, Jake brushed a light kiss across her lips. She was married!

The cowhands approached to congratulate them, then headed out.

"I thought we'd have lunch at the Silverado with Shell and Loni," Jake said after thanking the judge.

"Then we'll return to the ranch. Hank and Nolan can take care of things until we get back."

They had discussed taking a honeymoon, and both agreed it wasn't a good idea. Jake couldn't afford the time away from work, and this wasn't exactly the kind of marriage that started with a glamorous honeymoon.

Brianna glanced at Shell. He'd stood silent and straight beside his father during the ceremony, and she wondered how he and Loni were feeling. She knew Shell wished he and Loni were standing up before the judge. Did the romantic younger woman have any idea what she was rejecting? Life in New York could be exciting and fun, but it could also be lonely. Loni would be turning her back on a lot when she left.

"That sounds lovely," Brianna said when no one else spoke.

"Loni and I'll catch up with you," Shell said as they walked down the corridor, reaching out to snag Loni's arm. She looked startled, then wary.

Jake merely nodded. "We'll see you there."

LONI WATCHED the newly married couple walk away. "What do you want, Shell?"

"What I've wanted all along, Loni. But I'm starting to understand we don't always get what we want. Or we have to do things we might not want to do to get it. Jake didn't want to get married, but he did to keep the ranch. I don't know if I could have done that with some stranger. I'm asking you again, will you marry me?"

Loni bit her lip and slowly shook her head. "I can't," she said.

He nodded and released her arm. "I figured you'd say that. It's the last time I'm asking. I hate for my kid to be born to parents who didn't marry—I know how that goes. But I can't make you. I'll provide for the baby, and I want to spend time with him. I don't want him not to know his father."

Loni looked away, her heart clutching. She didn't want to marry, but to think he'd never ask again made her feel frightened. She'd thought he'd always want to marry her.

What if they *had* married? Would his love have cooled as swiftly? It was a good thing she'd made plans. She'd be so successful, Shell would come begging her to marry him.

She couldn't respond to his comments. She wanted the best for her baby, but she couldn't imagine taking an infant to New York. What was she going to do?

"We'll be late to the lunch," she said, walking down the hallway. Why did life have to be so hard? She didn't want to deal with any of it.

She glanced at Shell as he led the way to Brianna's car and hardened her heart. Her future was in another direction.

Shell no more wanted to live in a city than she wanted to stay in Wyoming. He belonged to the windswept plains, chasing his own dreams. Still, Loni was sorry they would no longer include her.

JAKE GLANCED at his watch and looked down the street. "Where the hell are they?"

Brianna was aware of his growing impatience, but wasn't entirely sure it was due to Shell and Loni's delay in arriving at the restaurant. He had to be feeling as jittery as she was. They'd taken a huge step without a lot of foresight. She tried to quell her doubts. They were married. For good or ill. She refused to second-guess her actions. She respected Jake. Had lustful thoughts every time she looked at him.

Wouldn't that be enough to start?

"Did they know it was this restaurant?" she asked.

Jake nodded. "The Silverado's the only fancy place in town."

He hadn't really looked at her since she'd arrived at the judge's chambers—except just before he kissed her.

Brianna's SUV came around the corner just then, and Jake visibly relaxed. When Shell and Loni joined them, Jake asked what held them up.

"Unfinished business," Shell muttered. "All taken care of now."

Brianna glanced at Loni. The girl had a smile plastered on her face, but Brianna could tell she was not happy.

Lunch was more somber than celebratory. The food was excellent, but no one seemed to enjoy it. Brianna's nerves grew taut with apprehension as the minutes ticked by. She would spend the afternoon moving her things into Jake's room. Then dinner. Then...bed.

Her heart raced at the thought. She wasn't ready for this. Yes, marriage and a family were what she wanted. But the reality was scary.

"Storm coming," Shell said as he pushed away his empty plate. "I thought I'd ride up to the mesa and check that old line cabin, make sure it's tight for the winter in case we need to get up there. Take a sack of canned goods. I think there's hay for the horse. Maybe I'll head over to Ormsby's place afterward and stay the night."

Jake nodded. "If Nolan got that last bit of fencing taken care of this afternoon, we should be in good enough shape to hold us for a while. Until something else snaps."

"Or unless the rain washes something out," Shell grumbled. He fidgeted with his fork, glanced at Loni, then away. "You ready to go?" he asked her.

She shook her head. Just then the waiter brought a small white cake and with a flourish placed it between Jake and Brianna.

"Oh, how lovely!" Brianna was delighted and immediately knew the cake was from Loni. She smiled at the younger woman. "How did you manage this?"

Loni grinned. "I have connections. You can't have a wedding without a wedding cake. You two have to cut it and make a wish."

"Isn't that what you do when you blow out candles on a birthday cake?" Jake asked.

"You can wish on a wedding cake, too," Loni insisted. "Go ahead and cut it. After we have cake, I'll be ready to leave with Shell. But you two don't have to hurry back if you want to do something around town for a while."

"There are things that need doing at the ranch," Jake said.

"On your wedding day?" Clearly Loni was offended by the idea.

"I have things to do, too," Brianna said, wanting to start as she meant to go on. And siding with her husband was one way to do that. "We've had a lovely wedding, and this is wonderful. Thank you, Loni. I really appreciate it."

Brianna and Jake cut the cake and shared with others in the restaurant. Congratulations were given, and Brianna was introduced to a dozen or more people from Sweetwater. She couldn't keep all their names straight, but made an effort. They would be her neighbors.

As they drove home a short while later, Brianna tried to relax. The day had gone surprisingly well. She'd worry about the rest as it came.

Jake changed into his work clothes and then showed Brianna where he'd made room for her things in the closet and dresser.

"If you need anything else, let me know. I can bring in another dresser if you need the space," Jake said, looking around the room as if seeing it for the first time.

It wasn't the master bedroom. That had been his grandmother's, and he didn't want to sleep there.

He studied the bed, wondering if she was thinking the same thing he was—tonight they'd sleep together in that bed.

Or not sleep. They might make love. He rubbed the

back of his neck, feeling the tension rise a notch. He hoped she wasn't going to be like some martyred Victorian, lying back and thinking of England.

For the first time he could remember, he was nervous about sex. This wasn't some one-night stand. If things didn't go well, he'd have to live with it for the rest of his life.

"This will be fine. I'll move my things and see if I need any more room, but I don't think I will. I don't have a lot. Where shall I put my computer?"

He swung around. "You brought a computer? Why?"

"To keep in touch with friends, for one thing. I keep my accounts on it, and I thought it would come in helpful here."

"Doing what?"

"I don't know. If nothing else, I like browsing the Internet. I'm not exactly swamped with activity here, you know. Every time I've asked to help this past week, you brushed me off."

He had. But she wasn't a rancher. It would take more time to teach her something than to do it himself or have one of the men do it. Besides, once she was pregnant, he sure didn't want her outside doing hard physical work.

"The house needs care."

"It doesn't take long with Loni and me working together to dust and vacuum."

"She won't be here long. She keeps saying that once she has the baby, she's leaving. Wish I knew what she and Shell talked about today," he said.

"Her leaving, probably. Or maybe seeing us get married had him asking her again. Maybe I could fix things up a bit around here," she said slowly.

Jake felt uneasy with her casual suggestion. "No. I told you that on the first day."

"It's my home, too, Jake," she said reasonably. "I'm not talking about putting on an addition, only new curtains and some paint. Or are we to keep this place exactly the same way your grandmother had it?"

Her question stopped him. He didn't want to do anything as Elsa had. Surely new curtains and a coat of paint wouldn't entitle her to a portion of his ranch if they divorced.

Hell of a note, thinking of divorce on his wedding day. He looked at Brianna, struck by her way of looking right into his eyes. He didn't think she had an ulterior motive. She just wanted to fix up the place. Nesting. Didn't all women want that?

"It is your home, too. Do what you want—within reason. But leave the office alone."

He itched, suddenly, to get out of the house. Being so close to her, smelling the sweet fragrance that seemed to cling to her skin, was driving him crazy.

She nodded.

"I'll be back for dinner." He headed out, then paused in the doorway, looking back. Should he kiss her goodbye now that they were married?

"I'll be fine. Enjoy your afternoon," she said.

Jake strode to the barn, feeling uneasy. He knew a normal wedding day wouldn't have the groom going off to work. But there was so much to do and the storm predicted would be the first of many. Time was running out. Before long, winter would hit and they couldn't afford not to be ready.

BRIANNA CHANGED into jeans and looked around the bedroom. Today was definitely not the wedding day of her dreams. But as a practical wife to a rancher, it would have to do. She gathered up an armful of her clothes and carried them to Jake's room. Hanging them up in the closet, she studied his clothes, touching the suit he'd worn that morning. He had so few clothes, a couple of pairs of jeans slung over hangers, a half-dozen shirts. No designer suits or leisure wear. Just practical and durable clothes.

She was glad she'd shed most of her New York wardrobe. It would have been totally out of place in Wyoming.

By four, she'd finished. The bedroom still had Jake's stamp on it, but she'd put a few things on the dresser and changed the bedding. She'd also lit a vanilla candle to cover the smell of cattle and hay. Someday she'd probably get used to the smell, but that day hadn't arrived yet.

Brianna went to the kitchen to see if Loni had started dinner. She was surprised to find the younger woman sitting at the table, sipping hot chocolate, a pensive look on her face.

"Is something wrong?" Brianna asked.

Loni shook her head.

"What's for dinner? Shall I get it started?"

"We're having steak. I thought it would be a fitting

celebration. The baked potatoes will need to go into the oven soon. The rest I plan to have Shell—'' She stopped abruptly and for a moment Brianna thought she was going to cry.

"He and Jake were the ones who grilled the steaks when we had them before," Loni said, rising. "I thought Jake shouldn't have to cook on his wedding day. But I guess, since Shell's gone, he'll have to do the steaks. Shell left about an hour ago. I saw him ride out."

"I guess he thought celebrating at lunch was enough," Brianna said. "Didn't he say he was going to check out some cabin and then ride on to a neighbor's?"

"I don't know if he's ever coming back," Loni said.

"What happened?" Loni's comment startled her. Had Shell and Loni had a major fight? She thought he was just going for the night.

"He asked me to marry him again today. When I turned him down, he said he wouldn't be asking any more. Not that I care. Good riddance. He was always pestering me about that. Maybe he'll stop now." Her tone was defiant, and Brianna wondered…

"So going up to check the mesa was just an excuse to get away?" Brianna asked.

"I guess. I don't know if he plans to come back at all. He might move on. He's said over and over he doesn't feel any tie to Elsa Marshall's land."

"But if Jake inherits it, it would become his father's land. And at least a portion would go to him one day."

Loni looked at her. "Do you think Jake will leave part of the ranch to Shell?"

"Of course. Why wouldn't he? Shell is his son. Just because he didn't know about him until he was a teenager doesn't mean Jake doesn't care about him." Jake had said as much to her, but she doubted he'd said anything to Shell. The boy still seemed too prickly about their relationship. What they needed to do was sit down and have a serious talk to clear things up.

"I can handle dinner. You shouldn't have to on your wedding day," Loni said.

"I have nothing else to do. I'll scrub the potatoes. Why don't you make some of your biscuits, and this time I'm watching so I can get that down pat."

Dinner was no more celebratory than lunch had been. The men were tired. As soon as they finished, Hank and Nolan excused themselves and left.

"I'll do the dishes—on that I insist," Loni said. "And, Jake, I swear I'll throw a hissy fit if you go work on accounts on your wedding night!"

He raised his hand. "No accounts tonight." He looked at Brianna. "Want to sit on the porch?"

She nodded, surprised and pleased. It was cool, but as they had on other nights, they bundled up in jackets. Slowly they were talking through things. Maybe tonight she should tell him her real reason for fleeing New York.

When they stepped out onto the porch, Brianna stopped. "It's raining!" she announced, walking to the edge and watching as the drizzle soaked the ground.

The fresh clean scent of rain filled the air. She spun around and smiled at Jake.

"Don't you need the rain?" she asked.

"If it stays like this, it'll be good. It's the heavy downpours that cause flash floods." He stepped beside her and looked out over the dark landscape. "At least it isn't snow."

She shivered slightly, glad for the warm jacket. "It feels colder tonight. Is that because of the damp?"

"Yes, but the temperature is dropping. There'll be snow on the peaks come morning. Are you too cold to stay out?"

"I probably can't stay out for long," Brianna said, wishing he'd move closer and offer her some of his warmth.

Her heart pounded. Only a few more hours and they'd be going to bed. She tried to breathe, but felt panic rush through her. She wasn't ready for that! Could she tell him how she felt? Ask him to wait a little longer—just until they knew each other better?

Stupid, she thought. He needed an heir as soon as possible. She couldn't picture him waiting for her convenience.

"Brianna?" Jake was beside her. She looked up, just barely able to see his eyes in the faint light spilling from the windows.

"What?"

He lowered his head and kissed her lightly. Pulling back, he brushed his thumb across her lower lip. "We need to get the first time out of the way."

"Like that first kiss," she said, her heart racing.

"Sort of." He brushed back her hair, pulled her into an embrace and kissed her again. This was like none of his other kisses. Now he was a man intent on seduction.

Brianna relished the sensations that swept through her. Her own mouth opened, and she leaned into the kiss. The cold was forgotten, the rain a memory. The only reality was Jake and his kiss.

He fumbled against her jacket, slipping his hand beneath the heavy fabric and seeking the soft weight of her breasts.

Heat and desire built. Brianna tilted her head back when he moved to kiss the pulse at the base of her throat.

"Let's go inside," he whispered.

"Yes," she responded. If this was his idea of getting that first time out of the way, he had her vote.

He ended the embrace as if reluctant to be parted for the short distance to their bedroom.

Brianna turned to the house just as she heard Jake's name being called. Nolan burst onto the porch.

"Jake, Shell's horse came back without its rider."

CHAPTER SIX

"WHEN?" JAKE ASKED. "What happened?" Brianna felt a clutch of fear. It couldn't be good news—Nolan looked too upset.

"Don't know when. Hank heard something and we tossed to see who'd go out to check on it. I lost. Found Shell's horse bumping against the corral door. He's soaked, so he's been in the rain for a while. I tied him up, didn't even take off the saddle. Came for you right away."

"Let's go." Jake jumped down from the porch and headed for the barn at a run, Brianna following as fast as she could.

"Could he have fallen?" she asked when she caught up with Jake as he stopped by the horse.

"Either that, or he didn't tie the horse and something spooked him. Horses usually head for home if they bolt." The gelding stood docilely in the drizzle, his saddle gleaming with moisture, his head hanging.

Jake spoke to the horse and ran his hands over him. He paused on one leg. "Scratched up pretty badly here. Must have stumbled and fallen. Might have thrown Shell if he wasn't paying attention."

"Figure we can find him tonight?" Nolan asked.

"I'm sure going to try. If he's injured, the weather won't help. Although, he could have been near the line cabin and found shelter."

Brianna didn't say anything, but even a city dweller knew of the dangers of exposure—especially if rain and cold temperatures played a part.

"What can I do?" she asked.

"Go get some blankets, a thermos of hot coffee and maybe one of soup if you can make it quick. I'm going to saddle up, get some rain gear and head out. He was going to the mesa, so with any luck, I'll find him."

Jake untied the reins and led the horse into the barn. He stopped and called Brianna, who'd already started for the house.

"Call Ormsby's place just to make sure Shell isn't there. The number's in the address book near the phone."

Brianna nodded and walked quickly to the back of the house. The warmth of the kitchen contrasted sharply with the cool night rain. She hoped Shell wasn't lying injured in the rain. He'd be freezing.

She hurried to start the coffee, then emptied some canned soup into a pan. It was a good thing she'd learned how to use the old stove.

"What's up?" Loni came into the kitchen.

Without thought, Brianna said, "Shell might be in trouble. Jake and the men are going out to look for him. Can you tell me where the thermoses are? Jake wants to take some hot stuff with them. Oh, and I need to call Ormsby to make sure he's not there."

"What do you mean in trouble? He was going up

to the line cabin and then on to Ormsby's,'' Loni said, her voice tight with fear.

"His horse came back without him and has an injured leg. Jake's afraid Shell is hurt somewhere.''

Loni gave a small cry. ''I'll call the Ormsbys. Thermoses are in the cupboard over the refrigerator.''

The coffee seemed to take forever to brew, but Brianna knew it couldn't be hurried. She filled the three thermoses she found with hot water, waiting until she could fill them with the soup and coffee.

Jake strode in, his shoulders damp, his hair glistening with water.

"It's almost ready,'' Brianna said.

"He's not at Ormsby's,'' Loni added, joining them. ''Carl said he hasn't seen him in weeks. Jake, he'll be okay, won't he?''

"He's probably walking home now, cursing that blasted horse every step,'' Jake said. ''We're taking an extra mount so he can ride the rest of the way. I need to get my slicker and cell phone.''

In only moments, he was ready to leave, the thermoses tucked firmly under his arm. Brianna and Loni stood on the back porch, watching Nolan and Jake head out, a third horse led by Jake. Hank was standing by in case Jake needed more help later.

"He'll be okay. Shell's really savvy about the range,'' Loni said, watching long after the men had disappeared from view.

Brianna gently turned her toward the house. ''He'll be fine, and even better when his dad catches up with him. Come inside—you'll get a chill.''

"I just…I can't believe anything would happen to him," Loni said, looking over her shoulder worriedly.

"You know Jake will do his best for Shell. We may all be worried for nothing."

They kept vigil in the kitchen for hours. Finally Brianna was able to convince Loni to go to bed. She promised to call her the moment she heard anything.

Brianna went up to Shell's room and turned down the bed, just for something to do. She kept a kettle of water just below a boil, fixing herself a cup of tea, and hoping every noise she heard was Jake returning.

Once she flung a jacket over her shoulders and dashed to the bunkhouse. The rain had grown stronger and could no longer be called a drizzle. Hank was awake, watching an old movie on TV. He looked up.

"They back?" he asked, rising.

"No, I just wanted to see if there was anything else I could do. Waiting's so hard."

"Not anything either of us can do. If they need the truck, I'll head out. But Jake hasn't called."

"Want any coffee or anything?" Brianna asked.

"Naw, thanks, anyway. I have some here but I'm getting plumb tired of it."

She returned to the house looking in the direction Jake and Nolan had ridden, hoping to hear sounds of their return. But all she heard was the rain pounding the eaves.

Around two, Brianna was so tired she lay her head on the kitchen table. Some wedding night, she thought tiredly. Who would have expected her to spend it alone, worrying about her new stepson? She closed her eyes....

"Brianna?"

She opened her eyes and slowly sat up. She felt stiff. Jake was standing beside her, his slicker dripping on the floor.

"Shell?" she asked, realizing they'd returned.

"We found him. Hank's getting the truck ready. I'm taking Shell to the hospital. I think he'll be fine. He was tossed when the horse stumbled on some rocks. Knocked him out for a while. I think he's broken his arm, too, but he's arguing about that. Go on up to bed. We're all fine, or will be as soon as we get him to the hospital."

"I can go with you," she said.

"No need. Go to bed. I'll be back as soon as I can."

"Drive safely, then. The roads will be slick."

Amusement danced in his eyes as he looked at her. "Yes, ma'am."

"I'll worry."

"That's a novelty. Anyway, riding at night on rain-slick hills is more dangerous than county roads," he said. Leaning over, Jake kissed her lightly. His lips were cool. Brianna wished he'd lingered long enough for them to warm. But she blinked, and he was gone. She turned off the kettle, set the kitchen to rights, and then went to bed. At least Shell was safe and reasonably whole.

When Brianna woke some time later, she wasn't alone. Jake was beside her, asleep. His arm was over her waist, pinning her to the bed. His face was half-buried in the pillow. The side she could see looked more relaxed in sleep than she'd seen before, though still with that rugged look she found so appealing.

His hair needed a trim. Now it looked like a kid's—poking out every which way. Not that he seemed to care.

Suddenly he opened his eyes.

"Shell?" she asked, turning and feeling his heat beneath the sheet and blankets. Their first morning together. Talking about things in bed. It felt surreal.

"Slight concussion, a broken arm, wrenched shoulder, bruised ribs and hip. But he'll be fine."

"Oh, sure, he's probably out riding the range right now."

"He better not be!"

"What time did you get home?"

"A couple of hours ago."

"How late is it?" She looked around for a clock, but couldn't find one. His arm tightened slightly against her waist.

"First time I saw you last week I thought you were too thin." His hand trailed over her ribs. "You need to put on some weight—especially with winter coming." His thumb rested on the side of her breast.

Brianna caught her breath, her eyes drawn to his.

"With any luck, I'm sure I'll be bigger than either of us can imagine in a few months' time."

"With any luck." He kissed her, his hand sliding down her body, finding the hem of her nightgown and easing it up. When bare palm met bare leg, Brianna felt the jolt to her toes.

She tried to relax, but the blood was already rushing through her veins. Jake's mouth was doing wonderful things. The attraction that had flared into desire the first day she saw him grew and filled her every cell. It seemed right, as if she'd been waiting her entire life for this man....

PURE BLISS, she thought dreamily as she savored the afterglow of their lovemaking, the lethargy, the warmth, the drifting between waking and sleep. It hadn't been the wedding night she'd thought she'd have, but their marriage was truly consummated now.

"Are you all right?" Jake asked.

Brianna nodded. She wanted to say something, but wasn't sure what. Would he make a comment about their new status? There had been no words of love, of commitment. She hadn't expected any.

"Good." He lay beside her, pulling her close and drawing the sheet and blankets back over them. Brianna nestled her head against his shoulder, feeling safe and cherished. *And so a marriage starts,* she thought as she drifted back to sleep. Had their family started, as well?

When she awoke again, Jake was gone. Moving her hand to his pillow, she could feel the warmth. He hadn't been up for long. She decided she ought to get up, too. There was no telling how late it was.

Gathering her things, she dashed to the bathroom— only to find the door firmly shut. She could hear the shower running. Was Jake in there? She considered opening the door to join him, but she wasn't that daring.

A few minutes later Jake came back to their room. He seemed surprised to find Brianna awake, sitting up in bed.

"What time is it?" she asked. "We need to get a clock for the bedroom."

"After one. I want to get some work in before it gets too late."

"One in the afternoon?" She jumped up. "Good grief, we slept the day away."

"Which is why I need to get going."

"It's still raining."

He nodded. "Ranching doesn't stop because of the rain."

"How's Shell?"

"I checked before I took a shower. He's still sleeping. The doc gave him painkillers and antibiotics. Sleep is the best thing for him right now."

"Do you want me to fix you something to eat?" Brianna asked, feeling self-conscious in the nightgown she'd hastily pulled on before heading to the bathroom. Jake was fully dressed. It was more intimate than she expected, sharing a room with a husband. Having a casual conversation as if they'd been doing this for years.

"I'll grab something on the way out. See you at dinner." He hesitated at the door, then left.

Brianna wished he'd said something to bridge the awkwardness. Or maybe she should have—but what?

BY THE TIME dinner was ready, Brianna had convinced herself she was comfortable with the change from guest to lady of the house. Loni had deferred to her regarding choices for dinner, a change from yesterday. But when the men trooped in, Brianna felt awkward.

Shell had been in his room most of the day, so she was surprised to see him join them. His left arm was in a cast, and he walked a bit more deliberately than normal.

"Can I get you anything, Shell?" Loni asked quietly.

"Nothing special. I'll have what everyone else is having."

It soon became apparent that he would need help cutting his roast beef. When Loni moved to take his plate, he asked Jake to do it.

"I feel like a blasted two-year-old," he grumbled. The bruise on his forehead was purple and nasty-looking. Brianna wondered if he should even be up, but after that comment decided not to ask. He was a grown man, after all.

"Tell us what happened to you yesterday," Nolan said once the first inroads into the meal had been made.

"Fool horse shied at something. I never saw what. It was up in some shale when he slipped and I got tossed off like some rank tenderfoot."

Brianna thought he should be thankful he was in as good shape as he was. When she glanced at Jake, she saw his concern. But he kept quiet and she took her cue from him. More things to get used to, she thought.

After dinner, Jake said he was going to the office. Shell joined him. That left Loni and Brianna in the kitchen to do the dishes.

"I hope he's going to be okay, but he's so stubborn he'd never tell anyone if he wasn't feeling fine," Loni said, plunging her hands into the soapy water.

"Shell?"

"Of course. Guys have to be so macho about things. Stoic and all."

"I've heard most men make terrible patients. I trust Jake questioned the doctor. He'll be fine."

Loni nodded, and Brianna watched in surprise as the girl's eyes filled with tears.

Brianna stopped drying and put her hand on her shoulder. "Are you okay?"

Loni nodded and tried to smile. "It's hormones. I don't have any reason not to be terrific."

"It was scary," Brianna offered.

"Things like that happen on a ranch. Why he couldn't—" She stopped abruptly. "Never mind. I can't wait to get out of here!"

"It'll happen soon enough," Brianna murmured.

"Did you tell your friends about me?" Loni asked.

Brianna nodded.

"You don't think they'd mind showing me the ropes in New York, do you? I expect to sell some paintings right away, so I'll have some money. Maybe they can tell me the best place to look for an apartment."

"They'll be happy to show you around, introduce

you to other friends. You can tell them all about my move to the wilds of Wyoming.''

"But not how crazy I think you are," Loni said with a small grin.

"Oh, I don't know. They thought I was totally nuts when I left. Your view will only convince them they were right," Brianna said with a grin of her own.

"Should I tell them you're happily married?" Loni asked with a sly sidelong look at Brianna.

Brianna felt her face flush as she remembered making love with Jake that morning. She was truly married. And happy enough so far, or at least content.

"Absolutely." She wasn't sure her friends would believe it, but it would go a long way to reassure them she'd made the right decision.

Loni went to her room after they finished in the kitchen. At loose ends, Brianna headed for the office. Shell was sitting opposite his father, his legs stretched out in front of him. Jake was behind the desk, several stacks of paper in front of him. He looked up when Brianna appeared in the door.

"Do you need something?"

"Not really. I came to see what you were doing. Am I interrupting?"

"No." Shell stood. "You two probably want to be alone. I'm heading for bed, anyway. Another night's sleep, and I'll be ready for work in the morning."

"Take some time off," Jake suggested.

"I'd go crazy sitting around the house all day. I'll be careful and won't use my left hand. I don't need a nursemaid." Cutting off any argument, he left.

"He proves what I've always heard. Men don't make good patients." She crossed to the desk and glanced at the mess. "Bills?"

"Invoices, estimated tax forms and a few forms the government requires of ranchers. I hate paperwork."

"It's a necessary part of the business, I guess."

Jake nodded.

She perched on the edge of the desk and studied him. "If you work outside all day and work here all evening, when do you have time for other things?"

"Like?"

"Visiting with friends, going to the movies, watching TV or a hobby or something."

"When I get the place in the black, there'll be time enough for other things."

"I could help."

"How?"

"Doing this." She waved her hand at the of paperwork.

"I'm managing."

"You should automate."

"When I get around to it."

"I'm used to computers. Did a lot of cost analyses for the projects I headed up and a lot of projections for increased revenues. I'm not an accountant, but I do understand profit and loss and I could help with the accounts. Plus, I brought my laptop with me. If you explained the forms, maybe I could do them, as well. I could do it during the day and let you have some free time at night."

"Out of the question," Jake said firmly.

"Why?"

"I didn't bring you out here to keep the books."

"No, you brought me here to be a broodmare."

"Not that, exactly." He looked almost embarrassed.

"It's exactly like that. Well, let me tell you, Jake Marshall, I'm not going to sit around and do nothing for nine months even if I do get pregnant right away. If you don't want me helping you here, I'll find work in town or start my own business. Otherwise I'll go bonkers, and what kind of mother would that be for your precious heir?"

"I thought you were going to fix up the house," he said.

"Within reason. However, even if I spend a week on every room in the place, that'll take what, a couple of months? Gee, that'll be rewarding."

"If you wanted to work so much, you should have stayed in New York."

"I couldn't—" She stopped. Damn, she shouldn't have said that.

He went on alert, his eyes narrowed as he studied her.

"You *couldn't?*"

"Not and find someone to marry and have children with," she said quickly, hoping he'd not push the issue. "And anyway, I'm married to you now. The question is not about working in New York, but working here. You can't expect me to sit around and do nothing all day!"

He leaned back in his chair and rubbed his hand

over his face. "No, I guess not. I hate to stick you with the paperwork, though."

"I won't mind. Just because you hate doing it doesn't mean everyone else does. I'll see how it goes. If you don't like how I do it, I'll stop. Then you can take it back over—but I really think you'll like what I do." She hoped she could talk enough to get him to forget her slip.

"I'll try it for a month," he slowly. "There is a program I used down in Texas that's perfect for ranching operations."

"Tell me the name and I'll get it. Then I can get started as soon as it's loaded on my computer."

He gave her the name of the program and then said, "At the end of the month, I'll review everything and we'll reassess."

"Fine. You want to start explaining things right now?"

Jake shook his head, standing. "Right now, I want to take you to bed. We didn't get our wedding night."

"We had the morning after," she said, once again feeling the sexual tension build. When he stepped closer, it was all she could do to refrain from grabbing his hand and running for their bedroom. She'd had other lovers in her life—not many—but she'd never felt like this with any of them.

He cradled her head in his rough hands and tilted her face up to his, studying every inch of her skin, her eyes. "So we did. But I want a long dark night with just the two of us, no interruptions, no demands, nothing but you and me."

She gripped his wrists, feeling his pulse with one hand. It was pounding almost as fast as hers.

"Then let's go to bed, Mr. Marshall."

"I thought you'd never ask, Mrs. Marshall." He lowered his head to kiss her.

CHAPTER SEVEN

BRIANNA SNEEZED a second time. The dust she was trying to dispel had had years to accumulate. No reason to think she'd be able to clear it in one swipe. She surveyed the living room. The curtains had been taken down—almost dissolving in her hands they were so old. She'd bundled them into the trash. The windows would have to wait, though their dust-covered panes blocked a lot of the sunlight.

She tackled the last of the shelves, sneezing once again. The task would have been more fun if Loni had kept her company, but the girl had wandered off to her studio to paint. She wanted to build her portfolio, she explained to Brianna, so she'd have enough for a showing.

Brianna switched on the vacuum again and cleaned another portion of the faded carpet. Her mind wasn't on her work, but on Jake. Last night had been so exhilarating.

"And then took off at first light like it was a one-night-stand," she muttered, annoyed all over again.

Any thought of cuddling and becoming better acquainted had disappeared when he got up, dressed and headed out to the barn.

Granted, Brianna knew he had work to do, but a few more minutes with his new wife wouldn't change much—at least not on the ranch. But it would make a world of difference to Brianna.

"You knew how it would be," she reminded herself as she switched off the vacuum. "It's only been a week."

"What's only been a week?" Shell asked, leaning against the doorframe watching her.

Brianna swung around. "You startled me."

He shrugged. "Where's Loni?"

"Painting."

"What's only been a week?" he repeated.

"My being here."

"Do you talk to yourself a lot?"

Brianna nodded.

Shell took in the changes in the room. "It looks cleaner," he offered.

Brianna surveyed her work. "There's so much to be done. I want to paint the room a soft cream, with country-blue trim. Get a new carpet and see if the furniture can be professionally cleaned. If not, then I want new furniture."

"Yeah, well, don't hold your breath. We can't even get the hay we need to carry us through the winter. I don't see Jake springing for new furniture—especially when we never use this room."

"You probably don't use it because it's so awful. Once it's fixed up, you'll love it."

Shell shrugged, his eyes mocking. "Maybe he's not into spending a fortune just to placate his new wife."

Brianna squelched a hot retort. It was important that she fit in. Antagonizing Jake's son wasn't going to help. She took a breath and nodded. ''I'll ask him about it.'' Then she eyed him curiously. ''Is your arm feeling better?''

''It's okay.''

''Aches?''

He nodded once.

''But your other arm is fine. You could help me move the furniture, couldn't you?''

He raised his eyebrows, then slowly amusement replaced the mockery. ''If I wanted to, I sure could, *Mom*.''

Brianna blinked, then laughed softly. ''I don't think so, bucko. 'Brianna' will do just fine. Grab the end of this sofa and help me move it over to the window.''

For the next hour Shell helped Brianna clean the living room. She felt he spent the entire time studying her, but she was glad for the help and didn't challenge his quiet assessment.

''Damn, that's the third nail I've broken this morning,'' Brianna said studying her fingertip. She nibbled the edge, trying to round it. Glancing up, she caught Shell's stare.

''What?''

''You're not what I figured you'd be,'' he said, sitting on the arm of the club chair he'd just moved for her. ''I figured a city woman who would harp on the lack of things to do around here, like theater and clothes shopping. And turn tail and flee the first time she had to do anything like work.''

"City women keep house, too, you know. I worked hard in New York, didn't spend my day sitting around doing nothing."

"After work, then."

She thought back to the long days she'd put in at the ad agency, the weekends spent traveling, meeting with clients. Nights had been for sleeping for the most part, or catching up. The weekends she didn't travel had been spent shopping for food, doing laundry and trying to make time for Steven. How had she become so consumed by work that she let all the wonderful things New York had to offer slip by?

She dusted her hands. "You know what, Shell? I'm taking the rest of the day off. We've got a good start on this room. I'll fix lunch, then read a book until time for dinner." With that, she turned and left. She didn't have to cram her entire future into one day. The rooms would wait. The chores would always be there. Time to take care of herself.

Relax, slow down, that was what the doctor had told her. She'd delayed long enough. Time to put her new lifestyle in action.

Reading proved harder to do than she'd expected, though. She'd pulled a porch chair closer to the wall of the house to shelter her from the cool breeze, but the book couldn't hold her attention. She kept thinking of all she'd given up by focusing on her career. The damage to her own health was only one result. It was time she made an effort to enjoy the everyday things around her.

JAKE STEPPED into the kitchen and stopped at the door. Loni was setting the table. Brianna stood by the stove, stirring something in a large pot, her face flushed with the heat. He took a breath, startled at the desire that hit him. He wanted to cross the room and turn her to face him. To kiss those rosy lips, bury his face in that sweet-smelling, silky hair. To feel her soft curves against him. And take her up to bed—to hell with dinner.

Dammit, he hadn't felt like this since he was a randy teenager.

"Hi, Jake," Loni said, watching him curiously.

He nodded a greeting, eyes on Brianna as she looked up. Her smile let loose a new flood of feelings. He knew so little about her, but liked what he did know. He was dirty and dusty from riding all day. But he felt a surge of energy at the thought of the two of them in bed together.

"Hi. Dinner will be ready soon," Brianna said. "You have time for a quick shower. Want me to come up with you?"

He glanced at Loni, then back to Brianna. "If you want." They didn't have time to make love before dinner. But he'd enjoy the novelty of her company while he was changing.

"Do you mind if I leave the rest with you?" she asked Loni.

"I can manage. Go visit with Jake."

"The sauce is all ready."

"I can manage, Brianna. I'll dump the spaghetti into the boiling water when I hear the shower stop."

Almost afraid to look at her as they walked up the stairs, Jake could smell the light flowery fragrance she always wore. It reminded him of last night. Not that he needed any stimuli to remember. He'd relived those hours all day long.

"Shell helped me clean the living room," she said.

"So he took the day off, after all," Jake returned. "I thought he was going out with Hank." He pushed open the door to his room—their room—and allowed Brianna to precede him. She brushed by him as she did so. Deliberately?

"His arm was aching. Riding jarred it too much, I think. Anyway, his good arm was strong enough to help me move furniture." She turned and looked at Jake. "He's going to help me paint the room in a day or two. If that's okay with you? Can you spare him from the outside work for a little while? I think he plans to ask you himself. I can't figure out if he wants you to say okay or no, which would give him an out."

Jake shrugged out of his shirt and tossed it to the floor of the closet, adding to the pile already there. "He'd tell you if he didn't want to help. We're pushing to get everything done before the weather changes, so he'll be asking to know if I can spare him, that's all." Jake pulled off his boots, longing to just lie down on the bed. Last night hadn't exactly been conducive to sleep.

Brianna settled on the bed, bunching up the pillows behind her back and leaning against the headboard. "Can you?"

He'd lost the thread of conversation. Could he what? Kiss her? Make love to her again?

"What?"

"Spare Shell. Isn't that what we're talking about?"

Jake nodded, heading for the shower before he gave in to his baser instincts.

Brianna was still on the bed when Jake returned minutes later, a towel wrapped around his waist. He'd forgotten to take clean clothes into the bathroom with him. Now what? Get dressed with Brianna watching?

"If you're shy, I can leave," she said, her eyes brimming with amusement.

"Not shy," he replied, letting the towel drop.

He heard Brianna's breath catch. The sound sent a surge of heat just where he didn't need it. But it was too late. He wanted her. Dinner could wait; he couldn't.

He knelt on the bed and tugged her body gently until she was supine.

"Dinner?" she whispered, her fingertips already making designs on his arms.

"The good thing about spaghetti is it gets better and better the longer the sauce simmers. They'll save us some." He leaned closer and kissed her. Instantly Jake forgot they were supposed to be trying to make a baby. He could think only of Brianna and the pleasure he wanted to bring her—and the pleasure she'd surely give him.

IT WAS PITCH-BLACK. Brianna stared into the night, wondering what time it was. They hadn't made it to supper. But it had been hours since she'd eaten, and she was hungry. Could she slip out of bed without waking him? She knew he was tired. After last night and tonight, Jake needed his rest.

Slowly, stealthily, she eased over to the edge of the mattress.

"Going somewhere?" A lazy voice came from beside her.

"I'm starving," she said, leaning over to switch on the bedside lamp.

His towel was still beside the bed. Her clothes were scattered everywhere. Brianna let herself remember his kisses, his caresses and the wild explosion of sensations he'd created. If she ate quickly, she might be back before he dozed off again.

"I'll get up, too. I skipped lunch," Jake said, flinging back the covers.

The cold night air hastened their dressing, and in moments, they were headed for the kitchen.

Loni had left it spotless, but Brianna found the leftover spaghetti and sauce and quickly heated them. The French bread was gone, not surprising since she remembered how much the men liked bread.

Jake didn't speak as they ate, but Brianna didn't care. The food was delicious. She savored every bite.

When their hunger had been sated, she said, "I tried to make sense of your accounting system today."

He seemed to withdraw. "And?"

"It's confusing. The ledgers are not set up the way I would have done them. Do you mind if I simplify things?"

He shrugged. "Just don't lose anything."

"Shell said you need money for hay."

"We'll manage."

"I have—"

"No!"

She knew his views on her helping financially, but there was such a thing as stupid pride. Was there a way to do it without his knowing? Or without risking his ownership of the ranch? She made a mental note to check into that.

"What do you want to name the baby?" she asked.

Jake blinked. "A bit premature, isn't it?"

"Just wondering. You didn't get input into Shell's name. I thought you might have something in mind."

"I haven't thought about it."

"Me, neither, but maybe we should." She finished the last of the spaghetti. If she hadn't become ill and Steven had proposed, she would have accepted, not realizing until it was too late that he didn't want children. She shivered, thinking how she might never have had the family she longed for.

"Cold?" he asked. "I'm finished. We'll let the dishes soak and head back to bed," Jake said

"It won't take two seconds to do them. I don't want Loni to face a dirty sink in the morning," Brianna said, rising to carry their plates to the sink. "You go on up, I'll be along once I'm done."

"I'll wait."

Brianna glimpsed his reflection in the window over the sink. He was watching her. She quickly washed their dishes and utensils, conscious of his attention. It was as if they were an old married couple, spending a quiet evening in the kitchen, content with each other's company. The reality was so different.

THE NEXT MORNING Brianna and Loni headed for town to buy paint and the paraphernalia needed for the living room.

"Don't know why you're bothering—no one'll use it," Loni said, obviously in a cranky mood. "The men like their place in the bunkhouse, Jake disappears into the office every night, and Shell spends his free time in his bedroom."

"That's because the living room's so awful. Once it's fixed up, they'll want to spend time there, because it'll be nice. Especially if I put in a TV," Brianna said.

"I'll never stay home in the evening when I move to New York. I'll find a coffeehouse and hang out there once my painting's finished for the day. Or a trendy bar. Once I start having showings, I'll have to appear at the galleries to satisfy my fans."

Brianna smiled, remembering how much trouble Steven had with some artists showing up for the opening of a new exhibit. They simply refused to leave their ateliers, so he'd had to make up excuses. Sounded as if Loni, however, was more interested in the social aspect of painting than the art itself, but maybe she misjudged the girl. Hadn't she wanted more when she'd been nineteen?

"Tell me more about the Village," Loni said.

"I'm getting tried of talking about New York all

the time. You tell me more about Sweetwater. That was the deal, we swap information.''

''I know, but there's nothing to tell about this backwater,'' Loni whined. ''You've seen it. What's to know?''

''Then tell me about the neighboring ranches and the people who live on them. Tell me what you know about cattle and beef prices, and the cost of hay. What do people do for fun in town? Are there church socials or things like that?''

''My mother and my aunts are really into that kind of stuff. Typical rancher's wives. You'll fit right in.'' With a theatrical sigh, Loni began to talk about the ranches in the area.

They stopped at the post office when they first reached town. Loni glanced out the window, then hunched down in her seat. ''That's my aunt Maggie going in. I'll wait here for you.''

Brianna gathered the envelopes to be posted and headed inside. She checked their postbox, gathered all the bills, flyers, catalogs and journals. It had been several days since anyone had picked up the mail. Heading back to the car, arms full, she was intercepted by a middle-aged woman with brown hair. Her face was friendly.

''I'm Maggie Sorenson. You're Jake Marshall's new wife, aren't you?'' the woman said.

''How do you do,'' Brianna said, smiling politely. ''That's right, I'm Brianna Dawson—I mean, Marshall.''

''Loni with you?''

"In the car."

"She's my niece. Have she and that Shell made up yet?"

Brianna shook her head.

"That girl needs a reality check. What's she planning to do with a baby on her own, and her with no job? He's a nice enough boy, though her folks are a mite set against him because of his mother. But if they saw her happy with him, they'd come around. You tell her that, will you?"

"If you think it'll help."

"Probably not. She's always been a stubborn girl. She doing okay with the pregnancy?"

"Fine, I think. She and I aren't close, you know. We just met a week or so ago," Brianna said.

Maggie fumbled in her purse, coming up with a notepad. She scribbled on it for a moment, then tore off a page and handed it to Brianna. "This is my home phone. Let me know if I can do anything. And call me when the baby comes, will you?"

"Okay."

"Welcome to Sweetwater, Brianna. Hope to see you around." With that, Maggie left, glancing at the SUV where Loni was, but moving away from the post office without stopping.

"I met your aunt," Brianna said when she got in. Dumping the mail in the space between them, she looked at Loni. "She seems nice."

"She is. Did she ask about me?" Loni wanted to know. She sounded hopeful.

"Yes, she did. And she thinks you should marry Shell."

"If she does, she's the only one in the family. My folks would have a hissy fit if I did."

"They'd rather you be a single mother?"

"No, they want me to give the baby up. Which I'm thinking of doing. It would be too hard to go to New York with a baby. How would I manage?"

Brianna said nothing. The irony of the situation was almost too much. She wanted a baby, wanted to start a family. So much so that she'd traveled thousands of miles to marry a stranger. Here Loni was pregnant by a man she obviously had feelings for, and yet she was thinking of giving up her baby.

Brianna suspected Shell would want to raise his son or daughter—which seemed to Brianna to be the best solution. At least the child would have its father's love and commitment.

After buying the paint and brushes and other things she needed at the hardware store, Brianna stopped at the library. She quickly found the agricultural section and stocked up on several books that looked easy enough to understand, while providing the information she wanted about basic ranching practices.

That afternoon, after sorting and putting in order all the bills she could find, she began to input the information in the new accounting program. It was mindless work, but important. Once everything was in, she could draft a profit-and-loss report. Then Jake would have a better idea of exactly where he stood and what needed to be done next. She had a vested interest, after all. The ranch would one day belong partly to her child.

Dreamily Brianna leaned back in the chair. Could she already be pregnant? Could a baby be growing beneath her heart at this very moment?

If not, it wasn't for lack of trying.

Was that all it meant to Jake? Trying to have a baby? She hoped their lovemaking meant more. It was starting to mean more to her.

She sat up abruptly. No! It didn't mean anything beyond the chance to make a baby. True, he was the most thrilling lover she'd ever had, but it was the novelty of the situation, that was all. She refused to fall for a man who'd made it clear love wasn't in the picture. A comfortable relationship—that was what she wanted. Nothing more.

Attacking the stack of invoices with a vengeance, she tried to quell her wayward thoughts.

LONI HEARD the laughter when she entered the house. She'd been painting and wanted a break. The sound of voices came from the living room. She recognized Shell's deep tone. And Brianna's soft one.

For a moment jealousy struck her. Brianna had spent a lot of time with Shell since she'd bought the paint three days ago. They worked several hours each day on the living room, and it was starting to look lovely, just as Brianna had predicted.

But it was the time with Shell that Loni envied. Not that she wanted to spend so much time with him. But since his announcement at the courthouse, he'd either ignored her or went out of his way to avoid her.

She had always been used to his attention. Used to his eyes following her when she worked. Used to his trying to be alone with her. She'd loved him so much—until she'd gotten pregnant. He'd ruined all her plans.

Shell could have spent some time with her. With his broken arm, he wasn't riding much these days. He could have visited her in the studio. Sat with her after dinner. But no, he spent the time with Brianna.

She walked down the hall, pausing at the door to watch. The walls were freshly painted, and the trim was almost completed. Brianna was standing in the middle of the room, shaking her head and laughing. Shell had paint in his hair, on his face and on his shirt.

"I hope you rope cows better than you paint," Brianna said.

"I'm doing this one-handed. Give me a break." Shell turned, threatening Brianna with his brush. He caught sight of Loni and stopped, his expression closing instantly. He turned back around and finished the bit of trim he was working on.

"I'll be out of here soon," he said abruptly.

Loni met Brianna's eye when the older woman looked to see what had caused Shell's change.

"Hi, Loni, what's up?"

"I came to see what you were doing," she said. "It looks nice." It hurt to have Shell shut her out.

"I've about decided to junk this furniture, or at least store it in the attic or something," Brianna said. "I thought getting it cleaned would work, but sitting on it is like sitting on concrete. I want something comfy to sink into at the end of the day.''

"Jake isn't one to coddle himself," Shell murmured.

"And you are?" Brianna teased.

"Might give it a try," Shell said.

"Great! You can come shopping with me. Test out the furniture so I can get a man's point of view."

"Get Jake."

"Right, I can just imagine him giving up his ranch work for a day and going to town to sit in a bunch of different chairs," Brianna said.

Shell glanced at her. "He might if you asked. But I'll do it if he won't."

Loni felt another pang of jealousy that he'd do something for Brianna. It was childish of her. She'd told him she didn't want him, so why begrudge him happiness because he took her at her word?

"Want to help?" Brianna asked Loni.

Loni was surprised to realize she did want to help. But more, she wanted to be included. She was lonely. While that might be the fate of a famous artist—look at Shell's grandmother, she'd been alone much of her life—Loni liked to be with people.

"Sure." She glanced at Shell, but he ignored her. Still, it was better to be in the same room with him being ignored than alone in her studio. She smiled at Brianna. "Where do I start? I'm a painter—I think I can do better than Shell."

CHAPTER EIGHT

THREE WEEKS LATER the redecorating project was almost finished. Jake had not gone to test the furniture, but Shell had. Brianna felt she was making progress getting to know the younger man. Though he was still quiet and self-contained, he talked more readily, and once or twice even made a joke.

But it was Jake who continued to fascinate Brianna. He remained distant by day, warm and loving by night. It was as if once the lights went out, he morphed into someone else. She wished she could capture some of that closeness during the daylight hours, but until then, she would cherish the nights.

Being held in his arms, as she was now, was special. She felt desirable and feminine. But she wanted more. More than just fabulous nights of passion and sex. She wanted to feel they were drawing closer as a couple, as a family.

"So tell me what exactly it is you did today," she said. "Since you've been short a man with Shell out of commission, things might be piling up. I want to go out with you at least once while the weather is still nice. Can I help somehow?"

He had come home tired and hungry, just in time

for dinner with the rest of the men. Once finished, he and she had spent the evening going over accounts in the office, talking politely as strangers. Now they were alone in bed, and she wanted to talk.

Jake had gradually revealed some of his hopes for the ranch over the past few nights. Giving voice to his dreams wasn't easy, she could tell.

"You can't do what Shell does," Jake said in response to her plea to join him. "He works hard enough for two men. His arm is better. Only a few more weeks and the cast'll be off."

"I wouldn't try to replace him, just help out if I can. Or at least go out and see what you do all day. Besides, I want to see all of the place I'm calling home," she said, her hand resting on his chest. Idly she trailed her fingers back and forth over the heated skin. Surely she could do *some*thing—it might strengthen their relationship. Brianna wanted to belong in the worst way and was frustrated because she still felt like an outsider.

Jake was silent for a long moment, then gave his characteristic curt nod as his fingers captured hers.

"We saddle up at dawn."

"I know that. I've been the one making your breakfast, in case you've forgotten." Loni was sleeping in later these days. A sign she was drawing nearer delivery?

He gathered Brianna closer. "Actually you'd be surprised what I remember. Loni will have to clean up after breakfast, then—I don't want to wait. Tomorrow I'm heading for the farthest part, so I want an early start. I'll make one last check of fencing and water holes before winter. Rain is predicted next week. And snow won't be far behind. Some years we've had it by now. So if you're determined to go, now is the best time. Once you get pregnant, no riding.''

"Give me a break. Women can still do things while they're pregnant.''

"If they're used to riding and all, sure, but you're not. And we wouldn't want to risk the baby.''

"Yes, boss,'' she said sassily.

"I thought you had plenty to do with painting every room in the house and doing the accounts,'' Jake said. "Why the sudden desire to ride out?''

"It's not so sudden. I want to see more of the ranch.''

"Why?'' His voice was suspicious.

"Why not? This is my home, too, isn't it? I'd like to see all of it. And see the cattle, the fencing that takes so much work, and maybe get to know my husband a little better.'' She said the last in a rush, as if worried about revealing too much.

"To better assess the ranch's value?''

She needn't have feared his reaction to her personal comment. He was too focused on the blasted ranch.

"I'm not calculating your net worth. I can figure that out by looking at the books. And right now, I'm more solvent than you are,'' she said with some asperity.

"Right now most of the world is. But that'll change once the ranch is mine.''

"But not for a while. According to Shell, it'll take

a few years of good luck to pull this place out of the red.''

"Then that's what we'll have. Been talking about the ranch to Shell?'' His hand covered her waist as if staking a claim.

"We talk while he helps me out. What's going to happen with him and Loni?''

"I'm hoping the baby will bring them together,'' he said slowly.

Brianna was surprised. "Jake, she's planning to go to New York once the baby's born.

"What?'' He sat up, dragging the covers with him. "When did she tell you that? I thought she just wanted to move to town.''

"She's been pestering me about New York since I arrived. Apparently your grandmother told her she had talent, and she's convinced she's the next great American painter.''

"She can paint here. We've given her free use of Elsa's studio.''

"She seems set on going to New York,'' Brianna said.

"That's dumb. She doesn't know anyone there. She'd never make it. Heck, I don't even think she has enough money to get there, much less find a place to stay or a job.'' He was quiet a few seconds, then turned to lean over her, resting on his elbow. "Wait a minute. You haven't encouraged this, have you?''

"No. Well, not exactly.''

"What does that mean?''

"I mentioned her to a few friends, and they've of-

fered to help her out if she moves there. I didn't en-
courage her—she didn't need any encouragement.
She's bound and determined to leave Sweetwater.''

"Dammit! She's nineteen. She'll never make it in
New York or any other big city, despite what you've
led her to believe. Are your friends prepared to take
care of her? A young girl could get into a lot of trouble
on her own. Stop feeding her ideas!''

Brianna wished she hadn't brought the subject up.
But she wasn't one to back down when she'd done
nothing wrong.

"You left home at a younger age, and I was on my
own when I was nineteen. She'll make it if she wants
to.''

"Maybe. I thought once the baby came, she'd
change her mind. What's she planning to do—dump
the baby on Shell?'' Jake asked in an ominous tone.

"Actually she's mentioned adoption—for a couple
to take the baby.''

"Shell would have something to say to that! He's
the father. He has some rights. And I'm damn sure he
wants to be a part of his kid's life. If only to make up
for my being absent from his. At least he has that
choice. I never knew he had even been conceived until
he was fifteen years old.''

Brianna reached out, wishing she could assuage the
sorrow she heard in his voice. She rested her palm
against his chest, feeling the steady pounding of his
heart. She breathed in the scent of him. Only a few
moments ago they'd been as close as two humans
could ever be physically. She wanted to capture that

closeness emotionally, as well. Instead, it seemed as if she'd just made him angry and sad both at the same time. She wished she could change things.

Was she falling in love with Jake Marshall?

Only a few months ago she'd thought she'd loved Steven.

Or had that been just habit? Not once could she remember a time when he'd made her feel half as feminine and exciting as Jake did every night. Nor caused her to want to smooth things out for him.

"Tell me," she said softly.

He eased back down on the pillows, keeping her close as if he needed to be touching her. "His mother was Shelly Bluefeather. She was a senior with me in high school. We were a couple that last year. She was fun, lively and smart. She had plans to go to college on a scholarship. She wanted to become a lawyer and help her people."

He fell silent, lost in thought. Brianna felt a small prick of envy. No convenient relationship for some future goal, just the two of them as a couple. Had he been attentive, fun to be with? She remembered him from the summers on the Garretson ranch. A wild and randy cowboy. He'd changed a lot over the years.

"And then?"

"We became more than friends. But I wasn't staying. My grandmother made my life here hellish. I was counting the days until I graduated. In fact, I would have cut out earlier, except for Shelly. She persuaded me to graduate. 'At least have that diploma,' she'd say over and over."

"So you graduated and left?" Brianna said.

"Yeah, left the day after. I worked some different ranches for a while—mostly to get the entry fees for the rodeo circuit. That's why I was on the Garretson spread those summers you came to visit."

"Shelly got pregnant and never told you?" Brianna thought if nothing else the woman should have asked him for child support. Seeing the efforts he made now, the overtures he made toward Shell, Jake would have honored his responsibilities to his son. He would have enjoyed watching him grow, sharing his values and standards. Heck, he probably would have married Shelly and given her and Shell a home.

"She never told me. I don't know why. At first maybe it was because she didn't know how to find me. I came home when my dad died, saw her briefly. I guess Shell was about five. I didn't meet him then. She never said a word. People in town must have known, but no one ever said a word. She told Shell the truth just before she died. Told him that she never wanted to tie anyone down. Hell, she was the one who ended up tied down. Never went to college like she wanted. Ended up waiting tables. Just another Native who didn't get to live her dreams. She should have told me!"

"I agree. She should have told you. I'm sorry you didn't get to see Shell grow up."

"Yeah. Me, too. I'll do things differently with our baby. You won't have to worry about that."

"You'll make a great father, Jake. I'm not worried a bit."

Well, maybe just a little, but not because of Jake. Because of her TIA. What if the doctor had been wrong and she didn't have a normal lifespan ahead of her? How would her child manage with only one parent?

Just as she had growing up. As Shell had. And Jake. At least her baby would always have its father.

"Babies do best with both parents. Loni won't leave. But you stop filling her head with the thought of going to New York," he said.

"I won't talk about it with her if you don't want me to, but I didn't fill her head with anything. She's been determined to leave since I met her. I think you and Shell are ignoring the obvious."

"We'll see," he said, moving his hand up to her breast. Brianna forgot about the conversation as she responded to his touch.

BEFORE DAWN the next morning, Brianna wondered if she really wanted to see the ranch that much. She hadn't had enough sleep. Not that she was complaining. Jake was a generous and inventive lover. A woman could get addicted to his lovemaking. She wished she could be as close to him in other ways.

Shoving such thoughts aside, she dressed hurriedly and went to the kitchen to start breakfast while Jake readied the horses. Her excitement built. She'd loved riding when visiting her uncle. Since she'd been here, she'd ridden twice, not going far from the house, and was pleased to see riding was indeed something one never forgot. But the stiff muscles reminded her it was also something best done frequently to keep limber.

Loni wandered in, rubbing her back. She was dressed, but looked half-asleep.

"Good, I'm glad you got up early today," Brianna said. "I'm going out with Jake. Can I leave the breakfast dishes for you to do?"

The eggs were about ready, bread was toasting in all four slots of the large toaster. The juice had been poured and the bacon and sausages sizzled in the pan. Brianna glanced back at Loni and asked, "Are you okay?"

"Yeah, just couldn't sleep too well last night. I'll do the dishes, no problem. I wonder if the paint fumes are making me sick. I feel queasy."

"I can stay home today if you like," Brianna said. She didn't want to leave Loni if she was coming down with something. Yet she was dying to go out with Jake—just the two of them. She hoped to find some way to get him to be more open and welcoming during the daylight hours.

"No, I'll be fine. Though why you'd want to go out is beyond me. It's freezing cold, and all you're going to see is cattle and barbed wire. Look at a picture."

Brianna smiled and turned back to the eggs. "I want to feel the wind in my face, feel the cold air and smell the cattle on the range." She glanced almost shyly at Loni. "I also want to see what Jake is doing so I can picture that when he's not around."

Loni studied her for a moment. "You're falling for him."

Brianna shook her head. She wasn't ready to admit that aloud before she told Jake. And she couldn't tell him until she knew him better. "No, but we are bound together in marriage. Don't you think I should know more about him?"

"I still say you'll leave come spring. Or before. The winters here are brutal."

Brianna had a number of projects in mind for the winter. Used to constant activity and deadlines, the quiet life wasn't for her. Sometimes, quite frankly, she was bored. But now wasn't the time to go into all that with Loni.

Hank and Nolan came in, bringing the cold with them. Jake followed a moment later.

"Ready to go?"

"As soon as we eat!" Brianna said with a wide smile. She served up the hearty portions and sat down just as Shell entered.

"I'm going out on the range today," she said.

"Taking your place," Jake said.

Shell looked startled, then amused. "As if."

"She wants to see more of the spread," Jake explained.

Shell shrugged. "I can ride out with you if you like. Bring her back early when she gets tired."

"I'm not going to get tired," Brianna said. She didn't want to make an issue of it, but she was hoping to have Jake to herself.

"I'll bring her back if she can't do the entire day," Jake said easily.

Shell looked thoughtfully between the two of them and shrugged again.

Twenty minutes later Brianna mounted the gelding she'd ridden before. He was easy to ride, and she appreciated that no one was after her to prove herself. Her experience at the ranch in Jackson Hole was not enough to enable her to keep up with working cowboys.

She'd packed a lunch, including chocolate-chip cookies she'd baked yesterday. Jake had had several for dessert last night, so she knew he liked them.

It was cold. Her breath formed a cloud before her, and her cheeks tingled. But her jacket was thick and the leather gloves kept her hands warm.

"You going to be okay? You're not too cold, are you?" Jake asked as he swung up onto his own horse. Brianna couldn't help noticing how at home he looked, as if he and the horse completed each other. He nudged his mount, and they started toward the hills.

"I have on tons of layers. If it gets warm, I can take some off. If not, I should be fine all day. Where are we heading?"

"One final sweep at the far west boundary. The last time anyone checked, the fence was okay, the main body of the herd had moved to lower levels and there wasn't a problem. It'll be the first part hit with snow, and the last to have it melt, so this will be our only chance to check the area for months—unless we learn of a break. You up to a long ride?"

"Sure," Brianna said, hoping it was true. She

wanted to spend the day with him, no matter what it took.

They didn't speak as they rode, so Brianna was able to look around her, absorbing the stillness broken only by the sound of their horses. The grass was brown and dry. In the distance several dozen cattle grazed. Clouds built along the horizon. She knew rain was predicted in a few days. These clouds wouldn't be a problem except to block the sunshine and make it feel colder.

By the time Jake called a lunch break, Brianna had shed her jacket. The day had warmed up considerably, and it was delightful to be riding. She had begun to question Jake about various operations on the ranch, trying to understand the entire process—especially as it related to the bills and accounts she'd been working on.

"The aspect we need to change the most is the cattle. Establishing which bulls produce the better stock, lowering the average age of the herd, increasing the yield," Jake said, dismounting. "That's where forecasting would come in handy. Maybe you can get that computer of yours working on something like that before winter ends."

"I've got the accounts under control and ran those reports I told you about. We should look them over together one evening, and you can see if the budget I've devised will work."

Brianna gauged the distance to the ground. She'd enjoyed the ride, but she wasn't sure she could get off the horse. Gritting her teeth, she stood in the saddle and swung her leg over. But when her foot searched for terra firma, there was nothing. How tall was the horse?

Finally she kicked out of the other stirrup and landed with a soft thud. She knew enough to lock her knees before she sank into a heap on the ground.

"Are you okay?"

"Just out of practice. I'll be fine, don't worry."

Jake came around and reached for her reins. "I'll tie them up over here while we eat."

She pulled her saddlebags free and hobbled over to a relatively flat area. She sat down, grateful for the chance to rest. The sun was high in the sky, warm on her head and arms. It was hard to believe this was November in Wyoming. She'd expected snow by now.

Once they began to eat, Brianna looked at Jake. "So tell me about your friends. I want to start meeting them. Maybe invite them over for dinner from time to time."

"Don't have time for socializing," he said, stretching out on the dry grass and tipping his hat over his head.

"Yes, you do."

He looked over at her. "I know you must be bored, but there's a lot to do if we're to turn things around. And meaningless socializing isn't on the agenda."

"First of all, it isn't meaningless. And second, you do have the time. You have a wife now. I've caught up on the accounts, which means you don't have to work all day outside and then work all night in the office. And third, when we have these children we've talked about, they'll want friends and playmates. We might as well establish good relations with their parents now.''

"You forget, I left town right after high school. I'm not much on letters, so I lost touch with most of the guys I knew.''

"All the more reason to get started. Surely you have one or two friends you'd like to renew acquaintance with,'' she persisted. "I'm not complaining, but I do get tired of Nolan, Hank, Shell and you talking nonstop about cattle, beef prices, hay availability and vet bills every night. You need a break from work, too.''

"There's too much to do.''

"Well, it's all going to be there waiting to get done. Don't burn yourself out, Jake. I know what that's like.''

He looked curious at that statement. "Do tell,'' he invited.

Brianna knew she ought to tell him the full story; putting it off wouldn't make it go away. But still she hesitated. She didn't feel they'd yet built the kind of relationship that could withstand problems. If Steven dumped her after their years together, how fast would Jake send her packing?

"I only meant that I worked long and hard and never got caught up. No matter what, there's always more work waiting. Take time to enjoy what you've accomplished. Visiting with friends or expanding your life in other directions can only be beneficial to your workday.''

"Miss Pop Philosopher.''

"Maybe, but I want to do this. So give me some names."

Jake balanced himself on one elbow. "Brianna, I'm almost forty years old. Anyone graduating with me would have kids who are teenagers now—not playmates for babies we might have."

"So they can baby-sit."

He was silent for a moment, then spoke. "I heard Jim Ramsey married a few years ago. I think he has a toddler."

"And you two were friends?"

"As much as with anyone. We hung out together during school. He went to the university after we graduated. Runs a spread on the other side of town, works it with his father."

"Who did he marry?"

"Some woman from Laramie. She's younger."

"Like me and you."

"Probably not like me and you," Jake said wryly. "I think her name is Diane. Ask Loni, she'll know."

Brianna tucked away the names. She'd call in the next day or two to invite them to dinner. Time she began to put down roots and made some friends of her own here. What better place to start than with the wife of a friend of Jake's?

He began eating a cookie. "Good."

She smiled. "I love them, too. My mother and I used to make them on rainy days."

"Good tradition to start here, but don't just wait for rainy days."

Brianna was already thinking about the dinner she'd

have. She wondered if she would have to include everyone. She glanced at her husband. The man was not strong on social amenities. For a second she remembered Steven and how urbane he was. Of course he was used to wining and dining prospective clients and nervous artists.

She shook away the image and focused on the day. It was beautiful. Though the air was cool, the sun felt warm on her face. She glanced at Jake. He was still resting on one elbow, legs stretched out, gazing off across the range.

Remembering his kiss and caresses every night, Brianna's breathing grew shallow. Would he kiss her here? They were alone.

But sad to say, outside the bedroom he never seemed to notice her. He was so consumed with pulling the ranch out of the red he scarcely noticed anyone.

A distinctive chirping sounded.

Jake reached into his buttoned pocket and pulled out a cell phone.

''Marshall.''

Sitting up, he looked at Brianna. ''Slow down. Say again.''

He frowned and looked away. ''You're kidding…. Okay, tell the doctor you're the father and want in…. No don't say anything or do anything else. Ignore him. I'm on my way.'' Clicking off the phone, Jake stood hastily and stuffed it back into his pocket.

''Is something wrong?'' Brianna asked, scrambling to her feet.

"Loni's having the baby. Her water broke just after we left, and Shell took her to the hospital. Now she won't let him in the room with her, and he wants to see his baby born." Jake strode to the horses, snagged the reins and led them back to Brianna.

She hadn't needed to be told they were leaving. She had everything back in the saddlebags by the time he returned.

"Some damn fool lawyer is there saying Loni is giving the baby up for adoption."

"I told you she was thinking about it."

"Well, she's done more than think about it, she's made arrangements. But she can't do that without the father's consent, and the whole county knows Shell's the father. I'm heading in to see what I can do."

"I'm coming, too."

Jake waited for Brianna to mount her horse, then swung into his own saddle. "We'll need to ride a lot faster in than we came out. Can you manage?"

"Of course," Brianna said, hoping he didn't end up with another patient needing to go to the hospital!

CHAPTER NINE

THREE HOURS LATER Jake and Brianna entered the hospital. They hurried to obstetrics where they found Shell standing by the window of the waiting room gazing out. Nearby sat a man in a suit, briefcase beside him.

"Shell?"

He turned, relief evident when he saw Jake. He glanced at Brianna, and she was shocked at the anger he displayed.

"Did she have the baby?"

"Not yet. It'll be a while, the doctor said. She still refuses to see me. And this guy won't take no for an answer," he said, pointing to the other occupant of the waiting room.

"Thomas Payne." He stood and nodded briefly to Jake and Brianna. "Loni Peterson contacted me a couple of weeks ago about giving up her baby when it was born. I'm here to protect my client's interests."

"Jake Marshall, and the father of the baby will take it. There will be no adoption."

"There's no guarantee that's what my client wants," Payne said. "She was clear she wanted a nice family for the baby. Maybe there's a reason she doesn't want it left with the father."

"Not a reason that'll stand up in court," Jake said. "Shell has a steady job and lives with my wife and me. There will be plenty of adults to watch over the baby and take good care of it."

"And love it," Brianna put in, coming to stand beside Jake.

He glanced at her briefly, then nodded. "And love it," he repeated.

Thomas Payne looked at the couple, then Shell, who'd moved beside Jake. "I can't answer for my client at this time. Does she know the full situation?"

"Of course she knows," Shell said.

Jake put his hand on his son's shoulder in warning. "We'll have our own attorney contact you about this," he said.

"Mmm." Payne glanced at his watch. "Very well, as long as you don't badger my client, I'll wait to hear from your attorney. But do tell Ms. Peterson to call me so I can make sure any discussions are agreeable to her. If not, we will proceed, and if it comes to a custody case, then so be it."

"It won't come to that," Jake said.

The three of them watched the attorney leave. Then Jake turned back to Shell. "Was he giving you a hard time?"

"Not after I talked to you. I just shut out what he was saying. Before that, he tried to badger me into signing some waiver."

"Loni didn't discuss this with you?"

"You know she's barely speaking to me these days," Shell said in frustration, running his good hand through his hair. "I thought we had time. She wasn't due for a couple more weeks. Hell, we haven't even bought a crib."

"We have time to get a crib," Brianna said. "The baby won't be going home for a day or two, will it?"

"Don't talk to me about this baby," Shell said menacingly. "You're the one who told Loni you'd set her up in New York. She can't wait to leave. If you'd stayed the hell away, we wouldn't be in this mess!"

"That's enough," Jake cut in. "We can take this up with Brianna later. I'm going to call John Lieberman and get him going on this."

Brianna was hurt by Shell's attack. And Jake's brushing it aside. What was she doing here? Could she help with Loni?

"Can I see her?" Brianna asked. ·

"Probably," Shell said. "Aren't you her great benefactor? Ask the nurse at the desk." He turned back to the window, shoulders rigid with anger.

Brianna crossed to the nurses' station and asked if she could see Loni.

"Are you a relative?"

Brianna nodded. Future grandmother of this baby made her a relative, sort of. Suddenly she remembered. "May I make a call? I want to let her aunt know."

"Sure."

Brianna called Maggie Sorenson. She hoped the other woman would be as happy to hear from her as she'd implied.

She was. "I'll be right there. How's she doing?"

"Fine, last I heard. I'm going in to see her as soon as we hang up."

"I'll call her mother and let her know," Maggie said. "No matter what, Loni is her daughter and she deserves to know."

Brianna thanked the nurse for the use of the phone and headed to the labor room.

Loni looked lonely and sad in the high bed. Her eyes were closed and she was curled up as much as she could.

"Loni?" Brianna said softly.

The girl's eyes flew open and her face lit up. "Oh, Brianna, thanks for coming. I didn't know this would be so hard."

"How are you doing?"

"I'm okay between contractions, but when they come, it's awful. I never knew it would hurt so much." Just then she tensed and gave a low moan, gripping her stomach.

"Breathe through it," Brianna said, remembering deliveries she'd seen on television. Shouldn't Loni have taken some birthing classes or something? Brianna knew *she* would when the time came. She did not want to go into this blind.

"It's…all I can do…to breathe…period," Loni said, rocking back and forth. "This *hurts!*" The word trailed away into a wail. She lay quiet for a moment, then said, "The doctor told me the baby won't be born for a while yet. Why does it have to take so long?"

"Nature's way. Loni, Shell wants to see you."

"No," she said quickly.

Brianna brushed her hair back from her face. "Why not? He cares about you. And this is his baby, too."

"He doesn't care about me. The last time he asked me to marry him he said he wasn't going to ask again."

"After you turned him down, you mean? After you had turned him down at least a dozen times already? A man has his pride, Loni."

Was the girl playing hard to get? That could be dangerous with a man like Shell. Did Loni want to marry him?

"I don't want to get married," Loni said, as if she'd heard Brianna's questions. "I'm going to New York."

"So his not asking any more is a good thing—reduces your stress."

"My stress is off the scale," Loni said as another contraction hit.

When it passed, Brianna sat gingerly on the edge of the bed. "Loni, Shell needs to be a part of this. More so than most men. Think what happened to him. He wants his baby to know its father. Think how proud he'll be to be able to tell his son or daughter he was there right from the very beginning. No matter your feelings in this situation, think about the future and about your baby and its daddy."

Loni turned her face to the wall. "I don't want him around. I want the baby to go to a nice family."

"It's not going to happen. If you don't want the child, Shell does. And he has a nice home to bring the baby to. Though it still needs more work, in another year you won't recognize the place."

"And you won't be there if you don't hurry up and have a baby yourself," Loni flung out.

"Shell needs to be here. He needs to be a part of this," Brianna said firmly. "You have to let him share this, Loni. Or you'll have regrets the rest of your life."

The younger woman was quiet, until another contraction hit. Then she took a deep breath. "Okay, if he's so sure he wants to be a part of this, fine by me. You'll stay, too?"

"If you like. How about Jake? He's going to be the grandfather."

"Gee, I feel like I'm a circus performer on display. Why not? The more the merrier." She clutched Brianna's hand. "But you promise to stay. Don't let Shell browbeat me."

"Seems to me you're the one who's got him over a barrel," Brianna said. "But I promise to stay."

"The lawyer said Shell won't sign papers to let the baby be adopted."

"No, he won't," Brianna said gently. "How could you plan something like that without telling him? He wants you and the baby, but if he can't have you, he at least wants his child."

"You'll have most of the work with the baby if he takes it to the ranch. Are you willing to do that?" Loni asked, her grip still tight on Brianna's hand.

"Loni, I've given up my former life for just that purpose. I'll take great care of your baby. And when I have one, they'll grow up like siblings. We'll always love your baby," Brianna promised.

By the time Shell, Jake and Brianna had washed up

and donned hospital gowns, Loni was ready for the delivery room. Once inside, the process didn't go as fast as Brianna had assumed. Loni was struggling with almost nonstop contractions. Gasping between them, she railed against Shell, blaming him for everything.

He took it all calmly and soothed her as best he could. And he was there when their daughter was born, taking her from the doctor before the cord was even cut.

Brianna clutched Jake's arm, tears filling her eyes when the little girl let out a lusty cry. She was covered with fluid, her sparse hair matted against her scalp, but she was adorable. And from the look on Shell's face, the most perfect creature in the universe.

She glanced at Jake, startled to see his eyes looking suspiciously bright.

He glanced at her and then put his arm around her shoulders, drawing her close.

"Next time we do this, it'll be me," Brianna said softly.

LONI WAS ALONE in the double room. It was late, almost midnight. She was supposed to be asleep, but enough light came in from the hallway to make sleeping difficult. She turned over on her side, almost surprised again that she didn't have the baby to consider.

Her daughter. She'd glimpsed her briefly when Shell held her. Brianna had been right. The adoring look he'd given the baby had once been directed at her. But she'd thrown it away.

A tear seeped between her lids. She blinked rapidly.

She had a higher calling. She was going to be a famous artist. When the baby was older, she could come to New York to visit her mother. They'd go to museums, art galleries, eat at fancy restaurants and see Broadway shows.

But that was a long way in the future. Right now, Loni missed her baby.

Her aunt Maggie had been waiting to see her when she'd left recovery. She'd invited Loni to stay with her if she wanted. Loni did want. No sense spending a lot of time with the baby only to leave in a few weeks.

Loni would grow used to being alone. She'd have her painting. Wouldn't her daughter be proud of a mother who was world-famous?

She frowned when she thought about Elsa Harrington Marshall. Her fame had not brought that family happiness. Loni needed to make sure she didn't make the same mistakes. She wanted her daughter to look up to her and see her as a huge success.

Maybe she should go see the baby. The nurse had asked about bringing her in for feeding, but Loni had refused. So the hospital staff was taking care of the baby until the morning when the pediatrician said he would release her.

It might be her only chance to see her baby for a long while.

She climbed down from the high bed, feeling shaky and wobbly. She drew on the robe her aunt had brought and slowly walked out of the room. The nurse at the station didn't notice her. Loni turned toward the nursery.

When she drew near, she saw Shell, leaning against the window and gazing at the babies. She hesitated, then stepped forward. Another thing she'd have to get used to—dealing with the father of her child.

He glanced over when she stopped beside him.

"How are you feeling?" he asked.

"Fine. What are you still doing here?"

"Just watching Ashley."

"Ashley?" There were two babies in the nursery.

"My daughter."

"Ashley? You named her Ashley without even asking me?" Loni ignored the pinprick of hurt at hearing him call the baby *his*.

"Ashley Shelly Bluefeather. Named her for my mother and for…" He stopped.

"For what?"

"For the phoenix."

"The phoenix?"

"You know, the bird that rises from the ashes."

"Why would you do that?"

"Because we made a mess of things. Destroyed a wonderful relationship and burned our bridges. Yet this baby is a miracle. One I'm in awe of. She's the best thing to come from it all. So I thought I'd call her Ashley. You didn't have a name picked out for her, did you?"

Loni shook her head, suddenly feeling sad and guilty. Her own daughter, and she hadn't even picked a special name for her. But Shell had. Tears blurred her vision as she looked into the bassinet. Not that she could see much—the baby was swaddled in a blanket, lying on her side. Only one cheek and the fuzz of hair could be seen. Black, of course, like Shell's.

"Your aunt said you plan to stay with her now," Shell remarked after a while.

"Yes." Until she left for New York. Somehow the enthusiasm she'd once felt was missing. Probably because of all she'd gone through. Once she was back on her feet, she'd rediscover the thrill of anticipation.

"We'll send your things there."

"I don't mind coming out to the ranch. I need to get my paintings, too."

"We can pack them up and send them. Maybe crate them for shipment. Elsa had all the materials for crating."

"You don't want me at the ranch?"

"What's the point?" Shell asked. "You and I are finished. Ashley won't know who you are yet—she's too young. Brianna can see you in town if you two want to hatch some other plan together."

"What are you talking about?"

"Well, like her getting you to New York."

"She offered to give me the names of some of her friends, but that's all. She thinks I'm crazy to leave this place for New York. But I have to go."

"So go. Bye, Loni. Have a nice life." Shell walked away.

Loni watched him, panic flaring again. It was like at the courthouse. Only this time it was for good.

She turned back to the babies, wishing she could

hold her daughter—just once while she said goodbye. But she couldn't. Loni returned to her lonely hospital room, hoping she was making the right decision.

"THAT'S SHELL coming home, isn't it?" Brianna said at the sound of the kitchen door opening and closing. "What's going to happen with them?" She and Jake were in their room, but sleep proved elusive. Brianna kept replaying the emotional high from the birth of the baby. Amazed by the different goals she and Loni had.

She shivered, comforted by Jake's presence, despite his lack of support earlier. What would it take to convince both men she wasn't out to sabotage their lives.

"I don't know," he said. "But I wish you hadn't offered Loni any help in moving to New York. Tell her you changed your mind. She needs to stay close. Maybe in time she'll come to realize she needs to be a part of her baby's life."

"Jake, I would tell my friends to ignore her if I thought it would make a difference. But I don't. She's bound and determined to go. I truly thought it was a pipe dream. That once she saw her baby she'd want to stay. Maybe the difference is she was raised with both parents and doesn't realize how it feels when one is missing. You and Shell and I only had a single parent. And in Shell's and my cases, that parent died far too young. I would never leave a child of mine."

"But if Loni didn't have any support, she'd have to stay," he argued.

"Would she? Maybe she'll have it all. I think her paintings are good."

Jake shrugged, shifting the covers a little. "Good enough to make a living? The point is—"

"The point is you don't like her decision. Well, I don't think much of it, either. But it's her life. I think you're thinking more about Shell than Loni."

"Actually, I'm thinking about the baby. What kind of woman leaves her child?"

"What kind of woman keeps her child under her thumb, squeezing the life out of him, turning from her own grandchild?" she countered ruthlessly. "Who knows why people do things? I don't think forcibly keeping Loni here is going to make her a good mother. Not if she resents every moment."

Shell's door closed down the hall.

"He's hurting," Jake said softly.

"I know. And I think she's hurting, too. But neither you nor I can make things right for them. They have to live their own lives."

BRIANNA HAD BREAKFAST ready when Jake entered the kitchen the next morning. She'd made a big batch of hotcakes, knowing how hungry the men were all the time. He poured himself some coffee and went to sit down.

"Good morning," she said.

He nodded and sipped the coffee, looking at the table. "Where are Hank and Nolan?"

"Since it's pouring rain outside, I think they decided to fix something to eat in the bunkhouse," she said. "Isn't that what they did last time it rained so hard? Are you planning to work in this?"

Jake shrugged. "There're always things to be done."

Shell came in, but immediately crossed the room and reached for his hat.

"Where're you going?" Jake asked.

"Breakfast is ready," Brianna said.

"I'm heading for the hospital. I want to see the baby again."

"Eat first," Brianna suggested, dishing up eggs and hotcakes and adding several slices of bacon and sausage.

"I'm not hungry."

"Might as well eat—visiting hours aren't for a while yet," Jake said.

Shell glared at his father, ignoring Brianna. He returned the hat to the hook and sat down. He ate as if he was alone, eyes firmly on his plate.

Brianna heard the echo of his heated accusations. Was he planning to ignore her in retaliation for her perceived crime? Wouldn't *that* make their home life comfortable.

DESPITE THE RAIN that continued to fall, the furniture she'd ordered was delivered that morning. The two deliverymen were willing to cater to her need to see the sofa in first one spot, then another. She thanked them with hot coffee and cookies, something she would never have thought to do in New York.

When they left, she returned to the living room. She'd hung the curtains a couple of days ago. Now with the new rug and furniture, the room was the way she'd envisioned it. Would anyone else care?

She wanted some artwork for the walls. She couldn't believe Elsa had left nothing for her family. Would Steven give her a deal if he could locate one for sale? It seemed fitting that Elsa Harrington's home should have one of her paintings.

The phone rang, and she hurried into the office to answer it.

"Jake there?" Shell asked.

"No, he left right after you did this morning. I haven't seen him since." Did he expect her to jump to do his bidding after the way he treated her? Brianna glanced at the clock. It was almost noon. Would Jake and the others be coming in for lunch? She doubted they were far from the house in this rain.

"He's not answering his cell phone. But maybe you're the one I should be talking to, anyway. Ashley can come home today. And I need so much stuff."

"How nice."

"Come on. She doesn't have anything. I can't even take her unless she has a car seat!"

"Then go buy one."

"I don't know anything about baby stuff."

"Neither do I."

"You're a woman," he said. She could hear the desperation in his tone.

"And that gives me a baby-furnishings gene? I don't think so. You've known you were going to be a father for months. Why didn't you get things before now?"

"I thought we had time. Look, this isn't getting us anywhere. Find Jake and tell him to call me here."

She heard the back door. "Tell him yourself. I think he just walked in."

"Jake!" Brianna called. When he appeared in the doorway, she held out the phone. "It's for you."

She left the room when she heard him speak. Today should have been a joyous time, a new baby coming home. A little girl to love and watch grow to adulthood.

But Brianna had a hard time mustering any enthusiasm. She was not a part of the family, just someone living in the house.

Jake appeared in the doorway. He glanced around. "What's all this?"

"I ordered some new furniture, and it arrived today."

"I told you we didn't have any extra money for stuff like this. Send it back."

"*I* bought it. If and when I leave, I can take it with me if you don't want it."

He went still. "Leave? Are you sulking because of this morning?"

"No, I'm not sulking. But I don't want you to panic, thinking I was trying to worm my way into the ranch by buying a couple of pieces of furniture."

"Am I that paranoid?"

"You tell me."

"Shell needs help."

"And that concerns me because…?"

"You *are* sulking."

She jumped up and put her fists on her hips, glaring at him. "If I am, I have reasons. Jake, I'm your wife. You should have stood up for me this morning at the hospital."

"Shell was right."

"No, he wasn't and neither are you. Can either of you honestly say that my arrival was the catalyst that Loni needed to decide to leave Sweetwater?"

"If you hadn't offered—"

Brianna held up her hand, palm out. "Stop, answer my question yes or no."

"Your arrival and talk about New York put that destination in her head."

"Before that?" she persisted.

"She's talked about leaving since before she knew she was pregnant," Jake admitted. "Shell used to complain about it when they first started dating."

"So maybe I'm not responsible for everything that's gone wrong lately."

"I never said that."

"No, but you never challenged Shell when he said it."

"He's under a lot of pressure now. He didn't mean it."

"You never stood up for me," she said slowly. "If I can't rely on you to defend me, how can I rely on you for bigger things?"

CHAPTER TEN

"TRUST TAKES TIME," Jake said.

"I agree. Maybe one day I'll learn to trust you," she said.

Jake didn't like her response. But when he looked at the situation from Brianna's point of view, he could see he'd let her down. She hadn't brought about the circumstances they were in. Shell had been pestering Loni for months to marry him; she'd always said she was leaving. Why hadn't he reminded Shell of that?

Because it was easier to think Brianna was the culprit and join forces with his son. He wanted a tie that would be stronger than the one he and his father had. But alienating—no, *hurting*—Brianna wasn't the way to strengthen anything.

"I apologize," he said.

Her look of surprise should have amused him, but it only made him feel guiltier. If he didn't readily and willingly come to her defense, what kind of parents would they be? Maybe he needed to reexamine their marriage. If trust was lacking on both sides, they were in for a hell of a time.

"Shell said the doctor's releasing Ashley later this afternoon. She can come home, but he needs a baby seat for the car."

"He needs more than that," Brianna said, slowly lowering her arms. "What about a crib and diapers and bottles and formula and all that goes with a baby?"

"I told him we'd go get that stuff," Jake said warily.

"We?"

"I don't know anything about baby stuff."

"Neither do I," she said.

She'd shown such an even temperament since she arrived, he was surprised to learn she was going to be difficult about this. Was it her way of paying him back? Another aspect of marriage that would take getting used to. Time to start building bridges.

"I told him we'd get it."

She shrugged, looking around the room. "So go. You might want to get a rocking chair. I don't think you want the ones from the porch in the baby's room. It would be nice to rock the baby when feeding her."

"Come with me, Brianna."

For a moment Jake thought she'd refuse. But finally she nodded. "Okay, but don't expect me to be the expert in this."

"We'll learn together."

She smiled, and her face lit up and her eyes sparkled. He'd give a lot to see more of that smile.

"Good practice for when we need the stuff for our baby, huh?" she asked.

They'd been married for a month now. And still no sign of pregnancy. He wondered how long it took to find out once a woman conceived.

And what were his options if she didn't conceive? Lots of women couldn't have children. Wouldn't his grandmother have had a field day with that? But there was no evidence Brianna could or couldn't have children. They'd just have to keep trying.

If they didn't have to get the baby's car seat, he'd take her upstairs right now. The inclement weather reduced the workload, giving him more time to indulge in other pursuits....

"Did you want lunch before we leave?" she asked.

Jake turned away, afraid the tight feeling of his jeans wasn't due to shrinkage. He was fantasizing about taking his wife to bed and she was thinking about lunch.

"Yeah, let's eat first. It'll take a while to get to Laramie, and I'm already hungry."

"Laramie?"

"Sweetwater doesn't have any department stores, as you've seen. We need to go to a bigger town."

"Of course, and Laramie is how big?"

"Big enough."

IT WAS LATE AFTERNOON by the time Jake and Brianna arrived at the hospital. Brianna waited in the truck while Jake went to find his son. Shell was in the nursery, holding Ashley, giving her a bottle. Jake took in the tiny baby and his son's awkwardness. The boy was too young, he thought, even though he himself had been even younger when Shell was born. How had Shelly managed? Again came the awareness of how hard it must have been for her. Guilt over never contacting her flared inside him.

"How is she?" he asked.

"She can go as soon as she's finished eating," Shell said. "The nurses told me what to do. I just hope I can remember everything. Did you get a car seat?"

"Yes. I already set it up in your truck. We also bought a few books on raising a baby."

Shell looked beyond Jake. "Where's Brianna?"

"Outside. She's not too happy with you right now."

"I got that from the phone call."

"She has a point."

Shell nodded. "Maybe. I've been thinking about that since I talked to her earlier. Loni is bound and determined to leave. Brianna just made it easier. But easy or not, when Loni decides on something, she goes for it flat-out."

"She still here?"

"No, she left this morning with her aunt Maggie. She's staying there for a little while. I told her we'd send her her things."

Jake waited a moment, then nodded. "I'll head for home with Brianna. We have a lot to set up for this young lady. I'll get Nolan or Hank to give me a hand with the crib. We'll try to have it all ready when you get there."

"Thanks."

Jake didn't want to leave without saying one more thing.

"Did you know Brianna's father never acknowledged her? That her mother's parents kicked her out when she became pregnant and never spoke to her again?''

Shell went still. ''No, I didn't know that.''

''Her mother died when she was eighteen. There she was, just starting college on a scholarship, alone in a big city. The only relative who'd had anything to do with either of them was her uncle Buck, and he died six months before her mother.''

''So she should know more than anyone how important it is for a baby to have her mother,'' Shell said.

''Or she should know more than anyone how hard it is to be young and alone in a big scary city with no family or friends. Loni's going to go. Maybe Brianna just wanted to help. Think about it. And while you're at it, think about who's going to take care of this baby when you're working.''

Jake headed back to the truck. When he stepped outside, he looked around in disgust. It had begun to snow. Winter was setting in. If Brianna didn't conceive soon, he'd lose the ranch.

He'd worry about that later; right now he'd better see about finding a way to get enough hay to ride out the winter. If the weather turned really bad, he didn't have enough to keep the cattle alive. Beef prices were rock-bottom right now, but the only way to come up with ready cash was to sell some stock.

He headed for the car, wishing the hay was the only concern he had. If the breach this morning between Brianna and Shell wasn't healed soon, it would be a cold winter inside, as well as out.

He slid behind the wheel and realized how cold it

was in the cab. "You should have turned on the engine and run the heater," he said as he started the truck.

"I'm fine," Brianna said.

"Shell is feeding Ashley. As soon as they're done, he's heading for home. He said the nurses told him what to do. I told him we bought some books."

"Mmm." Brianna stared out at the falling snow.

She seemed so distant. With the baby coming home, he expected more excitement.

"You going to help set up?" he asked once they were on the road.

"I'll wash the sheets and blankets while you figure out the crib. Then I can make the bed fresh for her. You did get batteries for the baby monitor, didn't you?"

"We about bought out the store. There couldn't be a thing we forgot."

"We'll know soon enough. Was Loni at the hospital?"

"No. She'd gone home with Maggie."

"Why didn't she live with Maggie, instead of you, before the baby was born?" Brianna asked.

"Her aunt was out of town when her folks threw her out. She had nowhere else to turn, so we offered. Once with us, I guess it was easier for her to stay. She likes Elsa's studio, remember."

"Will she be coming to get her paintings and all her clothes soon?"

"Shell said we'd send them."

"I can take them to her if you want. Are you sure

she wouldn't like to come and get them? And see Ashley?''

''I'm not sure of much right now. We'll see what happens in a few days. She may leave for New York by the end of the week, for all we know.''

Brianna fell quiet and Jake wished he hadn't said the last bit. It reminded him, and her, of that morning.

BY THE TIME Shell arrived, the crib had been erected and the sheets and blankets washed. The bed Loni had used had been dismantled and was lying against the hall wall. The dresser was cleared and filled with clothes and diapers, its top lined with a pad.

Brianna was putting together a mobile of brightly colored animal figures to hang over the crib when she heard Shell's step on the stairs and looked up.

Jake was positioning the rocking chair near the window. They'd drawn the heavy curtains against the cold. Brianna still thought the room was too cool for a baby, but unless they cranked up the heat for the entire house, this room wasn't going to get much warmer. They'd just have to make sure the baby was dressed warmly and covered snugly in bed when she slept.

Shell carried in the baby carrier; Ashley was fast asleep.

''We're home,'' he said needlessly.

The next few minutes passed in a whirl as first Shell, then Jake, then Brianna held Ashley. When put in her crib, she still hadn't awoken.

"She's okay, isn't she?" Shell asked, leaning over the crib.

"Asleep," Brianna said. "Babies sleep soundly."

He glanced at her. "I thought you didn't have a special baby gene."

"No, but I read some of one of the books while I was waiting for Jake at the hospital. There's lots to be learned."

"We'll practice on Ashley, so we'll have it down pat when our own kid arrives," Jake teased.

Shell started to respond, caught the amusement in his father's eye and merely shrugged. "I hope babies are sturdy."

"First babies have to be. Most parents don't come with built-in knowledge. It's on-the-job training at best," Brianna said, awed at the tiny perfection of Ashley Bluefeather.

Her arms ached to hold her close, to keep her safe from all of life's blows. And if she felt like this about Ashley, how strongly would she feel for her own child?

So what if she didn't have the perfect marriage. To have a baby to love would be enough.

The incident at breakfast that morning set Brianna to thinking about her future. She'd come into this marriage believing she and Jake would meld their lives and grow closer.

She wasn't sure that was going to happen. Jake was too distant and unwilling to share himself. And that made her realize that she'd need more in her life if she was going to stay in Wyoming.

True, her doctor had told her to slow down, but to do nothing was not in her nature. There was no way she could retire at thirty-four!

BY THE END of the following week, she knew she would love being a mother. Ashley was a wonderful little girl. She slept on schedule, ate whenever it was time and even stayed awake for a while each day to entertain Brianna. Though she suspected she was supposed to be entertaining the baby.

Shell took over after dinner, bathing the baby and spending time with her in the newly redecorated living room. It was the warmest room in the house, and Brianna was delighted when Jake and Shell gravitated there every night after dinner.

She'd finish the dishes and then join them, sitting on the sofa and watching the baby, listening to their discussions concerning the ranch.

Brianna remembered her plan to get to know Jake's friends. It had been put on hold while they got used to the new member of the family. But if she wanted to put her idea into action before it became difficult to get to the ranch because of snow, she had better start calling soon.

The phone rang.

''I'll get it,'' Jake said, heading for the office.

The silence was a bit awkward when he left. Brianna stayed as far from the baby as she could when Shell was around, not wanting him to think she was usurping his place. But how could there be anything but benefit when a child was loved?

Jake returned a few minutes later, a scowl on his face. "Maggie Sorenson wants to talk to you, Brianna."

"Who?"

"Loni's aunt."

"Oh." Brianna hurried to the office and picked up the phone. "Hello?"

"Brianna, it's me, Loni. I got my aunt to call because I was afraid Shell or Jake would hang up on me."

"Oh, Loni, how are you doing?"

"Okay. I've been up and around for a few days. As long as I don't do much, I'm fine. Still tired, though."

"Are you calling about your paintings? Jake said they could crate them and ship them to New York for you if you'd rather. Or we can take them to your aunt's."

"Actually, I was calling about the baby," Loni said hesitantly. "How is she?"

"She's darling. We all love her to bits. Did you want to come by and see her?"

"I guess not."

Loni's voice seemed to lack conviction on that point.

"A short visit couldn't hurt," Brianna said.

"Is Shell still real mad?"

"I don't know that he's mad at all. You should see him with the baby. He's really smitten. And Jake almost has to order him to let him hold his granddaughter. I would never have suspected it of such macho cowboys."

Brianna heard a sniff on the other end. "Are you all right?"

"Yeah, just postpartum blues. Aunt Maggie says everyone gets them. Maybe I'll come out next week— to see which paintings I want. Some are early efforts and probably not worth anything. I need to get my paints and some clothes."

"We put your things in boxes. Ashley's room is the one you used to have."

"Oh."

Brianna waited, then heard a new voice.

"Hello, Brianna? This is Maggie."

"Hi."

Loni's aunt waited a moment, then spoke. "Honestly, that girl. She's moping around here like crazy, but refuses to go see her baby. It's not natural. She talks about going to New York. What's she going to do there?"

"Paint, I guess."

"If that's so dad-burned important, she could paint here. But I think it's a notion she took and hasn't let go of."

"Apparently Elsa told her she had talent."

"So? There are a million painters out there, but that baby only has one mother."

"Do you think she'd come to visit Ashley?"

"Is that what Shell named her?"

"Yes. It's pretty, don't you think?"

"I do. I'll see if I can get her to go out there, but there's no telling her much these days. I know my sister and her husband don't approve of Shell, but that's the wrong way to look at things. From all I've heard, he's a hardworking, responsible young man. Can't help who his parents are any more than little Ashley can.''

"He is a fine young man." Brianna looked up. Jake was leaning against the doorjamb watching her, his arms crossed over his chest. How long had he been there?

"Tell her she's welcome anytime. Come yourself. Ashley should know all her family.''

"Why, thank you. I might just do that next Tuesday, if that's okay with you. I'd love to see her again, maybe hold her. It's been twenty years since my youngest was a baby. Time flies.''

"I'll be home that day, so anytime.''

When she hung up, Brianna turned to Jake. "Did you want something?''

"Wondered why you were talking so long to Maggie. You invited her here?''

"Yes, I did. She sounds nice and she's Ashley's great-aunt.''

"I don't know if Shell's going to approve of that.''

Brianna was annoyed. "Then either make him like it or don't tell him. Are you two planning to deprive her of the rest of her family just because Loni didn't marry Shell?''

"Whoa, Bri, I didn't say *I* was against it, just thought he might be. Maggie Sorenson is a much nicer woman than Loni's mother. Though I suspect Susan Peterson is heavily influenced by her husband. But once the lawyers get everything nailed down, Shell will have total custody. So he gets to say if she sees her great-aunt or not.''

''Then I'll ask him myself so I can tell Maggie if she's not welcome.'' Brianna pushed past Jake and went upstairs. She was not going to be a party to keeping Ashley away from others who would love her. Brianna's own childhood had lacked family. She'd always envied kids with tons of aunts and uncles and cousins. The more the merrier, she thought.

She took a quick shower and dressed for bed. When she entered the bedroom, she was startled to see Jake already in bed, a baby book in his hands.

''Shell finished this one last night, so it's my turn,'' Jake said, holding it up so she could see the cover. ''You can have it after me.''

''Or I can read it during the day while you're out,'' she said, slipping beneath the cool sheets. She wished there was a way to heat the bed. Besides cuddling close to Jake.

She still wasn't comfortable initiating physical contact with her husband. Most nights he gathered her close, kissed her, and one thing led to another. But she knew it was just for the sake of a baby.

He lay the book down, flicked off the lights and reached for her. He was always so hot. And in only a few moments, could make her just as hot....

As she was drifting off to sleep, Brianna wished once again she and Jake could be this close during the day. She'd been here for more than six weeks. Surely—

A thought struck. They'd made love almost every

night since their wedding day, which meant it had been longer than six weeks since she'd last had her period. Could she be pregnant?

She almost laughed aloud. Of course she could be— Jake was doing all he could to ensure that! Suddenly impatient to know, she decided to go to town in the morning and get one of those home pregnancy tests. Ashley was delightful, but Brianna longed to hold her own child in her arms.

IT WAS SNOWING when Brianna awoke. She kept an eye on the accumulation as she prepared breakfast. Hank and Nolan were in and out fast, Shell didn't linger, and Jake got to his feet before she was finished.

"How can you all work in this weather?" she asked. "Won't you freeze?"

"I'm dressed for it. And we won't be out all day— too cold for that. But I want to check the amount of snow on the range, and the others have chores to do. You stay inside and keep warm."

"I thought I'd go into town today," Brianna said. She'd decided last night to say nothing to Jake until she knew for sure. No sense getting his hopes up if it was a false alarm. "Would someone be available to watch Ashley?"

"Later, maybe."

Brianna nodded. She wouldn't take the baby out in this weather. But if she waited too long, there might be too much snow for her to drive in. Living in New York, she had relied on cabs and public transit, especially in inclement weather. She wasn't sure she was ready to tackle the snow.

"We'll be back by lunch. Have something hot ready, will you?"

Brianna nodded. "Take care, Jake. It looks treacherous out there."

He paused by the door. Slowly he smiled. "I will."

Brianna remained in her chair for several moments after he left. That smile had been like a caress. She felt as fluttery as a teenager with a crush.

"Maybe it's hormones," she said aloud as she got up to do the dishes. Before finishing, she heard Ashley on the baby monitor. Her day had begun.

By lunchtime Brianna knew she wasn't going into town. Snow had fallen steadily all morning, and there was more on the drive than she wanted to chance. There was no telling if the snowplows had cleared the county roads yet. She tried to rein in her frustration. There wasn't anything she could do about it, but she wished she knew!

"We're staying in this afternoon," Jake said. "Shell can watch Ashley. I want you to go over the accounts with me."

"Fine," Brianna said as she made sure everyone had plenty to eat. She'd started the stew after feeding Ashley breakfast, and it was hot and filling. She made sure there were plenty of biscuits, as well. "I'm all caught up and have even run a few reports. I can show you how to pull up analyses on the computer program if you like."

Jake nodded.

When she finished up in the kitchen a little later, Brianna headed for the office. She was pleased with what she'd accomplished. And concerned when she'd realized just how much the ranch needed.

Jake stood by the window when she entered, gazing at the snow. It was falling so heavily the barn wasn't visible.

"Will we get snowed in?" she asked, crossing the room to join him. She shivered as she drew close to the window. It was colder there than in the center of the room.

"I think Elsa had storm windows. If we can find them and put them up, it'll save on heating," Jake said.

"Or we can just dress more warmly. Maybe I should have kept those heavy drapes in the living room. I didn't realize they were there for a purpose."

"I don't think they were. I think Elsa liked them."

"Ugh. For someone who had such talent for painting light romantic pictures, her decorating sense left something to be desired."

Jake turned to her, nodding. "You've done a good job, Brianna. The rooms you've done are, I don't know, welcoming, I guess. I like coming home at night."

The compliment meant a lot to Brianna—her husband was usually sparse with any kind of praise.

"I still want to hang some pictures on the wall, but that can wait. And I wish we had a small table for under the window."

"Check the attic, there might be stuff up there. Most

people living this far out rarely throw things away. Maybe a great-grandmother or someone had a small table that Elsa put away.''

''Do you always refer to her as Elsa?''

''I never felt she was grandmotherly, if that's what you mean. She had no use for Annie Colter's son.''

''But you were also your father's son.''

Jake shrugged and turned toward the desk. ''Tell me about this accounting setup, and let's see where we stand.''

The next few hours were spent discussing the situation on the ranch. Brianna learned a lot with Jake explaining things to her. As her knowledge grew, so did her appreciation for those who earned their living this way. It was a risky business, subject to the whims of weather and the marketplace.

Yet she could tell Jake loved the challenge. And she wanted him to inherit the ranch that had been in his family for generations. How horrible of his grandmother to threaten that. Elsa Harrington Marshall might have been world-famous for her paintings, but she sounded like a bitter, selfish old witch.

''What happened to your grandfather?'' Brianna asked when they'd finished going over everything. It wasn't quite time to start dinner, and she was curious about the man Elsa had married.

''He died when my dad was in high school—fell from a horse and hit his head on a rock.''

''Yikes, that's almost like Shell.''

''This isn't always a safe life.''

"So they didn't have any other children? Just your father?"

"Just my dad. But he loved the place and wanted nothing more than to run the ranch."

"Which he did."

"Not after he married my mother. Elsa threw a fit and my dad left. It was only when I was about fourteen that we came back." Jake leaned back in his chair and put his heels on the edge of the desk, crossing his legs. "My old man hit the bottle pretty hard after my mother died. Finally, after getting fired from about the fifteenth place, he decided to head for home. I don't know exactly what went on between him and Elsa, but we ended up staying here and he ran the place for her after that. Until he died a few years back."

"But you didn't stay," she said.

"No. I was young and restless and resentful of the old harridan. I wanted more than what my dad settled for."

"And what did you find?" Brianna knew the feeling—wasn't that why she was here? Looking for a family and roots. Her mother had been so lonely. Brianna didn't want history repeating itself.

"I found I was good at what I did. I met your uncle Buck for one. He was a big influence on me. And I found working for someone else isn't as good as working for myself, though the job as manager of the Bar-XT was close. I've only lived here for a few years all told, but the ties to the land go back to my great-great-grandfather. I thought I'd inherit when my grandmother died. The rest you know."

Brianna longed to go to him, to sit on his lap and wrap her arms around him. To let him know he would never be alone again.

She wondered what he'd do if she did just that?

"I called your friends and invited them to dinner next week. They're coming on Thursday. I thought to have something simple and easy to fix like a casserole so I can minimize my time in the kitchen and visit more," Brianna said. "Diane sounded nice on the phone. She said she hadn't been out here, but she knew Jim would know the way. I expect you guys to entertain us with reminiscences of your teenage years!"

"A big-city girl like you will be bored by the stuff we did."

She laughed. "Never happen. I'll be fascinated with every word."

CHAPTER ELEVEN

JAKE COULDN'T HELP himself. She was a fire in his blood. He knew their marriage was an arrangement both had entered into for different reasons, but their goal was the same. Make a baby. And what better time to work on that than a snowy afternoon when he couldn't work?

He was fooling himself if he thought that was the only reason. He just plain wanted her. Night and day. When they weren't together, he was thinking about her. When they were, it was all he could do to keep his hands to himself and not haul her up against him.

"I want you, Brianna."

Had he pushed his luck today? She looked almost shocked.

"Okay, then, cowboy. Lead the way." She rose and smiled at him. If he wasn't already so hot for her, that come-hither smile would be enough.

It was as if the hush from the snow permeated the house. The baby slept. Shell was in his room, for once with the radio on softly, as if in deference to his sleeping daughter.

Entering their bedroom first, Brianna turned and tilted her head slightly. "A departure for us, wouldn't you say?"

He nodded, his blood already pounding through his veins. The intensity of his feelings was a surprise. For years he'd been alone and satisfied with that.

She waited for him to close the door, then stepped closer, her eyes on his, her lips curled slightly in a sexy smile. He could watch her all day, though he'd rather watch her naked and in his bed than standing in her jeans and shirt.

Slowly, almost as nervous as a kid, he reached out to pull her into his arms. It had been easier these last weeks to make love in the dark. He didn't need to worry about guarding his expression or chance a knowing glance. But he wanted to see all of her sweet body. Wanted to watch her explode into climax and watch her in the afterglow, warm and slumberous.

He kissed her gently. Her response was immediate. No matter what the circumstances of this bizarre marriage, she held nothing back. In only seconds the kiss deepened.

He began to unbutton her shirt. He could feel her heart pounding against his fingers as they brushed her left breast. Her breath caught. He opened his eyes and found her watching him.

When her hand began to unfasten his own buttons, Jake wanted to rip off their clothes and feel her bare skin against his chest. But he slowed his fingers, stretching out the anticipation.

Eventually he slipped the unfastened shirt from her shoulders, entranced by the lacy bra she wore. Her nipples pressed against the lace, as if waiting for him.

He leaned over and captured one in his mouth. His

tongue rasped over the rough lace, wetting it and her. She moaned softly, holding his head closer as she arched into the kiss.

He moved to the other, giving it as much loving attention.

Brianna slid the shirt from his shoulders, her fingers rubbing his skin, increasing his temperature another five degrees.

He felt her muscles clench when he unfastened her jeans. Rubbing her belly softly, he wondered if he could hold on long enough to get their boots and jeans off.

It seemed to take forever to pull off her boots, slip her jeans down that silky skin and shed his own clothes. The sheets were cool when they lay down, but all he could think about was the softness of her skin, the heat she was giving off and the sweet taste of her when his tongue plunged into her mouth.

Just once, he thought whimsically, they'd have to take their time. But not now.

HE COULD SEE that the snow was still falling. There was no wind, and the flakes drifted down, fat and thick and silent. Brianna stirred and snuggled closer.

"Are you all right?" she asked.

He nodded. "Just thinking…how you're not what I expected," Jake said, his fingers still brushing her arm, as if to absorb the silky feel.

"And that was?" she asked drowsily. Her head rested on his chest, her arm was across him, and her fingers traced small patterns on his side. This wasn't the way he'd imagined spending a snowy afternoon. But it was perfect.

"I expected sophisticated, opinionated and cool."

"Mmm. Well, you're not what I expected, either, so we're even."

"And what did you expect?"

"A guy with no hair, a beer belly and who chewed tobacco."

Jake looked down at her in disbelief. "You didn't!"

She giggled softly. "I had fears just before I got here that you wouldn't be the same guy I knew as a teenager. I had such a crush on you then, did you know it?"

"Yeah. And so did your uncle."

"Uh-oh, did he say something to you?"

"Only threatened me with my life if I so much as touched you."

"Now look at us."

"Fortunately we're married, or he'd come from the grave to get me."

"Who would have thought?"

"Do you miss New York?"

"No. Well, maybe a little once in a while. But now with Ashley to look after, every moment is busy. I don't have time to miss things. Not that I had a lot of time to enjoy what the city offered while I was there. I worked hard. I miss my friends. But I e-mail them often."

"You haven't made a single complaint. I know this has to be a tough change."

"One I wanted, however, so it's not so tough. I still

have a long way to go to be a good rancher's wife, though, don't I?''

His arm tightened slightly. "I don't know, seems to me you have all this rancher wants."

Brianna smiled, wishing she knew for sure if she was pregnant. It would be fun to plan for the baby's arrival together. To think up names, talk about what they expected for their child.

Nagging thoughts kept coming through, however. Would they have afternoons like this once he knew she was pregnant? Were their nights in jeopardy? She loved their time in bed together—not only for the passionate lovemaking, but for the talking they did. It was the only time she felt truly a part of this marriage and ranch.

"So do you do this kind of thing every time it snows?" she asked playfully.

"I haven't in the past, but we could always start a new tradition."

"Good idea. Family traditions are important." She tilted back her head and reached up to kiss him. They still had time before dinner....

BRIANNA GOT TO town three days later with no difficulty. It had snowed for two days. Yesterday one of the men had cleared the driveway, announcing the county had cleared the main road. So today she was venturing into Sweetwater to buy groceries. She planned to stockpile a lot of nonperishables so that she wouldn't have to make a trip out again if the weather turned bad.

Her first stop, however, was the drugstore. She was driving herself crazy wondering if she was pregnant. She felt a bit tired, but that could be from waking in the night to give Shell a break from caring for Ashley.

She hadn't felt sick. Her breasts weren't especially tender. The only clue—lack of a period—could be explained by the move and the stress preceding it.

When she reached the drugstore, she became very conscious of the smallness of the community. She hoped for anonymity, but the druggist greeted her by name.

"I'm sorry, but I don't know your name," she stammered, shocked that he knew her.

"It's Fred Parsons. Recognized you right away from seeing you at the post office once, talking with Maggie. What can I do for you today? If you need a prescription filled, it'll take a little while, but I'll treat you to a soda while you wait." He gestured at the old-fashioned soda fountain at the side of the store.

"No, nothing today. I just came in to browse." She couldn't buy the kit. The entire town would know before Jake did. She couldn't do that to him. Would the grocery story carry the test kits? If so, maybe she could slip one into the basket and get out without much notice. Otherwise, she was heading for Laramie. It would take longer and she'd have to call home to let them know she'd be late, but no way was she letting everyone speculate before she knew herself.

The grocery store was crowded. Others were obviously using the break in the weather to stock up, as well. She filled two carts and part of a third, slipping in a pregnancy kit she found in sundries. When it was time to check out, she studied the clerks. Some were personable and chatted with the customers. One, however, looked like she had a steady diet of prunes. She rarely spoke to the customers, ringing up the items with little interest. That was her gal today, Brianna decided.

She nervously watched the clerk when the pregnancy kit passed by, but it might as well have been a box of tissues for all the notice the woman gave it. The bag boy didn't seem to notice it, either. He was too busy flirting with a girl two registers over.

Brianna felt as if she'd just made it through some hazardous assignment by the time she reached the truck. Once the bags had been placed in the rear, she took a moment to rummage around for the kit, then placed it securely in her large purse. She didn't want to chance anyone seeing it at home, either.

She had two more stops to make and then she was homeward bound. She swung by the bank, doing her business quickly, stopped at the feed store, and she was done.

When she arrived home, she found all the men out somewhere, except for Shell. He was feeding Ashley in the kitchen, talking softly to her. He looked up when Brianna arrived.

"If you wait a few minutes, she'll be finished and I'll help you bring in the groceries," he said.

"I'll get started, and if I bring them all in, I'll consider it good exercise," she said, wanting to get that done so she could slip away to the privacy of the bathroom.

It seemed to take forever to unload and put away the purchases. Shell was there constantly. Ashley sat in her infant seat, content and seeming to watch their every move.

Once finished, Brianna asked if he wanted her to watch the baby while he went to do something.

"If you don't mind," he said. "I have a couple of chores to do. Next week my cast comes off, and I'll be back on the rotation."

"Take your time. She and I will be fine."

Actually the baby was starting to fall asleep. Brianna took her up to her crib and covered her. Then she got the test kit and headed for the bathroom....

SHE WAS PREGNANT.

The possibility had been there for days, she acknowledged, feeling fluttery and shaky. But the reality was still startling. She was going to have a baby in nine months and be a mother for the rest of her life. Amazing!

She had to tell Jake. It would go a long way to reassuring him the ranch would soon be his.

Yet she hesitated. How would this change their relationship? Would he decide he'd done his bit and withdraw?

She'd think about it for a day or two. In the meantime she hugged herself giddily. *She was pregnant!*

TUESDAY MORNING Maggie called to say she'd be by around two o'clock. "I'm bringing Loni, if that's all right."

"Of course it is. I'm surprised she hasn't come out earlier."

"I guess something Shell said had her thinking she wasn't welcome there."

"Ashley is her child, too. Of course she's welcome."

Relieved the weather was good and that the men would be working in the afternoon, Brianna rushed through lunch.

"You in a hurry?" Jake asked as she whisked the empty plates away as soon as the men finished.

"Lots to do today," she murmured. She'd told Jake and Shell last week about Maggie's visit. But she didn't want to mention that Loni was coming, too. It wasn't that she was afraid he'd forbid it, exactly. It just seemed an easier way to keep harmony in the house.

"If the baby's going to be a problem, I'll stay in," Shell said.

"No. She's no problem. Besides, did you forget her aunt Maggie is coming?" The last thing Brianna wanted was a confrontation between Loni and Shell if they'd already ended things.

He frowned. "Should I stay around for that?"

Brianna smiled brightly. "I don't see why, unless you want to visit with her."

"No." He stood up and grabbed his hat and jacket, heading outside right behind Nolan and Hank. Jake remained a moment, eyeing her suspiciously.

"What's going on?"

She looked at him and smiled. "Not a thing you need to worry about. I baked a cake this morning to serve Maggie. There should be plenty left for dessert tonight," she said, hoping to change the subject.

He nodded and left.

"Whew, I'm not good at subterfuge," she murmured as she began to wash the dishes.

Ashley cooperated perfectly when Brianna changed her into the little red dress she'd bought her. No matter how high Brianna turned up the heat, the old house still seemed drafty and cool. She bundled Ashley in a soft blanket and held her while waiting for her guests. Soon she saw an unfamiliar car.

When it came to a halt at the front of the house, Brianna put Ashley in her infant seat and hastened to the front door, opening it when she heard them on the porch.

"Welcome," she said giving Loni a hug. "How are you doing?"

"I'm feeling fine," she said.

Brianna wondered at the truth of the statement when she noted the dark circles beneath Loni's eyes and the almost gaunt look to her. But she smiled and greeted Maggie.

The woman carried a wrapped present. "I brought a few things for the baby. I can't wait to hold her."

"Come in and I'll take your coats. She's in the living room. It's the warmest room in the house these days."

Loni handed Brianna her jacket and almost ran into

the living room. Brianna exchanged glances with Maggie and took her coat. "Has it been hard?" she asked.

"I think she misses that baby something awful, but she won't admit it."

They entered the living room together. Loni was on the sofa, holding Ashley in her arms, cooing at her, her eyes shining.

"She's bigger, isn't she?" she asked, looking at Brianna. "I'm sure she's grown some."

"Probably. She has a great appetite. She'll be ready to eat before long. You can feed her."

Maggie and Brianna chatted while Loni fed the baby. When it was time to leave, Loni made no move to get up. She'd held her daughter the entire time, except for a brief moment when Maggie had a turn.

"Loni, do you have any paintings that would be suitable for over the fireplace?" Brianna asked. "I want something special, and thought of your work."

"I might have something big enough that would go with the colors." She studied the wall for a moment. "Maybe a landscape. I did a couple of large ones, but they aren't as good as my smaller ones. Elsa always did small paintings, and I wanted to be more like her."

"Your style is your own," Maggie said. "And quite nice."

Loni smiled smugly. "Actually Elsa Harrington said I showed great promise. I've been working hard for more than a year now. I'm ready."

"When do you leave for New York?" Brianna asked, crossing to take the baby.

Loni watched with sad eyes as Brianna cuddled Ashley close. The baby soon fell asleep.

"I'm not sure. I'm not in that big a rush. Maybe I can come here next week and see the baby again."

"Any time, Loni. She's your daughter."

Loni blinked back tears and nodded. "Did Shell know I was coming today?"

"No. I thought it best if he didn't."

"You're probably right. Next time I come we can look through the paintings if you can wait that long."

"And I can ask the men to build the crates. Then when you sort what you'll be taking and what you'll leave behind, you can crate them immediately."

"That's fine. Thanks, Brianna." Loni got up and in only a few moments she and Maggie had left.

Brianna headed upstairs to put Ashley back in her crib, covering her warmly. She let her fingers brush the downy hair on her head.

"I think your mommy loves you more than she expected," Brianna murmured as she tucked her in. "She sure had love shining from her eyes when she was holding you today."

THE NEXT MORNING a huge tractor-trailer rig pulled into the yard, loaded with several tons of hay.

Jake watched in disbelief as Harvey Williams maneuvered the truck until he was in position to unload it in the storage barn.

Jake walked over.

"Morning, Harvey."

"Morning, Jake. I assume you want it in the barn.

Elsa always kept it here. Keeps it dry for the most part.''

''I think there's been a mistake. I didn't order any hay.'' Jake studied the truck. That was more hay than he would have ordered even if he'd had the money.

Harvey pulled out the order, scanned it quickly and shrugged. ''Paid in full. For delivery here.'' He handed Jake the sheet of paper. Glancing at it, he paused when he reached the name—Ashley Blue-feather.

''Dammit! Wait here, Harvey. Don't unload a single bale.'' Jake turned, clutching the paper in his hand, and stormed toward the house. He slammed into the kitchen. Brianna looked up from feeding the baby. The rocker had been pulled near the stove and she was watching the beans simmer, as well.

''What the hell do you think you're doing?'' Jake asked.

''Feeding Ashley?'' Brianna looked at the sheet in his hand and took a deep breath.

He held out the order slip. ''What do you know about this?''

''Oh, that.''

''Yeah, that. I told you no mingling of funds until we knew for sure if this was going to work.''

''I didn't mingle any funds.''

''Do you see how many thousands of dollars you spent on this hay? It goes back!''

''It's your hay, and you can do whatever you want with it,'' she said reasonably.

''What were you thinking?''

"Hmm, at which point? When you were being paranoid to believe that I was here to take over the ranch? Or when you were being stubborn and refusing to even consider another solution? Or when Ashley and I discussed my birth present to her and she said she wanted to help her grandfather and daddy?"

Jake stared at her, then looked at the baby.

"If you'll notice, the hay is from Ashley, not me," Brianna said mildly, shifting the baby to burp her. "And if Ashley wants to spend money on her daddy's ranch, then you tell her she can't."

"I told you—"

"Well, you aren't the ruler of the world. What Ashley and I decide to do, we'll do."

"It goes back!"

"Fine. You'll have a terrific credit with the feed store."

"They can refund you the money."

Brianna smiled. Jake didn't like the cat-ate-the-canary look to that smile.

"But I didn't give them a check, and you don't have the receipt. I doubt they'll be giving that much money to someone on your say-so."

"How did you manage that?"

"Cashier's check," she said with a grin.

"Hey, Jake, Harvey says the hay is for us." Shell entered, holding his hat in hand. "Says he can't wait here all day and we need to get it unloaded. Where did you get the money? I thought—"

Shell stopped when he looked between Jake and Brianna.

"Oh, man," he said softly.

"Your daughter bought it," Brianna said.

"What?"

"I gave her a present for being born. She and I discussed it and she decided to help out with the ranch. It's to be her home, right? And mine?"

Jake turned away, pride burning. He felt like a charity case. He didn't want or need Brianna's money. Just how much did she have if she could be so unconcerned about the cost of the hay? Glancing around the worn kitchen, he wondered again how much she'd given up to settle here.

Had he been paranoid? Had he not considered her feelings about belonging, being a part of the ranch? Jake knew he didn't trust women. He never had after seeing his grandmother in action. But Brianna was not Elsa Marshall. Maybe she had done just what she said, giving the ranch a shot in the arm and helping ensure her own future here.

God knew, he needed that hay. If they had any shot at getting the ranch into the black, they needed every steer and heifer to be standing come spring.

She came over to him, holding Ashley between them.

"Just tell Ashley thank you, Jake, and go unload your hay. I'm not trying to take away your home. I'm only trying to make it mine, too."

CHAPTER TWELVE

THURSDAY, Brianna spent the morning cleaning every room on the first floor of the house, except the office. It was the first time Jake's friends would be visiting and she wanted to make a great first impression.

As she studied the living room, she was struck again by the bare walls. Even if she got a couple of pictures from Loni, it wouldn't be enough. Maybe she'd look in the attic as Jake had suggested.

No time for that before their guests arrived. She'd decided on pot roast for dinner. Cooking everything in one pan would enable her to visit with the Ramseys. She didn't like the idea of staying in the kitchen. On the rare occasion when she entertained in New York, she'd had food delivered. No such luxury existed here.

Brianna found she liked cooking, remembering many of the things her mother had taught her, even though she hadn't used them much in the past decade. The men were always appreciative.

She ran up to change in plenty of time to be ready when Jim and Diane arrived. She was putting earrings in her lobes when Jake entered their bedroom.

He stopped a moment and looked at her. Brianna turned, holding her breath. She hoped she'd chosen appropriately. It was important to her to make friends here. The long skirt was soft and feminine. The silk top was elegant, yet comfortable.

"No one said this was a dress-up dinner," he said, stepping inside and beginning to unbutton his shirt in preparation for his shower.

"This is casual," she said, looking back into the mirror. Was it too much?

"I expect Diane will wear jeans. I know Jim will."

"Oh." She bit her lip in indecision. She wanted to present a gracious setting, but if she was going to look out of place, maybe she should change into jeans. Or maybe wool slacks.

"You look pretty," Jake said, coming up behind her, gazing at her in the mirror. "Gussied up like a city slicker. Is that how you dressed in New York?"

She nodded. "For a quiet evening in."

"A world of difference between there and here."

"I guess I'll change."

"Naw, leave it. Too bad Loni can't see you—she'd would love it. It would fit her idea of sophisticated. Give her something to strive for when she moves."

Brianna wondered if Jake didn't like sophistication, but it was getting close to the time his friend and wife would be arriving. She hoped she didn't feel too out of place with their guests. She'd come into this hoping to belong. So far she didn't feel she did.

Nolan had cleared the snow from the front of the house and Brianna turned all the lights on, hoping they'd use the front door, instead of the kitchen door as the family did.

When the doorbell rang a few minutes later, she looked at Jake in surprise. "I didn't even know there was a doorbell."

"Not used much," he said, heading for the door.

Brianna followed, standing back a little to watch Jake greet his old friend. Jim Ramsey was as tall and as muscular as Jake. He wore a thick jacket and the ubiquitous jeans. But they, like the ones Jake wore, were new and showed no signs of wear.

Diane Ramsey followed her husband in and smiled a warm greeting to Jake, then sought out Brianna. Her smile widened when she saw what Brianna was wearing.

"Told you," she murmured to her husband. "I'm so glad to meet the woman who snagged Jake Marshall. According to Jim, he was the perennial bachelor. I'm Diane Ramsey."

Brianna shook hands with both of them. Diane was also wearing a long woolen skirt with a matching sweater. "I thought a woman from New York wouldn't wear jeans when having company over," she murmured as they moved into the living room. She stopped in the doorway and looked around. "It's lovely. So warm and inviting."

Brianna was pleased by Diane's compliment and began to relax. She would fit in if she hung around Diane Ramsey!

Dinner went well, with even Jake loosening up a bit when he and Jim began to reminisce about their boyhood exploits.

"Shell should hear this," Brianna remarked after a

funny story about Jake's taking a foolish dare and breaking his arm as a result.

"Where is Shell?" Jim asked.

"He and Ashley are with the hands," Brianna said. "We invited him to join us, but he said he'd keep the baby away so we'd have some peace and quiet."

"You're a grandfather already," Jim teased Jake. "I'm way behind. My oldest is only two."

"I thought you just had the one."

Diane smiled sunnily and said, "So far, but I'm pregnant again. We expect this one in May."

Brianna wanted to blurt out her news. Her baby would be only a few months younger than Diane's. But she needed to tell Jake before anyone else. And she still hadn't found a way to do that without his bundling her off to the guest room for the duration.

Shell returned to the house just as Brianna was replenishing the coffee. Dessert had been eaten and they were moving to the living room.

"Any dessert left?" he asked. Ashley was fretful and he rocked her gently in his arms.

"I saved you a big piece of apple pie. It's in the oven keeping warm. There's ice cream, too," Brianna said, reaching for the baby. "Can I show her off to the Ramseys?" she asked.

"If you think they'd want to see her," he said, opening the oven for the pie.

"They'll love her. Won't they, sweetie?"

Diane and Jim fussed over the baby like long-lost relatives. When Brianna handed her to her grandfather, Jake took her with ease. He had never been around

Shell as a baby, or any others for that matter, but he had picked up the technique in no time.

Brianna knew he'd be delighted with her news. But it would change things, and she was still reluctant to do it any earlier than she needed to.

She brushed her hair from her face. It was warm in the living room with the fire Jake had roaring in the fireplace.

"Shell, come in," Jake said, spotting his son in the doorway, plate of apple pie à la mode in one hand.

"I'm going to have some dessert. If you want, I can take Ashley up first." He stayed in the doorway.

"No need, come in and eat here. You remember Jim Ramsey. Have you met his wife, Diane?"

"I'll get the coffee. I'll be right back," Brianna said once introductions had been made and Shell settled in one of the armchairs.

"I'll help," Diane said, joining her.

The kitchen was also hot. Brianna quickly checked to make sure she'd turned off the oven. She brushed her forehead again, feeling warm and a bit light-headed.

"Jim told me that Shell was Jake's son. Hard to believe he has a grown man for a son, isn't it? You can't be much older than Shell."

"Not old enough to be his mother, but still, there are thirteen years between us. Do you and Jim like cream—"

Suddenly everything went black, and Brianna crumpled onto the floor.

"JIM! JAKE! Help, I need you!"

Jake felt his heart stop when he heard Diane yell. He was on his feet and in the kitchen without thought, Jim and Shell right behind.

"What happened?" Jake asked, crossing swiftly to Brianna and hunkering down beside her. He touched her forehead, her cheeks. "She's so pale."

"She fainted. We were talking about cream for the coffee, and she just sighed softly and collapsed," Diane said.

"Call the doctor!" Jake snapped at Shell, reaching out to scoop Brianna up and hold her close to his chest. Standing, he turned to Jim.

"I'll put her on the sofa until we know more."

She began to stir, her eyes fluttering. Jake swallowed hard, feeling relief flood through him.

"What happened?" she asked, looking puzzled.

"It appears you fainted," Jake said, walking through the door Jim held and heading back to the living room.

"I can walk," she protested.

"Maybe, but I'd rather you didn't. Shell's calling the doctor. We might have to take you to the hospital. How do you feel? Did you hit your head when you fell?"

She closed her eyes, her head snuggled against his chest. "I felt light-headed and then everything went black."

Jake could hear the fear in her voice. He understood—he felt a little fear himself.

Carefully he laid her on the sofa.

"What can I do?" Jim asked.

"Nothing yet. Watch her. I'm going to see what the doctor—"

Shell entered carrying the portable phone against his ear. "Okay, she's awake." He held the phone to Brianna.

Jake sat beside her, his hand on her shoulder as if to provide reassurance.

"Hello?" Brianna gazed around the circle of concerned faces. Only Ashley, now held by Diane, appeared oblivious to the situation.

"I was hot, I remember that. Both the living room and the kitchen seemed like ovens. Then, everything just went black."

She listened for a moment, then looked up. "How long was I out?"

"Only a few seconds," Diane said. "I don't think you hit your head or anything, just sort of sank to the floor."

Brianna relayed the information, then nodded. "Tomorrow at ten. I'll be there." She clicked off the phone and handed it to Shell, avoiding Jake's eyes. "She says I should take it easy the rest of the evening and then see her in the morning."

Jake stood and paced to the fireplace and back. "I'm not waiting until morning. No one just passes out in the middle of a conversation for no reason. Your health is too important to wait until morning. I'm taking you in to the hospital. I want a doctor to examine you, not listen to a few words on the phone!"

Brianna reached out and caught his arm as he made to pace back to the fireplace.

"It's okay, really. It's not totally unexpected, Dr. Fleming said, given the circumstances."

"Oh," Diane said, smiling at Brianna.

"What circumstances?" Jake demanded.

"I was trying to find a way to tell you. I certainly didn't expect to do it like this," Brianna said, glancing around at the others in the room.

"I think that's our cue to leave," Diane said to her husband.

"Why? Jake might need help," Jim said.

"Jim, we need to leave!"

"I'm sorry the evening ended like this," Brianna said. "I had such a great time until I fainted. Please come again."

"You should come out and see us next time," Diane said, reluctantly handing Ashley back to Shell. "You can meet our little bundle of terror. Travis is a handful, but he's all ours."

The Ramseys left with plans for future visits, then Shell took Ashley upstairs.

Jake turned off lights and made sure the door was locked. He crossed quickly to Brianna when he returned to the living room. "Are you sure you're all right? I can run you into town now. Not wait for morning."

"Truly, I'm fine." She hesitated a moment, then looked at him. "I wanted to wait until just the right moment, but I haven't found it yet, and at the rate you're going, you'll work yourself up when there's no need. I'm pregnant. The doctor said sometimes pregnant women faint.''

"Pregnant?'' He appeared stunned. "Are you sure?''

"I took a pregnancy test, talked to Dr. Fleming on the phone and yes, I'm pretty sure.''

"Hot damn.'' He leaned back on the sofa, staring at the ceiling.

"I'm going to bed,'' Brianna said, standing. "Sorry for flaking out on you. What a stupid ending to a great evening. I like your friends.''

"I'll go up with you.''

"You don't have to.''

"You could faint again and fall down the stairs. If you won't think about yourself, think of the baby,'' he said sharply.

Of course his concern would be for the baby. Not that she would do anything to harm their child. But his focus would always be on their baby first and others second, if at all.

"I don't feel faint. I'm not feeling hot or lightheaded like before. And I really don't need an escort every time I go up or down the stairs.''

"Maybe we should fix up a bed for you down here, save you the stairs,'' he suggested.

"No. I want our room.''

"Our room?'' he said evenly. "Wouldn't you be more comfortable sleeping by yourself?'' he asked.

"All my things are in our bedroom,'' she replied, heading doggedly toward the stairs.

"They can be moved,'' he said.

"Darn it, Jake, do I have to spell it out for you?" She pulled away and turned to glare at him. "All right. I don't want to move out of our room. I want to keep sleeping with you. There, are you satisfied?"

JAKE STARED at her. Color was high in her cheeks. Her eyes sparkled. Her hands were on her hips and she waited, almost without breathing, for his response.

As if he was going to argue with her. She wanted to stay with him? Sleep with him?

"Hell, I thought you'd be glad to have your own space again."

"Well, I'm not."

"Well, then. Sure, stay. I mean, we are married and all."

"If it's no trouble."

He rubbed a hand across his face, wondering what to say that wouldn't screw things up.

"It's just...well, I thought you'd put up with enough."

"Put up with what?" she asked, relaxing her position slightly.

He remembered she should be getting into bed. "Need help?"

She shook her head.

"Then get on up and we'll talk there."

"I like that the best," she said.

"What?"

"When the lights are off and it's just you and me, talking in the night," she said, starting up the steps. He followed. One minute he was worried she was sick, the next elated to know she was pregnant. But her decision to stay in their room had him the most off-kilter.

"Was talking in bed the only thing you liked?" he asked when they reached their room. He had to hear the reality before he became dumb enough to weave fantasies about something he knew nothing about.

"No," she said softly, reaching for her nightgown.

"What else?"

She threw him a look and sank onto the edge of the bed. "Use your imagination," she said. "I could use a little help here, after all."

He was there in a second, feeling all thumbs and awkward male, but wanting to extend the conversation he was finding fascinating. He unfastened the zipper.

She pulled her top over her head and tossed it toward the dresser. It fell short, landing in a puddle on the floor. Brianna looked up at Jake and smiled slowly as she saw him look at the creamy tops of her breasts showing above the lacy bra.

"Maybe we should celebrate our new baby," she said huskily.

Desire flooded Jake, but caution held him back. "Maybe we should wait."

"For what?" Brianna pulled her nightgown closer and held it against her chest as if suddenly shy.

"The baby…"

"I understand people can make love almost until the baby arrives with no problems," she said. "Unless you'd rather not."

Jake stared at her. Was she crazy? He could hardly

do his work during the day without thinking about her. He'd have them go to bed at seven in the evening if he didn't think everyone, including Brianna, would consider him totally nuts.

From the uncertainty in her expression, he knew she hadn't a clue how she affected him.

They were even, then, because he hadn't a clue how he affected her. He would have bet the ranch she'd have been happy to conceive if it meant he'd leave her alone. Now she was making overtures. Women. They never ceased to amaze him.

Jake sat on the mattress next to her and gently tugged the nightgown away. Slowly he tangled his fingers in her silky hair and tilted her face toward his. When he kissed her, she sighed softly. He felt her breath against his cheek and didn't know what to think. Maybe thinking was overrated. At this point, all he wanted to do was feel—feel every inch of Brianna against him. Hear her soft noises when they climaxed together, talk to her just before falling asleep.

He reached over and flicked off the light, then proceeded to make love to his wife, the mother-to-be of his next child.

JAKE INSISTED on driving Brianna into town to see the doctor the next morning. She protested, but he was adamant.

"What if you fainted again?" he asked. That ended the argument.

They took Ashley with them, freeing Shell to work.

His arm was almost mended and he was using it more and more every day.

The snow sparkled in the bright sunshine, and Sweetwater seemed to glisten in the clear air.

"I'll go in with you," Jake said when he parked beside the building where the doctor's office was located.

"There's no need," Brianna said. "Why not take Ashley for a walk? She's bundled up well."

"Any reason I shouldn't go with you?" he asked.

Brianna hesitated only a split second before shaking her head. She needed to tell him about her TIA. She had put it off for too long now. Jake deserved to know. But she certainly didn't want to have the doctor question her and have him find out that way. She needed a way to tell Jake that wouldn't freak him out now that she was pregnant.

Her doctor in New York had said he didn't think there would be anything to worry about as long as she changed her lifestyle and reduced stress. Which she'd tried to do.

Brianna knew she'd do everything in her power to make sure she had a healthy baby. Having Jake worried every moment until then was not something she wanted!

Stepping into the waiting room, Brianna glanced around. It was almost full, women very obviously pregnant, others with toddlers in arms. She glanced over her shoulder at Jake and almost laughed at his expression. She knew he hadn't thought this through.

"Take Ashley for a walk. I'll be out when I'm finished," she said.

Just then the door from the office opened and Loni came through. She spotted Brianna and her face broke into a smile. Then she caught sight of Jake and froze for an instant, until she saw Ashley in his arms. Heading determinedly for them, she stopped only inches from the baby, her eyes never leaving her daughter.

"Can I hold her?" she asked, reaching out. Jake took a step back, tightening his grip on the baby. "Thought you'd be in New York by now," he said.

Every eye in the waiting room was on them. Brianna pushed Jake back out the door, Loni right beside her. Closing it behind her, she glanced around the lobby of the building. Fairly empty, just people passing through who were not paying any attention to the four of them.

"I just want to hold her," Loni said. "She is my daughter."

"Some claim you abandoned her. She's Shell's," Jake said.

Loni was clearly stricken. "I didn't abandon her. Don't ever tell her that!"

"What would you call it, then?"

"She's living with her father and grandparents. Isn't that what you wanted?"

"Don't," Brianna said, putting her fingertips over Jake's mouth when he opened it to say something else. "Don't say another word. You're making things worse."

"They don't get worse," he muttered, glaring at her.

Before Jake knew what she was doing, Brianna took Ashley from his arms and handed her to Loni.

She then linked her fingers with his and tugged him toward the office door.

"Jake and I have an appointment with Dr. Fleming. We'll be done in about a half hour. You watch her until then."

"Brianna," Jake warned, standing immovable.

"Come on, you wanted to see the doctor, so now's your chance."

They reentered the waiting room, the object of everyone's curiosity. Brianna took a breath, raised her chin and went to the window to let the receptionist know she was there.

No one in the waiting room said a word. Brianna glanced around and then looked at Jake. No wonder. Probably no one dared speak for fear he'd scowl at them the way he was scowling at her. She knew he'd have plenty to say when they were alone.

She'd been surprised to see Loni, but not surprised to see the hunger in her eyes when she looked at her baby. Brianna suspected the reality of being separated from her child was beginning to tell on Loni. For all her longing to escape Sweetwater, she was still here. And her less-than-enthusiastic response to Jake's questions had Brianna wondering even more if moving away was really what Loni wanted.

CHAPTER THIRTEEN

LONI DIDN'T KNOW what to do with the baby, besides marvel at how beautiful she was. She hesitated a moment when Brianna and Jake disappeared into the doctor's office, then took the first step. There was a bank of benches lining the wall in the lobby. Loni sat down, gingerly holding the baby.

"Hello, Ashley, how are you?" she asked in a low voice, brushing the soft rosy cheeks. "Are you warm enough?" The baby was bundled up in a pink-and-white fleece snowsuit and wrapped in a white blanket. The little knit cap on her head was hot pink and covered her forehead almost to her eyebrows.

The lobby was heated, but with the constant opening and closing of the outer doors, cool air swirled around them.

"I've missed you," Loni said, darting a glance around to make sure no one could hear her. "I didn't think I would, you know. But I do. I wish you could come to New York with me. But you're better off with your daddy and Jake and Brianna on the ranch." For a moment a wave of homesickness for the ranch rolled over her. Loni could scarcely breathe. She'd thought she'd been miserable on the ranch, with no other option than the life her mother and aunts had. She'd thought of nothing but getting away.

Now the time was right, and she still couldn't go. She held her daughter's tiny hand in hers, rubbing the tender skin with her thumb.

Ashley drifted back to sleep. Loni sat watching her, noting her thick eyelashes, her button nose. She didn't look much like either her or Shell, but was her own person. Loni wondered what she'd be like as she grew up. Would she be wild and carefree and into everything on the ranch? Would she love horses and cattle, or hate them as much as Loni had?

Though she hadn't always. Riding had been her passion until she'd discovered painting at fourteen, when her aunt had given her a set of acrylic paints. She and her cousins had spent long, lazy summers riding to the swimming hole or coming into town to get ice-cream sodas at the drugstore. She'd been in the Christmas pageant at school every year, sometimes only as an angel, but several times with a speaking part.

Would Ashley love the Christmas pageants? Would she and her friends spend summer afternoons swimming in the river or lazing beneath the cottonwoods?

Or would she be rebellious and troublesome as Shell had been growing up? With only Shelly Bluefeather to raise him, he'd been out of control. It was only after her death that he'd met his father. Jake had put down some strong rules and changed Shell's behavior a bit.

Loni caught back a sob. She missed Shell in ways she hadn't expected. Living in the same house but holding him off, she'd thought she could walk away when the time came. But being apart from him now, she wondered if she could. She longed to see him. Hear him say something, anything, even an insult.

Was she making a mistake? Giving up all she had here to go to the city to prove…what? That she could be rich and famous? Would anyone care? Her parents liked their lives. Shell liked working on a ranch. Even Brianna, who once had all Loni wanted, had given it up to come to marry a stranger and live in Wyoming.

"Why, Loni Peterson, is that you?"

She looked up into the face of Mrs. Abernathy, her fifth-grade schoolteacher.

"Hi," Loni said, smiling politely.

"I heard you had a baby. A little girl?" Mrs. Abernathy leaned over and looked at Ashley. "She's beautiful. I guess I'll have her in my class in a few years."

Loni nodded, realizing she knew a lot about how her daughter would grow up. Ashley would have some of the same teachers she and Shell had had. Participate in the same events, follow the traditions that were ingrained in residents of Sweetwater. There was a certain reassurance in knowing that.

She bet residents of New York never ran into their fifth-grade teachers.

"What did you name her?" Mrs. Abernathy asked.

"Ashley. Shell named her. Her daddy," Loni said, wondering what reaction she might get.

"Tell him hi for me, will you? I haven't seen him in a long time. He was always a secret favorite of mine. Guess it wouldn't hurt to let him know that now.

But, of course, at the time, I had to be impartial. But teachers always have favorites."

"I'll do that," Loni said, surprised at the reaction. Maybe not everyone viewed Shell as her parents did.

"I have to run—I have an appointment. See you at parent conferences one of these days." Mrs. Abernathy smiled and headed toward the bank of elevators.

If she stayed, Loni would be going to parent conferences, attending school plays, cheering Ashley on in sports events. Joining in the fun of Friday-night football games at the high school each fall.

Instead, she'd be in New York. A world away from Sweetwater, Wyoming. A world away from her daughter.

"I CAN'T BELIEVE you grilled Dr. Fleming like that," Brianna said as she and Jake left the doctor's office.

"I just wanted to know some things."

"Some things? Good heavens, there's nothing else left. You asked about everything."

"Just to make sure I keep the baby safe."

That stung. She wished Jake cared as much about keeping her safe. Of course he did—but only because she carried their baby.

"I still think I can go riding," she said.

"Nope, not until after the baby comes. Anyway, the weather isn't that good for pleasure riding."

"I'm not staying in the house for the next several months."

"You could slip on the snow or ice."

"I managed fine for this long. I doubt I'll start falling now."

"No."

She stopped and looked at him, nailing him with her frown. "You are not the boss of me. I will do as I please. I'm not going to harm the baby, but I will not live like some pampered prisoner for the next seven months!"

"Are you pregnant?" Loni asked, joining them. Ashley was still asleep. "Of course you are. Why else would you be seeing Dr. Fleming? It didn't click when I first saw you. I only really thought about Ashley."

"I am, and this man thinks I should do nothing for the next several months but sit around and eat bon-bons."

"Fruit. Candy would be bad for you."

Loni laughed. "Cool. I'm happy for you, Brianna! Except now you'll have Jake on your case. He'll drive you crazy."

"He's already started. You should have heard the questions he asked the doctor." Brianna had been secretly flattered the first one had been about making love. She hadn't thought he'd ask such a thing of a stranger. Jake continued to surprise her.

"I'll take her," Jake said, reaching for Ashley.

Loni relinquished her reluctantly. She gave them both a bright smile. "Well, I'm heading back to Aunt Maggie's. I'll call you, Brianna, about coming to the ranch."

Brianna gripped Jake's arm before he could refute Loni's statement. They watched the girl leave.

"I don't want her on the ranch," Jake said.

"I thought I could invite whomever I wished to my home," Brianna said, relaxing her grip and slipping her arm through his. She checked Ashley, who was still sleeping.

"Dammit, of course you can. But…" He stopped and shook his head. "Do what you want. You will, anyway."

"Actually, if you really don't want her there, I'll honor your wishes," Brianna said. "But it was her home for a number of months. Don't make it so hard on her."

"She made it hard on Shell."

"Ah, the parent defending his young."

"You think that's silly?"

"No, I think it's wonderful. You are a terrific father, Jake. Shell's lucky to have you. I can't wait to see you with our child."

When he turned onto the graveled driveway some time later, he still heard Brianna's words echoing in his head. No one had ever told him he was a terrific father. He wasn't sure Shell would agree. But he was pleased Brianna thought so.

He glanced at her. She was asleep, leaning against the door. The baby in the car seat between them was awake, but quiet, her eyes staring at the rearview mirror. He'd missed so much of Shell's growing up. But he wouldn't miss Ashley's, or his and Brianna's baby's.

AFTER THE LUNCH DISHES were washed and put away, Brianna headed for the office. She had caught up on all the accounts for the ranch and was now working on getting all the information on the cattle input.

But first, she wanted to tell Connie and Nancy, have them spread the word to her friends in New York. She would even e-mail Steven, asking if he would look at Loni's paintings when she arrived in New York.

It felt odd to contact Steven. Even odder to be uncertain of his response. At one time she'd thought they were so close. How wrong she'd been. Still, for old times' sake, she hoped he'd give Loni a fair chance.

It was snowing again on Monday when Loni called to invite herself to the ranch.

Brianna worried about her driving in the snow, but Loni assured her she could manage. "I'll have my uncle's truck," she said, "and that way I can take the pictures back with me. He's got a camper shell on the back, so they'll stay dry."

"Come along, and bring a pizza when you come. I've been dying for one all weekend."

Loni laughed. "You already have cravings!"

"Just bring a pizza."

Shell came into the office on the last and waited until Brianna was off the phone.

"Jake said you could find the latest vet report. He wanted me to check on one of the mares."

"Just a sec." Brianna located the report in minutes and handed it to Shell. "That was Loni. She's coming out to get her paintings."

"And you're telling me because…?"

"I thought you'd want to see her."

"No. Thanks for the warning. I'll stay in the barn."

"She's not coming until after lunch, so you can at least eat with the rest of us at noon."

He nodded once and left.

Brianna shook her head. Obviously her attempts to patch things up weren't going to work.

LONI SHOWED UP a little after one-thirty. Brianna welcomed her into the kitchen and reached for the pizza box. "Thank you. I can't believe how much I've been craving pizza. I thought it was supposed to be pickles and ice cream."

"It can be anything. With me it was marshmallows. Is Ashley asleep?"

"Yes. She ate lunch around noon and went right to sleep. I'm sure she'll be awake before you leave, though. Want to see her now?"

"Yes, please." Loni jumped up.

"Go on, you know the way. We put her in the room you were using."

Sometime later Brianna had her fill of pizza and was staring out the window at the light snow. Shell was walking toward the house. Not able to resist, after all?

He entered the kitchen with a burst of cold air.

"Jake said I'm to help Loni if she needs help crating the pictures."

"I like what you've done to the living room," Loni said, entering. She stopped when she saw Shell.

"I still need something for the walls."

Loni shook her head, reluctantly looking at Brianna. "I doubt Shell wants anything of mine hanging on the wall. Every time he looked at it, he'd be reminded of me."

"Every time I look at our daughter, I'm reminded of you," he said. "I don't care what Brianna hangs on the walls."

"Your dad said there might also be some pictures in the attic. I haven't had a chance to look. Do you know of anything up there?"

Shell shook his head. "I've never been up there."

"Me, neither," Loni replied.

"Thought you'd be in New York by now," Shell said.

"I've come to get my paintings. Once I have them ready to go, I'll be off," Loni said.

"If that's all you're waiting for, then let's get them packed up," Shell said.

Ashley's wail came through the baby monitor on the counter.

"I'll go," Loni said.

"I'll go," Shell said.

Brianna said nothing. She sat back down and watched the two of them glare at each other.

"Both of you go. She's your daughter."

Brianna could hear them on the baby monitor when they entered the bedroom still bickering. She hoped Loni knew what she was doing. Brianna still thought the girl was a fool to throw away the devotion Shell had for her and to turn her back on Ashley. But it wasn't her life.

Suddenly the bickering ceased, and all Brianna could hear was Ashley's fretting. A moment later she heard steps on the stairs. Loni burst into the kitchen, tears in her eyes. "Let's go to the studio."

"What happened?" Brianna asked, rising.

"Arrogant male," Loni fumed, heading for the back door. "He kissed me."

Brianna heard Shell's voice crooning to the baby as she left the room following Loni.

She'd been in the studio only a few times. Loni had wanted to keep it to herself when she lived on the ranch, and Brianna had respected her privacy. She paused at the doorway, surveying the large light room. Canvases were still stacked against one wall, in several rows. Two easels were set up, one holding a partially completed painting.

Brianna studied the painting on the easel. It was a view of the mountains. Snow covered the peaks, drifting down like confectioner's sugar on the lower slopes. A sweep of open range was in the foreground, a lone derelict barn to one side. The painting wasn't finished, a third was only sketched in, but Brianna could feel the passion that had gone into the work. She wished Loni would finish it before leaving.

"You are talented," she said slowly.

Loni looked at the painting. "Do you think I'm doing the right thing? Moving away, I mean."

"I can't answer that for you. Only you know what's right for you, for your life at this point."

"I didn't expect to miss the baby so much. I didn't want to get pregnant, you know. It just happened. Then I resented Shell, though it wasn't his fault any more than mine. Making a baby takes two."

Brianna nodded. She didn't know what to say to Loni. Should she urge her to think her plans through some more? Or try to convince her to stay in Wyoming? Would that only get the girl's back up?

"Ashley is adorable, and I miss her every minute of the day," Loni said on a sob, struggling to maintain her composure. Brianna drew her into a hug, and that seemed to break down all Loni's defenses and she began to cry in earnest.

"I want to be with my baby," she wailed. "I should be the one changing her, feeding her, loving her. It hurts. I didn't expect it to hurt so much."

Brianna patted her back, praying for the right words. "Maybe you should spend more time with her. New York will wait, you know. It's not going anywhere."

"I've wanted to leave Sweetwater for so long. It's such a small place...nothing ever happens here."

"But your family is here and you can still paint. I've contacted my friend who runs a gallery. Maybe he can sell your paintings in New York. You could go there to visit."

"It wouldn't be the same."

"Then you have to decide. Ashley or living in New York."

Loni went to the sink, where she grabbed some paper towels, blotted the tears from her cheeks and blew her nose. "All great artists have to suffer."

"That's a bunch of bull," Brianna said, growing impatient. "Where did you ever hear that?"

"Elsa Harrington told me that. And she was considered one of America's greatest living artists."

"I know that, but from what I've learned about her since I've been here, she wasn't one of America's greatest mothers or grandmothers."

"No one understood her."

"Maybe she liked it that way," Brianna suggested. She wandered to the row of paintings leaning against the wall and looked at the first one, then flipped slowly through the entire group. The next-to-last one caught her eye—an old-fashioned still life with a worn Bible and faded flowers. It would be perfect on the living-room wall between the two big windows. She'd put a little pie-crust table beneath it. The painting demanded an old-fashioned frame, and maybe she could find one somewhere. She eased it from the stack.

"I'd like to buy this one from you," she said, turning to show Loni.

"You can have it," she said, scarcely glancing at it.

"Thank you, but I'll buy it. You're trying to build a career, remember?"

Loni shrugged. She sniffed again and shook her head. "I can't do this today. I'll have to come back."

"Come tomorrow. Shell's going into Laramie, so he won't be here. We'll bundle Ashley up and bring her here so you can spend time with her while you pick the paintings you want to ship."

"That would be great. Thank you, Brianna."

Brianna carried the painting to the house, wondering how much to pay Loni. Maybe there was a gallery in town or in Laramie that would frame it for her and could suggest its value. Where had Elsa shown her

work? Who'd brokered her sales? She bet Jake
would know.

Later that afternoon, with Ashley down for a nap,
Brianna ventured up into the attic.

The stairs were at the end of the second-floor hall.
When she reached the top, she saw that the attic covered the entire house, the roof sloped low on either
side, but she could walk upright in the center.

Dusty furniture, corded boxes, stacks of magazines
and old suitcases were everywhere. Brianna carefully
picked her way through, trying to get an overview of
everything there. It looked as if the Marshall family
had never thrown a thing away. A chair with three
legs was propped drunkenly against a stack of card-
board boxes. An old water-stained box was half falling
apart, its contents—old clothing—spilling out.

"Brianna, where are you?" Jake's voice came
clearly through the baby monitor she'd carried up with
her.

She went to the stairs and called down to him. He
had to be in Ashley's room for her to hear him so
well.

A moment later he appeared at the bottom of the
attic stairs.

"What are you doing up there?"

"I came to look for some pictures you said might
be here, or a small table," she said. "Come up, there's
something I want to show you."

He joined her in the dusty space. Brianna noted instantly that he took up a lot more room than she did.
His head brushed the ceiling even in the center.

"It's toward the far end," she said, leading the way. It was a cradle, and she reached out and rocked it gently. It moved smoothly from side to side.

"Isn't it lovely?" she asked. "Do you think we can take it down and fix it up for Ashley? And then for our own baby?"

"Ashley has a crib."

"This would be perfect in the office. I could work and have her with me. She wouldn't outgrow it for six months and then we can use it again. Please?"

Jake nodded and reached for the wooden cradle to carry it down. Brianna remained in the attic, looking behind boxes, continuing her exploration.

A few minutes later, Jake returned to the attic. She was half-hidden behind a stack of boxes, looking at several canvases stacked against the wall.

"Don't let anything fall on you," he warned, moving swiftly to her side. "We can wait on pictures, or you can buy some new ones. I don't think you should be up here right now. Too many things are precariously balanced and could fall on you."

"I'm fine. I'm almost done. I found a stack of paintings here. Three are already framed. Maybe we can use them." She maneuvered around the boxes and pulled off a dust sheet protecting the paintings. She caught her breath at the subject, a small boy playing near the river. For a moment she thought of Jake as a child. He would have had dark hair like this boy. Would he have been as lonely?

As Brianna continued to rummage around, Jake gazed around the attic. "What a bunch of junk," he said. "Someone should go through all of this and trash most of it."

"Are you volunteering?"

"No."

"I suspect that's why it never got done. No one wants to do it. Here's some other paintings. Can we take them downstairs where we can see them better? This light here isn't much better than candlelight. Do you think these are by your grandmother?"

"They don't look like it. Her style was romantic and light. These are dark. I'll carry them. Be careful going down the stairs—they're steep."

"I'm fine."

It took three trips to bring down the paintings Brianna had uncovered—fourteen in all. She had Jake line them up against the dining-room wall. Turning on the chandelier, she walked over to the first painting and studied it. The derelict wooden barn in the foreground reminded her of Loni's painting. But unlike Loni's, it was dark and somber.

"It's ugly," Jake said. "No wonder it was in the attic. It should have been tossed, not saved."

"It is ugly. We can get rid of it, then. No sense keeping paintings we don't want."

"First step in clearing out the attic?"

Brianna smiled at him. Jake felt his insides tighten. He had come in to check on her, but wondered what she'd say or do if he hustled her up to their bedroom and made love to her to ease the ache that seemed to be a permanent part of him ever since she'd arrived.

They didn't need to keep trying to make a baby, but his desire hadn't lessened.

After the way she'd been the other night, he began to suspect she wouldn't say no.

"This one is better," Brianna said, standing in front of another painting. "It doesn't fit in with what I'm trying to do in the living room, but it's a good painting. Maybe we can find a spot for it."

He shrugged. If he liked a picture, then well and good; if not, he didn't worry about it. Art wasn't something that interested him. A result of the relationship with his grandmother perhaps?

"I wonder if some of the colors would show better if they were professionally cleaned," Brianna murmured. "Who knows how long they were in the attic. I can see the dust on this one." She rubbed a fingertip across one of the paintings. "It's odd that some have frames and others don't."

"Maybe Elsa used the missing frames on other paintings. She could have acquired these just for the frames."

"I suppose."

"You could ask Bill Tyler. He's the man who used to show my grandmother's work. He has a small shop in town, his main gallery in Cheyenne and connections to galleries all over the state. If he doesn't do cleaning, he'd know who does. He can frame the ones you want." *Leave the damn paintings alone and pay attention to me,* he wanted to say. He ran his fingers through his hair. What was the matter with him? He'd come in to check on her, not—

"I bought one of Loni's today," she said, turning to face him.

That caught Jake's attention. "Why? To give her money to take off?"

"No, because I like it, and it'll look perfect between the windows. Anyway, I think she's having second thoughts. She misses her baby."

"She should have thought of that before making plans to leave," Jake said in annoyance. "If you would withdraw all the help you promised, maybe she'd stay."

"If she stays because she's forced, she'll always resent it. You can't *make* people do what you want, Jake. You know that."

"My grandmother pretty much did with my father."

"And you know how unhappy he was." She paused and looked at him questioningly. "Why did you come in? Do you need me for something?"

"Need or want?" he asked, his eyes never leaving hers. He saw her eyes sparkle, her lips lift in a slow smile.

"So, cowboy, just what is it you want?"

"You," he said, closing the distance between them.

CHAPTER FOURTEEN

BRIANNA DIDN'T GET to the cradle until after supper. It sat in the corner of the kitchen while she prepared the meal and fed Ashley.

"What's that for?" Shell asked when he came in.

"I'm going to fix it up for Ashley. Jake will put it in the office for me, and she'll be able to spend the day with me."

"She has a crib."

"Now she'll have another one," Brianna said, not planning to argue with him. Ever since Loni had left, he'd been like a bear.

At dinner, the cradle became the topic of conversation. "I had one as a baby," Hank said.

"Probably because cribs hadn't been invented yet," Nolan joked.

"I'm not that old, you ol' tomcat."

"Coulda fooled me."

"Maybe you can help me clean it up and find something to use for bedding until I can get to town to buy a small mattress," Brianna suggested to Jake, amused by the cowhands' banter.

"Jake doesn't want to be messing with some stupid cradle," Shell said. "If it's for Ashley, I'll do it."

"We can all work on it as a family project," Brianna said.

"I don't need any help."

"Families do things together. We could be starting a new tradition."

"You just want to clean it up because your own kid will use it in a few months."

"Exactly." Brianna beamed at him as if he'd spoken with warm intent, not with a nasty snarl.

Shell pushed back from the table, his meal half-eaten. "I'm not helping, you're not part of my family, and I'm not big on tradition. Maybe I should look for someplace else to live and work." He stomped out of the room.

"What bee got up his butt?" Nolan asked.

Jake shrugged. The rest of the meal passed in silence. As soon as Nolan and Hank left, Jake looked at Brianna.

"Family project?"

"Yes. And Shell's part of this family, too. Maybe you should make that clear to him. Our having a baby doesn't do anything to change his relationship to you or this family."

"He doesn't seem to want to be part of it," Jake said.

"Don't be dumb, cowboy. Of course he wants to be a part of it. Think about it. For the first fifteen years of his life, he didn't have a father. Now, even though he's living here, your focus is on someone else—someone not even born yet. How would you feel?"

Brianna stood up and collected Shell's plate, putting it into the oven to keep the food warm.

''Go talk to him, Jake. Tell him he's your son and no one will ever take that from him. That you want him here. Make him feel he belongs!''

She realized she must feel comfortable with him if she was willing to talk to him this way.

Was she beginning to have the sense she belonged? That she had a place on the ranch? Not just as the mother of the child that would allow him to inherit, but as herself. She wanted Jake to care for her because of who *she* was.

JAKE STARED at the woman he hardly knew. Would he ever understand her? She looked at him as if he'd done something wrong. Shell *had* to know he was part of the family—he was his son.

Brianna obviously expected him do to something. But what? Shell knew the score.

At last he tossed his napkin on the table, got to his feet and left the kitchen. Heading up the stairs, he hoped something would come to mind. He didn't relish facing Brianna again if he didn't resolve things.

Shell's door was open, the room empty. Jake headed for Ashley's room. He paused in the doorway of the dimly lit nursery, watching as Shell leaned over the crib, tucking in his baby girl, brushing his fingers lightly over her downy hair.

''I never got to do that,'' Jake said, leaning against the doorjamb, crossing his arms over his chest. Now he was here, and he still didn't know what to say.

Shell straightened and turned, his face in shadow.

"Would you have wanted to?"

"I think so. I cared for your mother a lot—she was my best friend. She should have tried to find me and tell me. I came back when my father died—she could have told me then."

"You never guessed?"

Jake shook his head. "Call me dense, but it never crossed my mind. I guess because I would have expected Shelly to tell me if we'd made a baby. I'm sorry I didn't get to see you when you were small."

Shell shrugged.

Jake took a deep breath and plunged on. "You're my son, my family. I'm so proud of you I could strut like a bull. Brianna said I needed to make sure you knew that. I'm not good with words, but I've wanted to make things right ever since I found out about you...."

"At least you didn't turn your back on me when you found out," Shell said grudgingly. "We had a good life in Texas."

"Did it change coming back here?" Jake asked.

Shell only shrugged.

"I considered giving up the ranch," Jake said.

That seemed to surprise Shell.

"Yes. But then I thought it better to stay. It'd be my revenge against that old witch. Once it's mine, it's mine to do with as I want, no strings. I'll be signing half over to you."

"What?" That staggered Shell, Jake could see.

"You're my son, so why not? You'd get it when I

die, but I don't want you waiting around the way I had to. You get half.''

"I thought you wanted a new baby with Brianna. She wants to be part of a family so bad you can almost touch it,'' Shell said. ''What about that baby?''

"Brianna had it tough growing up, like you did. Like I did. Seems to me the three of us should bond together, make more of the future than we had of the past. She's given up the most, I think. Changed her entire lifestyle, trying to find a place to fit in. It can't be easy.''

"It's too early to tell for sure, but I think she's going to be a good wife for you,'' Shell said.

"I think so, too. And a good friend to my son, if he'll let her. The thing is, I'm not much on family things. Didn't have any traditions—maybe came from having no mother around. But Brianna sets store by them. So maybe we should try.''

Shell remained still, as if thinking things through. ''Mom had us do things as a family. Women do set store by it, I guess.''

"Brianna's right,'' Jake continued, hoping he was saying the right things. ''We need to build our family ties. Strengthen them so Ashley won't have the problems we had. We'll give her a joyful childhood, with plenty of love to go around.''

"You're proud of me, huh?'' Shell asked.

Jake felt his heart melt. ''So proud I could bust. You have strong values and a good work ethic. Your mother was a terrific person and did a great job raising you. Wish I could claim some credit for it, but she did it all.''

"Yeah. She was special." Shell hesitated a moment, then continued, "You and I've been together six years—first time I knew you cared. I don't need half the ranch."

"Never said you needed it. I just plan to make you a partner."

"What about your new kid?"

"If any kid of mine wants to work the ranch, we'll see what we can work out. If not, you can have the whole kit and caboodle."

"Are you going to have more than one?"

"I think Brianna wants to fill this house with kids, to have so much family that no matter where she turns, there they'll be."

"That'll give Ashley plenty of playmates," Shell said, stepping forward. "Let's go do the family thing with your wife."

When Shell reached him, Jake wrapped his arms around his son for the first time, gratified beyond belief when Shell returned the hug. Just maybe, things would come right between them. Thanks to Brianna.

She was clearing the dishes when they entered the kitchen. Glancing over her shoulder, she took in their expressions. "Your dinner is keeping warm in the oven," she told Shell.

She looked at Jake and raised her eyebrows in silent question.

"We'll help you with the cradle when he finishes eating."

Shell sat down to eat the rest of his dinner. Jake poured himself a cup of coffee and joined him at the table.

"Why are all those paintings stacked against the walls in the dining room?" Shell asked.

"Brianna wants to put some of them up in the living room. I think it's her nesting instinct," Jake replied. "We found them in the attic."

"Where you found the cradle?"

Jake nodded.

"Think it was yours?"

"No. My folks didn't live here when I was born. It could have been my father's, though."

"Definitely a family tradition, then, having Ashley use it," Shell said, glancing at Brianna.

She turned around, her smile broad and contagious. "Yes. And as soon as you finish eating, we can get started. The thing needs a lot of work before it's clean enough for a baby. Ashley will love it. And I'll love having her in the office with me while I'm working."

"You don't have to be there all day every day," Jake said.

"I'm not. Just a few hours each morning. But it'll be fun to have her keep me company. I'm going to take the paintings to the man you recommended—Bill Tyler, right?—to see if he can clean them up and frame the ones I like. I hope they'll show better then. Who knows how long they were in the attic."

Brianna hesitated a moment, then added, "Loni's coming back tomorrow. She was upset today and didn't finish choosing which paintings she wants. I bought one from her."

"She's good," was all Shell said.

WHEN JAKE WAS ready to leave the next morning, he stopped at the back door and turned to Brianna. "You aren't planning to take the paintings in today, are you? Forecast is calling for flurries later."

"No, not today, just sometime this week. But I can drive in flurries, you know. It's blizzards that have me freaked."

He smiled. "They have us all freaked. I'll be working in the barn today. See you later."

Loni called at nine and said she was on her way— as long as Shell wasn't going to be there.

"No, he went into Laramie to do something for Jake. You might pass him on the road, but that's all. Come early and spend some time with Ashley."

"Thank you, Brianna, I'll do that."

Brianna took wrapped sandwiches and hot soup to the bunkhouse midmorning, asking Jake to eat with the men, explaining about Loni.

"I know you don't approve, but let me do this, please?" she asked.

"It's your house, too," he said. But she could see he was not pleased.

Loni showed up right at ten. She headed straight for the cradle and Ashley, then leaned down to pick her up.

"When did you get this?" she asked, studying the intricate carving on the headboard. The rich mahogany gleamed from the polish they'd given it last night. The bedding was topped by a frilly blanket that had been a gift from Loni's aunt Maggie.

"Found it in the attic. I went up yesterday to see if there were any paintings there I might want to use. I found a few. After they're cleaned, I'll know better if I want any of them. The ones I don't want, I'm getting rid of. You wouldn't believe all the junk up there."

Loni nodded. "Oh, yes, I would. If it's anything like my folks' place, there'll be stuff there owned by the Marshall who *built* the house. Things were hard to come by in the early days, so they saved everything. Every spring my mother threatens to clear out our attic, yet she never does."

They chatted about the possibility of ever getting rid of all the junk, about what to do with any paintings Loni didn't want to take, about Ashley and her schedule. Loni asked how Brianna was feeling, envious when she heard that Brianna had so far not experienced morning sickness.

"I was so sick at first I hated getting up in the morning," Loni moaned. "It isn't fair!"

Brianna laughed. "I'm enjoying it while I can. Who knows, I might still get it."

After lunch, they bundled Ashley into her snowsuit and were ready to depart for the studio when the front doorbell rang.

"Who in the world would be coming here today?" Brianna asked. Knowing that any neighbors would likely go around to the back, she headed for the door. She opened it—and froze. The last person in the world she expected to see on the front porch was Steven Forrest.

"Surprised to see me, love?" Steven asked as if they'd only parted yesterday.

"What are you doing here?" she asked, her brain seeming to shut down.

"I came to see you, Bri. Aren't you going to ask me in?"

She stared at the man she'd once thought she'd spend her life with. He seemed smaller than she remembered. His hair seemed thinner, or was it styled differently? His suit looked out of place on the rustic porch. For a moment she thought she might be hallucinating.

"Come in." Good manners overcame her surprise.

He leaned over and kissed her on the cheek. "I know you're surprised to see me. I got your address from Nancy. After your e-mail to me, I knew we had unfinished business."

"Uh, I don't think we do," she murmured, finding it hard to believe that Steven was actually in Sweetwater, Wyoming. He only left New York to go to London or Paris.

"Who is it?" Loni asked, coming in from the kitchen, carrying Ashley.

"This is Steven Forrest," Brianna said. "Loni Peterson. Steven is the one who owns the art gallery I told you about."

"Oh, you came all the way out here to see my work?" Loni looked stunned.

"Not exactly," Steven said. He turned to Brianna. "So this is the young artist you mentioned."

"Yes. She's heading to New York and I thought you could assess her paintings." Brianna felt totally confused. "What are you doing here?"

"I came to see you. See what you're up to and if you're ready to come back to New York."

"Steven, I'm married. I live here now."

"Don't be ridiculous, Brianna. How could you be happy here? Even I didn't realize how far off the beaten track this place was until I tried to make reservations. I had to drive from Cheyenne, which was the nearest city I could fly in to. There's nothing here for someone like you. Let's talk."

"Maybe I should leave you two together," Loni said uncertainly, looking back and forth between the two of them.

"We've said all we have to say," Brianna replied. She didn't want to be left alone with Steven.

He acted as if she hadn't spoken. "Look at this place," he said. He swept his arm around, stopping when he saw the dining room. "Why do you have paintings on the floor, instead of the wall?"

Trust Steven to get sidetracked by the paintings. He was an art connoisseur first and foremost.

"Look, Steven, it's nice of you to drop by. But I'm sort of busy now."

"Drop by? Brianna, I've been traveling for two days to get here. I'm not leaving because you're busy. I'll wait until you're free. Maybe I can help you hang those paintings."

"Most of them aren't even framed. I'm not sure which ones I want." She had an idea. "You could go with Loni to the studio and look at her pictures. Give her an assessment right here. That way she'll know what to ship and what to leave behind. Come back when you're finished, and then we can talk."

That would give her some much-needed breathing room. She had to think! She'd never expected Steven to show up in Wyoming.

His displeasure showed. Brianna remembered how he liked doing things his way.

"Please?" she said, wondering what she would do if he refused.

"Very well. But I'm not leaving until you and I have a serious talk."

"I'll take Ashley," she said, reaching for the baby. Loni relinquished her reluctantly. "Take Steven out and show him your work. You're lucky—not many people get a private assessment by Steven Forrest." Brianna tried to smile encouragingly for Loni, but was too distracted to tell if the smile was effective.

As soon as they left for the studio, she slipped on her own heavy jacket and carried Ashley to the barn. She wasn't sure if Jake was even around, but if he was, she wanted to be the one to tell him about Steven's unexpected arrival.

Jake was grooming one of the horses when she entered. A saddle sat nearby. He looked at her, his expression softening when he saw Ashley.

"Is this another family thing? Bonding with my granddaughter in the barn?" He dropped the currycomb and walked over to them, reaching out to brush a fingertip along the baby's soft cheek. Ashley tried to kick her feet, but they were wrapped securely in a thick blanket.

"Steven's here," Brianna blurted out.

Jake looked at her. "Who's Steven?"

"A man I knew in New York." She found herself reluctant to tell him that Steven was the man she'd been involved with.

"And why's he here?"

"To see me."

"To visit an old friend?"

Brianna couldn't hold his gaze. "I guess so."

"Where is he?"

"Loni's showing him her work. He's a gallery owner in Manhattan. If he takes her on, she'll have it made," she said.

"What do you want me to do? Come in and meet him?"

"Yes. Yes, that would be good." She gestured toward the horse and saddle. "Were you going somewhere?"

"Nolan found a problem with one of the wells. He called in. I was going out to try to fix it before the storm hits."

"Oh, well. That's more important. I think Steven will be here a while. He's looking at Loni's work. He owns a gallery in Manhattan."

"You said that. Should I be surprised that a man who owns an art gallery in Manhattan is here to see Loni's work?" Jake asked.

''Not exactly. I mean, I e-mailed him to ask if he'd look at her work when she got to New York. I didn't expect him to come here to see her. Me. Us.'' She was babbling.

Jake frowned. ''Are you feeling okay?''

''Yes.'' She shifted the baby. ''I'm sure Steven will be here for dinner—you can meet him then.''

CHAPTER FIFTEEN

WAS STEVEN SERIOUS about wanting her back? A little late, Brianna thought as she returned to the house. She was making a place for herself here. It wasn't all she'd expected, but she was growing to love the ranch and the pace of life.

Ashley grew fretful, and Brianna prepared a bottle. She took her up to the nursery to feed her, sitting on the rocking chair. Brianna delighted in the quiet time with the baby. It sure beat dealing with frantic clients or tight deadlines, she thought, smiling at the precious child.

"What do you plan to do with your life, pumpkin?" she asked softly. "I hope you find your niche right away and don't have to put up with all the turmoil that's going on around here."

When Ashley drifted off to sleep, Brianna settled her in her crib. She went back downstairs to make sure Shell hadn't left some dirty shirt somewhere, or Jake hadn't left the newspaper scattered around the living room as he occasionally did.

She looked again at the paintings in the dining room. She'd love to have one or two framed and hung—especially the one of the small boy. It reminded her of Jake.

"Brianna?" Steven called from the front door.

"Come in." At least this time she could be more gracious. She went to the dining-room doorway so he'd know where she was.

"How did it go?" she asked when he joined her.

"I gave her my assessment. She has some choices to make. What are these?" He looked at the first painting, picking it up and taking it to the window for better light.

"Who did this?"

"I don't know. We found all these in the attic. Only three are framed. I don't know if anyone ever hung them or not. Jake doesn't remember seeing them before."

He tilted the painting, apparently studying every detail. At last he put it down and glanced over at Brianna.

"How are you doing here, Bri? Wasn't your move a little drastic? The place is a dump. Did the cowboy marry you for your money? It looks as if he could use a major influx of cash."

Brianna bristled. "The ranch is doing fine," she said.

He looked at her for a moment, then turned back to the painting. "'Fine' and 'good' are very different." He put the painting down and lifted another one.

"Would you like some coffee?"

"Cappuccino would be nice."

"We only have regular coffee here."

Once again he looked surprised. "What happened

to the latte lover? How do you manage with plain coffee?''

She didn't tell him she drank only herbal tea these days. It wasn't important. Her future was vastly different now from what it had been when she and Steven had been a couple. She still felt a doubt or two, but for the most part, she was growing to love her life on the ranch—cranky stepson, aloof husband, no caffeine and all.

''I have French roast. Want some or not?''

''Yes, thanks,'' he said, turning back to the paintings.

Brianna took her time preparing the coffee. She also hunted up some cookies. If she'd known he was coming, she would have baked something.

She shook her head. Steven would be even more astonished to learn how much she enjoyed cooking and baking. In New York, takeout and eating out had been their preferred method of dining.

But that was the point, wasn't it? To change things from the way they'd been. The stressful, high-pressure lifestyle that had threatened her health was a thing of the past. And she had no intention of returning to it— or to him.

He was standing by the window gazing out when she came back. She glanced at the paintings. He'd stacked all but three in one pile.

Turning when she entered the dining room, he cocked an eyebrow at the items on the tray.

''Quite the domestic scene,'' he murmured.

''We can talk in the living room if you like,'' she

said, continuing on to the room she'd so lovingly re-decorated. Pleased with the result, she wanted to show it off.

Steven sat in the chair by the sofa. The one Shell often used. How different Steven seemed from the two men in her life now.

She served the coffee, then sat back on the sofa.

"I can't believe you really married the man. What were you thinking? Brianna, this isn't the life for you. A ranch in the middle of nowhere. No theater, no Star-bucks, nothing but endless land. And a lot of snow."

"I'm happy," she said, realizing it was true.

"Where is this cowboy you married?"

"He's a rancher. He's out on the range right now, working. But you can meet him later."

"Working in this weather? It's supposed to snow later."

"Work isn't halted because of weather. If you stay for supper, you can meet him. And his son and the other hands."

Steven glanced at his watch. "Actually, I was hop-ing to talk you into dinner in town. The hotel rec-ommended a nice restaurant."

"The Silverado."

"You've been there?"

"Sure. It's the only really nice restaurant in town. There's a café and a couple of saloons, but the Sil-verado has delicious food."

"Then come to dinner with me."

"I can't."

"Include your husband, if you like," he said, scowling at her answer.

"I'm the one who cooks here. If I'm gone, there's no one else, unless one of the men does it, and after a day out in this cold, I don't think I could ask that."

"You're the cook?" He couldn't have sounded more horrified if she'd told him she had leprosy.

Brianna was getting a little tired of his reaction. Had he been this stuffy and supercilious before and she hadn't noticed? Had Steven changed—or had she?

"No, I'm not the cook. I'm the wife of the man who owns this place. Part of what I do is cook for him and the crew. Wives have been doing that for centuries, you know." Who did Steven think he was to come and denigrate her chosen lifestyle? Brianna was starting to get angry.

"I can't picture you married," he said, "or stuck here in the boondocks. You belong in New York. Jerry and Suzi send their regards. They ask about you all the time." He was obviously attempting to disarm her.

Friends of Steven's. Brianna doubted they'd so much as mentioned her name. Surely he'd given them a long song and dance about her illness and his not being able to cope with seeing her that way. That was the line he'd given her.

"Tell them hi for me when you see them." When would that be? Surely he couldn't spend much time away from the gallery. "Who's minding the gallery for you while you're here?"

"Jackson. We're winding down an exhibit, then we'll be closed for a few days to set up the next. I'm displaying Carter Harris's work,'' he said importantly. Brianna remembered how excited he'd become about artists she'd never heard of. But it was his business, just as advertising had been hers.

She didn't miss it a bit. She knew, however, that Steven was very much a part of the art world, and could never walk away from it.

Their conversation turned to mutual friends, and then to what Steven had been doing since he'd last seen her.

She kept an ear out for Loni's return, but the afternoon progressed and the girl didn't appear. She wondered if she should check on her.

"Will you exhibit Loni's paintings?'' she asked.

"No.''

"Why not?''

"That's between the artist and myself. I have to head back to town shortly. I have some phone calls to make before the West Coast shuts down. Have dinner with me. We can finish talking over old times, at least. If you're sure you won't be returning to New York with me, then this will be our last evening together. You still mean a great deal to me, Brianna.''

She wanted him to mean a great deal to her. She'd devoted two years of her life to the man and hoped they would one day marry. She'd thought she loved him. But now, she felt nothing. And it made her feel vaguely guilty.

"I'll see.''

He kissed her cheek and left.

Brianna stood by the front door for several moments, until the cold forced her inside. She felt odd. One part of her relished the fact that Steven had come to find her. Another part realized it was far too late. The things she had once held dear no longer meant as much. She had new priorities. New dreams.

She should have told him about her pregnancy.

After checking on Ashley, she put some frozen stew on for dinner. Maybe she could serve the men and still go to Sweetwater to meet Steven.

Was she out of her mind? She was a married woman.

Jake could come with her.

"Oh, right, like that's ever going to happen—especially if he suspects Steven is the man I once thought I'd marry," she murmured.

But the thought of hearing more about Manhattan, about what mutual friends and acquaintances were doing was appealing. She did get tired of talk about cattle all the time. In truth, she was a little homesick for the life she'd left behind.

Jake returned around five. He stopped by the office on his way in. "Friend gone?" he asked.

Brianna was composing an e-mail to send her friend Nancy, reminiscing about their time together in Manhattan. She had once been as young as Loni and as full of dreams. For a little while that excitement had been enough.

"He had some business to take care of. He invited us to join him for dinner at the Silverado."

"What about the men?"

"I've made a stew. I'll put on some biscuits right before it's ready. We could still go in."

"Shell home yet?"

"No."

"Someone needs to watch the baby."

"If he's not home by suppertime, then we can ask Hank or Nolan. It's not as if she's going to do much more than sleep. Let's go, Jake."

He studied her for a few minutes. "Who is Steven?"

"A friend, I told you."

"That's all? There's nothing else between you?"

"Nothing." She could say that with all honesty. Any tie they'd once had was long severed. She felt a rush of gratitude that she had not wasted more of her life with the man. It was scary to have a TIA, but look how much worse her life could have been.

"I'm tired," Jake said. "I don't want to go out. I want to eat dinner and relax, not drive to town and visit with a stranger I don't know and have nothing in common with." He leaned against the desk and added, "You go if you want."

"Alone?"

"Why not? Didn't you do things on your own in New York? The roads are clear and the storm isn't expected until later. Go and enjoy yourself."

"I wasn't married then."

"For heaven's sake, you're not planning to run off with the man, are you? Or start some torrid affair."

"Of course not." She wondered what he'd say if she said yes. If he cared for her as much as she did, wouldn't he object to her having dinner with another man?

"Then if you want to go, go." He headed toward the stairs.

She listened as his footsteps receded. She wouldn't be so complacent if Jake wanted to go off for dinner with some old rodeo friend who showed up and happened to be female.

Showed what being in love did.

Startled, she stared into space. She loved her gruff husband. She only wished it was reciprocated.

After checking on the stew, Brianna went upstairs to change. She would go.

Jake sent her off early. He said he'd manage dinner and the baby.

Still, Brianna felt guilty as she drove carefully into town. She was shirking her duties. But she did want to get out, and with more snow predicted, she knew it could be several days or even weeks before she'd be able to visit Sweetwater again.

She parked her SUV at the hotel and went in, asking for Steven at the desk. When contacted, he invited her up. She declined. Dinner with an old friend was one thing, but going to his room… She was very conscious of what a small town Sweetwater was. She would not be a source of gossip.

He emerged from the elevator a few moments later, looking as out of place in the hotel as he had in Jake's home. His suit probably cost more than the desk clerk earned in a year; his gold watch was worth a small fortune. But it was his air of detached sophistication that gave him away. He would never be a good old boy, talking with friends and neighbors. He was into showing off his accomplishments and flaunting his wealth.

Not for the first time since he'd arrived in Sweet-water, Brianna wondered what she'd seen in the man for two years. Yet hadn't she bought into the entire concept herself when in New York? Her clothes had been expensive, her indulgences foolish, though affordable on her extravagant salary.

Life was for the living. Her illness had shown her that. Her priorities had changed, but she couldn't fault Steven for staying with what worked for him.

He drove the short distance to the restaurant, talking pleasantly about the most recent show he'd put on. Mentioning people she'd known.

By the time they'd finished the main course, Brianna had a headache and knew she'd made a mistake in coming. She was frankly bored with Steven's monologue on Steven. Whenever she asked about her New York friends or began to talk about her new life here, he'd steered the conversation back to himself.

She glanced at his watch. It was not even nine o'clock. She could be home in thirty minutes and tell her husband he hadn't missed a thing.

"You have a fortune in paintings," Steven said unexpectedly.

"What?"

"The ones I examined today are Elsa Harrington's. I think they must be from early in her career. The technique is more primitive. The colors are dark and less blended, and they don't resemble her later style. But they were definitely done by Elsa Harrington. When they're cleaned up and properly framed, they'll command top dollar.''

"Why didn't you say something this afternoon?"

"I didn't want to get into a lengthy discussion without your husband there."

"Are you sure?"

"Enough that I'm prepared to offer one hundred thousand dollars for the lot."

Brianna sipped her after-dinner decaf coffee, dropping her gaze so Steven would not suspect how interested she was in what he'd just said. Amazing. One hundred thousand dollars would go a long way toward helping Jake do some of what he wanted on the ranch.

She couldn't wait to get home to tell him. All the more reason to cut the evening short and leave.

"You haven't touched your wine," Steven said.

"I'm not drinking alcohol these days," she said.

"Vintage not up to your standards?"

"No, I'm pregnant and don't want to harm the baby."

He looked stunned. There was no other word for it. "That makes it awkward," he said a moment later.

"Makes what awkward?"

"I planned to talk you into staying the night. I know you can't really care for this rancher you married. You don't even know the man. We were good together, Brianna. I miss you more than I ever expected I would. Leave this cowboy and come back where you belong." He reached out to take her hand.

Brianna withdrew it instantly.

"Correct me if I'm wrong, but a few months ago weren't you the one who told me you couldn't cope with my illness? That it would be too hard on you to have to watch if I suffered a stroke and became incapacitated? I'm sure that was you."

"I was wrong. I love you, Bri. I want you to come back and marry me. We were perfect together. The baby complicates things, but we can work something out. Arrange a nanny to watch it on the ranch until it's grown, or something."

She stared at him in disbelief. She would have been overjoyed had he stood by her in the days when she was so afraid. But he had abandoned her completely. Now he wanted her back even after learning she was carrying another man's baby?

It was ludicrous. Especially the part where he wanted her to give up the child. She'd clearly never known this man at all.

"There's no point to this discussion. I'm already happily married. My husband and I are expecting a baby in the summer, and I have no intention of going back to New York with you. Or even staying the night!"

She snatched up her purse and headed for the exit. She heard Steven behind her when she stopped to get her coat. A glance over her shoulder showed he'd been held up by the waitress, demanding payment. Served him right if they thought he was trying to skip out on the bill.

Stepping outside, Brianna stopped suddenly. It was snowing. The storm had arrived.

It was six blocks from the Silverado to the hotel, where she'd left her car. She could have Steven drive her, or walk. She chose the latter, but walking on the snowy sidewalks in high heels wasn't easy. She slipped twice and barely caught her balance. Slowing down, she watched her step even more closely.

She was freezing by the time she reached the SUV. Starting it, she hoped the heater would kick in soon. Her feet felt like ice.

Without waiting she began the drive home.

By the time she left the lights of Sweetwater behind, she was creeping. It was hard to see where the road was in the endless swirling white reflected in her headlights. The windshield wipers kept the glass cleared, but piled the snow up until she was peering through a fan-shaped space.

Twice her car crunched on gravel, which let her know she'd drifted off the road onto the shoulder. Each time, she eased back onto the pavement and tried to judge where she was. Everything looked different at night, especially covered by a blanket of snow.

At last she recognized the fence lining the long drive to the ranch. As she made the turn, the back wheels lost their grip, and she had to fight for control. Shaken, she took a deep breath. Another couple of miles and she'd be home. Gripping the wheel tightly, she prayed she'd make it without mishap.

As she drove, visibility became increasingly worse. Suddenly the car skidded and slammed into a small embankment on the right. She heard the headlight break just as the seat belt grabbed.

Shaken, she tried to back the car up, but couldn't get traction, even in four-wheel drive. The front wheel was caught on something.

Great, now what?

She zipped up her jacket, turned up the collar and climbed out of the car. She felt in her pockets—no gloves. When had she last had them? No matter, she didn't have them now. Walking to the front of the car, illuminated by the left headlight only, she tried to see the problem. But the swirling snow and strong wind made it impossible to determine anything.

She debated her choices for a moment. No one knew when to expect her, so no one would be looking for her. And the SUV would soon be as cold as the outdoors. She turned and began walking toward the house. It couldn't be more than half a mile—if she stayed on the drive. Wandering off track was a possibility, but surely the barbed-wire fencing would keep her from going astray.

Her feet soon felt like ice again as they sank almost ankle-deep in the snow. Next time she went anywhere, she swore, she'd wear heavy boots, no matter how dressy the event.

As she stumbled along, she berated herself for going out to dinner. She should have stayed home where she belonged. Steven had been a totally different man from the one she remembered. Although, she admitted, his desire for the paintings had been familiar. She remembered other times when he'd talked about acquiring an artist's work. He always bragged about the fantastic deals he made. She should warn Jake to hold out for more. Surely Steven's first offer wouldn't be his best.

Shivering, Brianna peered ahead, trying to see the house. When she topped a rise in the road, she saw the house in the distance, all the lights on. Nothing had ever looked so good to her. Tears filled her eyes as she slipped on the wet snow. Regaining her balance, she went doggedly on. It was farther than she'd originally thought, but at least it was within view.

The first pain hit suddenly, low on her left side. She almost doubled over. The second, moments later, seemed to clench her entire abdomen. She sank to her knees, holding herself against the pain. Was something wrong with the baby?

She couldn't be losing the baby. Not now. Oh, please don't let her foolish decision cause a problem with her baby!

"Jake!" she screamed uselessly. With the wind blowing, there was no way he could hear her. Awkwardly she climbed to her feet and walked on, leaning over against the pain that seemed to crash through her in waves. She was still a couple of hundred yards from the house.

"Jake, please come for me," she said, feeling light-headed. She couldn't faint, not out here in the snow. She'd freeze to death if she lay unconscious for any length of time.

"Jake!" She yelled his name again, struggling to keep going. The house didn't seem to be getting any closer.

Suddenly the front door opened—she could see the spill of light onto the porch. A man stood silhouetted in the opening.

"Jake, help me!" she cried, fighting to stay upright.

He started for her at a run, and Brianna sank to the snow.

"Brianna, what are you doing here?" Jake reached her in seconds, kneeling in the snow, his arms reaching for her. "What happened?"

Another pain.

"Jake, I think I'm losing the baby. It hurts so much." She held her stomach, and he swept her up and hurried to the house.

"Where's your car?" he asked.

"It slid off the drive a little ways back. I had to walk. I couldn't stay there. But then, I felt these pains...." She trailed off as another struck. "Don't let anything happen to my baby."

CHAPTER SIXTEEN

"SHELL!" JAKE CALLED as he entered the house. Kicking the door closed, he headed for the living room. He placed Brianna on the sofa and pulled the afghan from the back to cover her. He took off her soaked shoes and began to chafe her feet for warmth.

"Yeah, what?" Shell came into the room and stopped dead.

"Call her doctor—the number's on the pad by the phone—and tell her we're taking Brianna to the hospital. Then go start the truck, but first, get something hot for her to drink."

She moaned softly, curling up as the cramps continued. "It's awful out. I could hardly see."

"You should have stayed in town when you saw how bad it was," Jake said. His hands felt warm against her icy toes.

"I wanted to come home," she said fretfully. She didn't dare tell him why.

Please don't let anything happen to the baby, she prayed, only vaguely aware of the activity around her. Shell brought her a cup of hot, sweetened tea, saying it was what his mother always forced down him when he was sick. He spoke briefly with Jake, then headed out to start the truck.

"I want it warm for you," Jake explained. "And it'll only take a minute or two, nothing that's going to cause a difference either way. Are you getting warmer?"

"Yes."

Jake could hear her teeth were chattering. She was curled up in a ball, trying to ease the pain, but nothing seemed to stop it. He felt so damn helpless. What if she lost the baby?

"Ready," Shell said. "I'll drive, you hold her."

"Ashley?"

"I'm right here," Hank said, stepping beside Shell. "I'll watch her—I have a granddaughter of my own, you know."

Jake grabbed his jacket, then lifted Brianna, coat, afghan and all, and carried her out to the truck.

He was scared. He didn't know enough about pregnancies to know if her cramping was a dangerous sign or something totally unrelated. But he did know that that kind of pain needed attention.

Shell drove as fast as conditions allowed, but it seemed to Jake as though they were driving through cold molasses. Time sped by and they were still far from the hospital.

Brianna clung to him, whispering over and over not to let anything happen to their baby. But he couldn't make that promise. What would happen if she lost the baby? Would they have time to conceive another before the deadline? Did he want to try again? It depended on what happened with Brianna.

He and Shell could find another place to work. They

could go back to Texas, or find someplace in Colorado or even Wyoming.

Would she stay with him if he was just a ranch manager, not an owner? Would she feel she was putting too much into her side of the bargain and not getting enough in return?

What if she left?

The thought was devastating. Was he only now realizing how much he cared for this gutsy lady? He couldn't lose her, not now! If something happened to this baby, he'd give her a dozen more. He wanted Brianna to stay. To remain his wife until they both died.

The lights of the hospital finally came into view. Shell drove right up to the emergency-room entrance and stopped. "I'll park and come find you," he said.

Jake nodded and climbed out with Brianna. Two nurses met them, one pushing a wheelchair. "Can she sit in this?"

He placed her in the chair, but she clung to his hand. "Don't leave me," she pleaded. "I'm sorry, I didn't mean for this to happen."

"I won't leave you. Come on, let's see if your doctor's here yet."

Despite his best intentions to stay with her, Dr. Fleming would not let Jake remain into the examining room. He was directed to the waiting room. He couldn't sit. He could only pace the narrow space, from the window to the door and back. Could he have done something during the ride in? Was there something they should have been doing all along?

Shell joined him a short time later.

"What happened?"

"I don't know yet. The doctor's with her." Jake stalked to the window.

"I saw her car on the ranch road on the way out. Did you notice it? She walked almost a mile in the snow."

"In high heels. Dammit, she should have taken boots."

"Or not gone."

"Or not gone," Jake agreed. He'd wanted to show her how open-minded he was. One of her friends had come to visit, so let her visit. But if he'd gone with her, she wouldn't have been caught in the storm. Had the walk in the cold caused these pains she was having? Or was there something else?

Time seemed to stand still. He wanted to see her.

Dr. Fleming appeared in the doorway. Jake crossed to her, fear like a living thing inside him. "How's my wife?"

"She seems to be doing okay for the moment," Dr. Fleming said. "We gave her something to stop the cramps. They were severe. I want to keep her overnight. See if we can figure out what caused them."

"She's not in danger, is she? Or the baby?"

"I don't think so."

"I don't want anything to happen to either of them, but especially my wife!"

"I understand. I'll do my best. At least it wasn't the earlier problem causing this one. She's still fine in that regard."

"What earlier problem?" Jake asked, confused. He hadn't known of any problems.

The doctor hesitated. "The TIA. We've been monitoring her closely because of it."

"TIA?"

The doctor sighed. "Maybe you need to talk with your wife. But not tonight. I've sedated her and she's being moved to a room. She'll be awake in the morning. You might want to go home and get some sleep."

"I need to see her," Jake said.

"She's asleep."

"I don't care. I need to see for myself that she's all right."

"Very well, but don't try to wake her. She needs the rest. We'll be monitoring her all night. If there's any change, I'll let you know."

"I'll be here."

"You can go home, no need to stay."

"I'll be here," he repeated. "I told her I wasn't leaving."

The doctor looked at him as if recognizing his stubbornness. "Try the maternity waiting room, then. They have more comfortable chairs. Give us a few minutes to get her transferred, then check in with the nurse on the second floor."

Jake turned to Shell. "I'll call in the morning—when I know more."

"I can stay."

"No need. Go home and let Hank get a good night's sleep. Ashley needs you."

"Okay. Call first thing. I hope she's going to be all right."

"Yeah. Me, too."

Jake waited ten minutes, then headed for the second floor. The duty nurse was expecting him and led him straight away to Brianna's room. Lying in the high hospital bed, she looked small and lost. Her fiery determination was missing.

He caressed her cheek. She was warm, no longer cold. The IV solution had stopped the cramps, eased the pain. Only time would tell if their baby would be all right.

"Get well, Brianna. Come home," he said.

He sought out the nurse. "I forget what TIA stands for," he said.

When she explained, he asked a couple of other questions, nodding when she explained things to him.

Why hadn't Brianna told him? Her entire change of lifestyle made sense now. But there was a risk in pregnancy. She hadn't mentioned that to him. There was a chance she could have a stroke. She'd put her life in jeopardy to give them the baby they both wanted.

But nothing was worth her life. Not the ranch, not the baby she wanted. They could find another place to live. They could adopt. There were other options. And he planned to discuss every one of them with Brianna as soon as she awoke.

Provided, of course, she wanted to stay with him. God, she had to! He couldn't lose her.

He went into the waiting room and sat down. After a long moment, feeling rusty, he began to pray.

BRIANNA AWOKE slowly. She opened her eyes and looked around in muted recognition. She was back in the hospital. After her attack last spring, she hadn't ever wanted to be in one again.

She was alone in the room. A monitor beeped softly beside her. Wires and tubes ran from both arms. Had she lost the baby? She was afraid to ask. As long as no one told her, she could still hope.

The blinds in her room were drawn, but she could tell it was morning. Either very early, or another overcast day. The light seeping under the bottom of the blinds was gray.

A nurse peeked in. "Good, you're awake. Your doctor left strict orders to let you sleep, but breakfast is ready, and your husband's been here all night worried about you. Ready to see him?"

"Jake's here?"

"Of course. Where else would a husband be? I'll help you into the bathroom, then I'll get him. After that, breakfast!"

Brianna wondered how anyone could be so cheery this morning. Slowly she covered her stomach with her hand, moving carefully so as not to tangle the tubes. Was the baby all right?

"Hi," Jake said from the doorway a few minutes later.

"Hi, yourself. The nurse said you stayed the night." Brianna felt her heart swell with happiness just seeing Jake. He looked tired, needed a shave and still wore the clothes he'd worn the day before. But to her he'd never looked better.

He came right up to the bed and took her hand. "Of course I stayed. You asked me not to leave. I wouldn't have, anyway."

"Did I lose the baby?"

"No. You and the baby are going to be fine." He squeezed her hand gently, reassuringly.

Tears filled her eyes, dripped down the sides of her face.

"Hey, that's the good news." He brushed away the tears.

"There's bad news?"

"Depends on your viewpoint. Bed rest for a week and then a very light workload. Doctor's orders. She'll be around to talk to you before she discharges you."

"Bed rest for a week?" Brianna couldn't imagine anything worse. She already felt as if she'd slowed her pace to a crawl. That would be a dead stop.

Still, she would do nothing to jeopardize her baby's health and well-being. A week she could do. Already her mind was figuring out ways to get things done without too much extra work on anyone.

"So I can go home today?"

"Either today or tomorrow. I think your doctor wants to make sure you're stabilized before releasing you."

"When is she coming to see me?" Brianna asked. Apparently the physician had told Jake a great deal. But *she* was the patient, not Jake.

He shrugged. "Some time today, I guess," was all he said, then fell silent.

The silence stretched out, and Brianna wondered if

there was something Jake wasn't telling her. Was the baby still in danger?

He had stayed the night. For her, or for the baby?

No matter. She was grateful either way. Steven hadn't visited her in the hospital when she'd been ill. And once she was home, he visited her only once, and that had been to say he wasn't the type of man who could deal with serious illness.

But Jake had stayed, even when she hadn't known it.

A knock sounded on the partially opened door, and Loni peeked around. "Brianna, I came as soon as I heard." She walked to the far side of the bed, glancing warily at Jake. "Are you feeling okay now?"

"I'm feeling dopey, but Jake says the danger is past. I haven't seen my doctor yet today."

"Gosh, I was so scared for you! What can I do to help?"

"How did you know she was here?" Jake asked, his voice losing its softness when he addressed Loni.

"I called the ranch to talk to Brianna. Shell told me. He didn't know how bad it was, only that you thought she might lose the baby last night. Gosh, that would be so scary."

"Guess I should let Shell know you're doing okay, Brianna," Jake said.

She squeezed his hand. "Go call him. By the time you get back, maybe the doctor will have come and released me."

"Not without my talking to her again," he said.

Brianna watched him leave, then smiled at Loni.

''Thanks for coming. You're right, I was scared silly last night. I was so afraid I was going to lose the baby. But Jake said if I take it easy for a while, things should settle down. I guess this is part of being a mother. You start worrying about them before they're even born, and it never stops.''

Loni fidgeted with her purse strap, not meeting Brianna's eyes. Brianna realized her gaffe, but she couldn't help how she felt.

''So what does taking it easy mean?'' Loni asked, perching gingerly on the side of the bed.

''Complete bed rest for a week, if you can imagine. I'll go bonkers. Not to mention worrying about who's cooking and cleaning, and I guess Shell will have to stay in and care for Ashley.''

''I can do that. I would be glad to help you out, Brianna. You've been so nice to me since you got here. Let me come and take care of things until you're back on your feet.''

''I thought you were leaving,'' Brianna said, surprised at the offer.

''I, uh, not just yet. I thought maybe I'd wait until Ashley is a bit older. I've talked to an attorney. Shell can't keep me from seeing my baby.''

''I don't think he plans to. We all thought you'd be gone. What about your painting?''

''Well, Mr. Forrest said to look him up when I'm in New York.''

''Oh.'' So Steven hadn't closed the door entirely.

''Let me come help you, Brianna.'' Loni's tone was

almost pleading. "It'll help me be closer to Ashley, too."

"I'll ask Jake," Brianna said. "It's still his house."

"But when you two have your baby, the place stays in the family, and you're family. So it's your house, too."

"Good morning, Brianna, how are you feeling this morning?" Dr. Fleming entered, accompanied by a nurse.

"Better than last night," she replied.

"I'll see you later," Loni said. "Call me and I'll be at your place in a flash!" She headed for the door and left.

While the nurse took the vital readings, the doctor questioned Brianna more closely about how she felt and what she'd been doing when the cramps started.

"Your blood pressure and other readings are strong. I don't detect any more turmoil in the abdominal area. I think you're going to be fine and carry this baby to full term. To be safe, I want to do a sonogram and a couple of other tests. If everything checks out, you can go home. I'll prescribe bed rest for a full week—that means you can get up to go to the bathroom and even sit up for a half hour or so morning and afternoon. But no work. No fixing soup, no making beds, nothing. If you can't promise that, I can't in good conscious release you."

Brianna nodded. "I promise."

Dr Fleming went on, "Then another checkup. I think everything will proceed normally, but we don't want to take any chances."

"I'll see she follows orders," Jake said from the doorway. "So you get sprung from this joint today, huh?"

"Later, after more tests and only if the results are within the parameters I want," the doctor said, smiling. "Go home and have a shower, Jake, and eat a good breakfast. With luck, we'll be finished here by the time you get back."

The doctor smiled at both of them and left, the nurse trailing behind.

"Loni offered to come and take care of the household until I'm back on my feet," Brianna said. "Apparently she's having trouble letting go of Ashley. I can't imagine why she thought she could just have that baby and walk away."

"Do you want her there?" Jake asked.

"I wouldn't mind. How do you feel about it? It's your house. She does know the ropes. It would be like things were before I came." A thought struck her. Nothing much had changed since she arrived. If she had slipped away with Steven, would anyone have noticed?

Jake, of course, because of the baby.

"I'll talk to Shell," he said. "If he's agreeable, I'll call her. I'll be back this afternoon. Call if you're released before I get back."

Brianna nodded, feeling bereft after he was gone.

LONI WAS ALREADY at the ranch when Jake arrived with Brianna. He carried his wife upstairs, over her protests, directly to the guest room she'd used when she'd first arrived.

Looking around suspiciously, Brianna noted the bed had been freshly made and was already turned down.

"We thought you'd be more comfortable here," Loni said brightly, plumping a pillow. "Jake said this way he wouldn't disturb you when he came to bed or left in the morning. You get to sleep in as late as you want."

Brianna felt stunned, rejected. Maybe Jake wasn't any better about being around an invalid than Steven had been. He'd just not been as forthright about it.

"Do you have everything you need?" he asked as he helped her remove her heavy coat.

Brianna nodded and stripped off the jeans and sweatshirt he'd brought for her at the hospital, then donned the nightgown Loni held and climbed into bed. It did feel good to lie down.

Loni lowered the blinds and dimmed the light in the room. "I'll be back to check on you soon," she said.

Jake followed her out, leaving Brianna on her own.

She turned on her side, back to the door, and tried to forget the wary look in Jake's eyes. He was afraid they'd lose the baby, she knew that. She was afraid of that, too.

And if there was no baby, there'd be no reason for him to stay married to her.

Brianna realized that was what she wanted—to be married to the man for the rest of her life. To build a future that would include the ranch, Shell and Ashley. And Loni. She was part of the family, too.

Brianna wanted to see Ashley grow up, see her graduate from high school. She'd definitely made some strides with Shell, even though he still blamed her for Loni's desire to leave. She wanted the chance to get to know him better, maybe even love him as Jake's son.

But mostly she wanted to stay with Jake. If she lost the baby, would he want her to stay? There was just so much to think about. Nevertheless, she closed her eyes and slept.

She awoke some time later. She felt better, not as drugged. After a quick trip to the bathroom, she stopped by the nursery to check on Ashley, but the baby wasn't in her crib. She was probably with Loni.

Brianna went back to bed and lay there, glancing around the room, wondering what to do next. Not even home a day, and she was already growing antsy staying in bed. Maybe she could spend the half hour she was allowed for sitting up in the kitchen, where she could visit with Loni.

For a glance at the small bedside clock told her the kitchen was where Loni would be now, preparing dinner. They'd all be sitting down to the meal soon. She would miss Nolan complaining about something, and Hank teasing him. She'd even miss Shell's grumpy face.

But mostly she'd miss hearing about Jake's day.

"Good, you're awake. I wasn't sure." Loni said, pushing the door wide open. She carried a tray laden with dinner. Jake was right behind her.

"You can sit up to eat," he said, coming over to help her with the pillows.

Once Brianna was settled with the tray across her legs, Loni hurried off. Jake remained, however, walking over to the window. He was quiet for so long Brianna began to wonder.

"Are you going to join me for dinner?" she asked.

"No, I'll eat with the men." He turned. "Are you feeling better?"

"Yes."

"Did you talk to the doctor again about fainting the other night?"

"Yes. She said that's normal in some pregnancies."

"Some, or ones where women have had a TIA."

Brianna's appetite fled. He was gazing at her with that implacable look he sometimes got.

"The doctor told you?"

"Interesting that my wife didn't mention it, isn't it? There's a definite health risk to someone who had a TIA and becomes pregnant."

"I checked with the doctor when I first became pregnant. She sent for my records, and we reviewed everything. I am not considered at risk for another TIA, if that's your worry."

"But you don't know that."

"Cut to the chase, Jake. What's the problem?"

"That you could have incapacitated yourself getting pregnant. That you might not be able to carry this baby to full term without problems arising."

Of course. He was worried she wouldn't be able to deliver a baby. And that would mean he wouldn't get

the ranch. There was not enough time, if she understood the deadline correctly, to wait to conceive another if she lost this one.

"Your concern is duly noted."

"What were you thinking to keep something like
that from me? You wonder why I don't trust
women...well, lady, there's a prime example. Don't
you think I should have been informed before now?"

"It's not an issue. It's my health and I'm taking
care of it."

"By putting your own well-being at risk and that
of an unborn baby?"

"Your precious baby will be fine!"

"I'm going to dinner," he said, walking from the
room.

"Jake?" she said as he reached the hall.

"What?" Reluctantly he turned to face her.

One thing she'd learned about families was that they
stuck together when the going got tough.

They weren't a family. They were a bunch of individuals living in the same house, and she didn't have
a clue how to change that.

"Those paintings in the dining room might have
been done by your grandmother. Steven offered me a
hundred grand last night to buy them all. I'd hold out
for half again as much if I were you."

CHAPTER SEVENTEEN

"WHAT?" JAKE HEARD the words, but he couldn't grasp the reality. He was thinking family, and she was talking about a fortune in paintings? "My grandmother gave all the paintings still in her possession to artist groups. There was a complete inventory done before she died, and they've all been distributed."

"These were the paintings we found in the attic. Steven's an excellent art appraiser. He wants to buy them."

"He called earlier," Jake said. "I didn't talk to him, and Loni hung up rather quickly. Nothing was said about buying paintings."

"Just watch out when you do talk to him," she said, dropping her gaze to study the food on the tray.

Jake waited a moment, but he could tell she was not planning to expand on the statement. He headed for the stairs, deep in thought. Brianna had paled when he told her he knew about the TIA. Was she feeling guilty? Why hadn't she told him?

Because she didn't care to, he decided. She was looking to make a home and family here on her own terms. They weren't growing close as she'd once said she hoped they'd do. To conceal a major problem like that showed him where he stood with her.

He flipped on the light in the dining room and headed for the paintings, amazed that they might be worth something. Picking up one, he looked at it closely. This painting had none of the romantic overtones, soft colors and plenty of light that had been Elsa's style. It was almost bleak, a drab scene of cattle and barren land. He peered closely at the lower right-hand corner. The small signature was almost undecipherable, but he realized finally that it was indeed Elsa's. He picked up another painting. This was totally different—a lone rider on a horse, the vast sweep of a Wyoming plain as background. The colors were muted, somber. The entire scene evoked a feeling of sadness. He turned it over. Lightly penciled in the corner were the words "My Son."

He studied the painting again. This was his father? Was this how Elsa, his mother, had seen him?

He swiftly went through the others. The one of a small boy he liked. He looked on the back, hoping for some other notation, but there was nothing. He knew the swimming hole. Had this also been his father as a child?

Could these paintings really be Elsa's? He'd contact her agent in the morning. And talk to his attorney about legal ownership.

Shell came through the swinging door from the kitchen.

"Loni's got dinner on the table," he said. "Thought you were still upstairs."

Jake put the painting down. "These were done by

my grandmother," he said. "Brianna said her friend wants to buy them."

"The one who's going to be showing Loni's work? I'd suspect his expertise if I were you," Shelly said cynically.

"She said he offered a hundred thousand dollars for the lot."

"Was he serious?"

"She said to hold out for half again as much."

Shell gaped at the paintings in utter disbelief. "If Brianna is right," he said, "it would go a long way to fixing this place up."

"Damn straight it would. Who would think a few flimsy canvases would be worth so much? A bull I can understand, but..." Words failed him.

"So you think it's on the up and up?"

"He called once. If he calls again, you can bet I'm going to talk to him."

"Brianna okay?" Shell asked, studying his father.

Jake nodded. He hadn't told the others about her TIA or that she'd kept the knowledge of the dangers from him. With any luck, no one else had to know he'd been made a fool of.

"I'm going in to town after dinner, if that's okay," Shell said. "A few of the guys want to meet at the Oak Bucket."

"Sure. Want me to watch Ashley?"

"She'll mostly sleep, but Loni will be here. That's why she came, isn't it? To take over for Brianna until Brianna's back on her feet?"

Jake nodded. He clasped his son's shoulder. "Hang in there, son."

"Aren't you going to tell me it'll get better?" Shell asked wryly.

"Hell, no. The best we can hope for is that it doesn't get worse."

LONI DIDN'T SPEAK much during dinner. She felt awkward being back with the others after all her grand talk. The only bright spot was that she got to spend as much time with her daughter as she wanted. And that was a huge bright spot. She had weeks to make up.

Once Brianna was back on her feet, Loni knew she'd have to leave again. But she wouldn't go far— just to town. She wasn't sure what kind of job she'd get, but as long as she could support herself she didn't care. If she got a nice apartment, she could have Ashley visit.

It wasn't the same as *living* with her daughter, but she'd thrown her chances away. And for nothing.

She listened to the dinner conversation with only half an ear. The rest of her attention was on the baby monitor. She'd put Ashley down just before dinner. The baby had been fussy for a little while, but quiet since.

"…on a hot date?" Hank was asking.

Loni looked at Shell. *He was dating again.*

And why shouldn't he? She'd rejected all his proposals. He'd told her loud and clear the day Jake married that he wasn't asking again.

He was moving on. Time she did, as well.

Only, she had nowhere to move on to. Not that she'd tell him that. Or anyone. Ashley was her reason for staying, and that was all anyone needed to know.

Tears threatened again when she thought of her mother and father. Of the family she'd let down. Of the foolish dreams she'd held above all else. Steven Forrest had shattered them once and for all when he said she showed definite promise but needed more experience. His final words had been to look him up in ten years—he wanted to see how she'd progressed.

When he finished eating, Jake stood. ''If that Steven Forrest calls again, I want to talk to him.''

Loni nodded, heartsick at how quickly Shell had found someone else. Was she someone who would comfort him? Ha, that was easy. Shell didn't need much comfort—he was far too self-sufficient. Was she someone who'd think he hung the moon? She'd once thought that. He'd never laughed at her dreams, while she'd scoffed at his. He'd always been devoted to her, and she had taken that for granted.

God, she'd messed up her life so badly she didn't know if she'd ever get it straight again.

Half an hour later, Loni cleaned the kitchen, then watched some television until it was time to feed Ashley her late-night bottle. After that there was nothing to do but get changed for bed. She couldn't sleep though, and wandered downstairs. The light had been left on over the sink for Shell when he returned.

She went to the back door and opened it a crack, standing behind the door to avoid as much of the cold

BARBARA McMAHON   271

air as she could. She listened for a long moment, but there was no sound of a truck.

Emotions held in too long bubbled up. She felt so lost and alone. Slowly she closed the door, leaning against it, resting her forehead against the cold wood. She'd had her chance at happiness and willfully destroyed it. She was only nineteen and all she'd hoped for was gone. She began to cry as if her heart would break. But that wasn't possible, for it already had.

Eventually she turned and grabbed a handful of paper napkins to mop her face and blow her nose. Maybe a cup of hot tea would help. It was her mother's remedy for almost everything.

The tea prepared, she sat at the table, sleep the furthest thing from her mind. Suddenly she heard Shell's truck on the drive. She should get to bed before he saw her. What if Shell thought she was waiting up for him? How pathetic.

On the other hand, she had a perfect right to be in the kitchen. She could say the baby had been up and she was just winding down before going back to bed. At least she'd had the sense to change and wasn't still wearing her jeans.

His step was light, but she could still hear him cross the wooden porch. The kitchen door opened, closed.

''Loni? What are you doing up?'' he asked, obviously startled to see her.

She refrained from looking at the clock. It had been after midnight the last time she'd checked; she didn't need to know anything more.

''I wanted some tea,'' she said.

He came closer. She could smell beer, but no perfume. Slowly she raised her eyes to find him staring at her.

"Have you been crying? In all the time I've known you, I've never seen you cry."

"Well, sometimes a woman does, you know," she snapped. She picked up her cup and stood. "I'll take this to my room with me."

"Is Ashley all right?" he asked.

She nodded, wanting to dash away, longing to stay. She wished they could be the way they were a year ago, so anxious to be with each other, filling those moments with lovemaking and discussions of their plans and dreams. Though, come to think about it, she'd talked more than he had.

"Did you have fun tonight?" she asked. Then wished she'd bitten off her tongue. She didn't want him to think she cared.

"Yeah. But it's later than I thought. I'll pay for it tomorrow. Jake doesn't let his men sleep in."

"I won't keep you. You need your sleep." She gripped the cup, but didn't move. He'd spent the evening with someone else. It shouldn't hurt after she'd refused him so often. But it did. If she could turn back the clock to a year ago, a month ago, she'd do things so differently....

"You okay?" he asked. That low sexy voice almost melted her bones.

She nodded, tears filling her eyes again. She held her breath, hoping she could keep them back until he left. But he didn't move.

She tried, she really tried, but a sob escaped.

"Loni?" He reached for her. "What's wrong?"

"Everything," she said, putting the cup down before she dropped it. Gripping his shirtfront when his arms came around her, she began crying in earnest again.

His strong arms felt so wonderful, and his soothing murmurs eased the ache in her heart. She felt safe with Shell, safe and loved.

"Shell, promise me you won't tell Ashley that I was going to leave her, please?"

"What do you mean?"

"I'm not going to New York. Or Dallas or anywhere. I'm staying right here in Sweetwater. I can't be apart from her while she's growing up. How could I ever have thought such a thing? Please don't ever tell her. Please?"

"I won't." He tightened his hold on her. "You're staying?"

She nodded, the tears slowing. If she could hold time still, she'd be happy for the rest of eternity.

"What happened to the world's greatest artist?"

"It isn't me. And probably won't ever be. He didn't think I was good enough."

"Ah, baby, I'm sorry."

That hurt even more. As mean as she'd been, he still cared about what happened to her.

Loni drew back and looked at him. "I bet you had more fun earlier with her than with a weeping woman like me."

"Her who?"

"Your date."

He was silent a moment. "There was no date. That was Hank teasing."

"There's nothing stopping you from dating," she said, probing the wound.

"Nothing except myself."

"You aren't dating?"

Shell shook his head.

Loni swallowed. "Why not?"

"Tried dating once. Look what happened. My feelings for you haven't changed, Loni. Not this quickly."

She almost couldn't breathe. Dared she hope? Her gaze couldn't hold his. Not with the crazy idea that had just popped into her mind. Her heart began to beat faster.

She slowly released her grip on his shirt, attempting to smooth the wrinkles with her fingers. "I know you said you'd never ask me to marry you again. But what if I asked you?"

BRIANNA DIDN'T KNOW how long she'd been awake, but it felt like hours. She'd slept too much during the day. She'd tried all the tricks, but nothing worked. She might as well turn on the light and read.

Just as she did so, she heard the baby. Ashley was fussing, but not yet crying. She could take care of her and let the others sleep. She'd had enough rest to last her a week.

In only a few minutes, she'd warmed a bottle and changed the baby. Lowering the light, she sat in the rocker. Soon Ashley was drinking noisily, her hand wrapped around one of Brianna's fingers.

Brianna loved this quiet time. She could rock a baby all day long, she thought. Ashley would soon go back to sleep, but Brianna wasn't ready to relinquish her anytime soon.

"It's just you and me against the world at this time of night," she said softly as the baby drank.

"Not quite," Jake said from the doorway.

"Did she wake you?" Brianna asked in surprise. "I thought I caught her before she really wound up." He looked forbidding, standing there in shadow. He'd donned jeans and thrown on a shirt, but he hadn't fastened the buttons. Her heart skipped a beat when she glanced at his chest, remembering the nights he'd held her while they slept.

"What are you doing up?" he asked.

"I couldn't sleep."

"Guilty conscience?" he asked sardonically.

"Too much sleep in the afternoon," she replied with spirit. She looked back to the baby. If Jake had come to berate her for not telling him earlier about her TIA, she'd get up and leave. She'd apologized. End of the matter.

"That's the point. The doctor said complete bed rest."

"You try it—it's boring. Besides, she also said I could be up a half hour morning and afternoon. This is my afternoon time."

"It's four in the morning!"

"So count it as morning time. Whatever. How much

risk can I be taking sitting in a rocker, holding an eight-pound baby?''

He shrugged, stepped inside and crossed the room to her side. Sliding down the wall, he sat on the floor near enough to touch her if he reached out his hand.

''How long have you been up?''

''Awake for at least an hour. *Up* for just a few minutes.'' The baby was already growing sleepy. Brianna took the bottle from her, brought her to her shoulder and gently rubbed her back.

''Steven Forrest called me tonight. You were right—he wants to buy the pictures.''

''Are you going to sell?''

''Should I?''

''Jake, they're yours. You decide.''

''I need to get Bill Tyler's assessment. He knew my grandmother's work better than anyone. If he likes them, I'll probably stick with him.''

She nodded, repositioning Ashley in her arms and slowly rocking.

''You don't care if your friend doesn't get them?'' Jake asked.

''Not particularly. Get the best deal you can. They're your legacy.''

''What happened last night that made you come home during a blizzard?''

She looked at him. She meant to make this marriage work, with or without Jake's help. It would be easier with his help. She just wished she felt he was trying.

''Steven sort of made a pass, and I took offense. I wanted to get home. I didn't know when I started out from town that the snow was so bad or that my car would slide off the road.''

''What's sort of a pass?''

''He wanted me to spend the night with him.''

''The hell you say!'' Jake sat up at that. ''What kind of friend is he, anyway?''

''Once I thought we were close. Subsequent events proved otherwise,'' she said. ''He's no more interested in a potential invalid than you are.''

''You'll always have a home here, but you need to take better care of yourself.''

''I'm taking perfect care of myself.''

''Now, but not always, huh? Tell me what happened with the TIA?''

''Why? So you can yell some more?''

''I have not yelled,'' he said with great precision.

''Maybe not in volume,'' she muttered.

''Brianna, you'd drive a saint crazy. What happened?''

She leaned her head back against the high rocker back and closed her eyes, remembering. She really didn't want to talk about it, but Jake deserved to know. Would it change anything?

''It was the scariest day of my life. I really thought I might die. I was only thirty-four and I figured I had decades left. What a shock when your body betrays you and shows how tenuous the thread of life is.''

''What happened?''

''I was at a staff meeting, briefing my team on tasks that needed to be done for a couple of projects. Suddenly I couldn't see. There was just a blank fog where once a roomful of people had been. I tried to say something but couldn't. Everything was garbled. I could hear myself, and I couldn't understand why the words I heard weren't the ones I was thinking.''

"God!''

"Fortunately one of my staff was a medic for the army reserve. He suspected the situation right away and had me on my way to the hospital before I could say anything else. The left side of my face was frozen. I felt like I had the flu—all weak and shaky. It seemed as if my knees wouldn't hold me upright when I tried to walk.''

She opened her eyes and glanced at him. "It was hours before I was stable and could talk properly again. Aphasia, they call it. Short-circuiting of the brain paths. Anyway, I was in hospital two days while they monitored me and ran a dozen tests.''

"What caused it?''

"After eliminating all the high-risk factors, like smoking, high blood pressure and obesity, none of which I have, the doctor said it was most likely my stressful lifestyle. I was living on borrowed time—like a rubber band stretched more and more until it snapped. I'd snapped. If I didn't make changes…it would likely happen again with more dire consequences.''

She paused, then added, "The irony is that I held the meeting to brief my staff because I was leaving for vacation the next day. My first in over a year.''

"So you move to Wyoming, cut back on stress and

live happily ever after," he said. "Just forgetting to mention that one minor detail to your husband."

"Would you have married me knowing that?"

He shrugged. "Who knows? That choice was taken from me."

"Now all we have to do is keep me going until this baby is delivered," she finished for him.

He looked at her, his eyes unfathomable. "That sounds cold."

"This whole setup is cold, if you think about it. Do you believe we're building a marriage? Starting a family? Or are we still two individuals on parallel paths?"

He was silent so long Brianna didn't think he was going to answer her. She felt hope drain away. If she didn't want an answer, she shouldn't have asked the question.

"You are going to be okay, right?" he asked.

"I think so."

"What part does Steven play in this?"

"He couldn't handle being around a sick person. But after hearing I was doing fine, he thought he'd come out here and see if we could take up where we left off. He wasn't happy when I told him no."

Jake got to his feet. "I don't need to know any more. Let me put the baby in her crib and you can get back to bed. You need to rest."

"I've gone over this with Dr. Fleming. She doesn't think I'm at risk with this pregnancy. I'm doing everything I'm supposed to. I can't explain last night, unless it was the cold or the strain of being with

Steven. But it wasn't tied to the other. I'm not an invalid, Jake.''

He lifted the baby from her arms and snuggled her against his chest until he placed her in her crib. Covering her with the light blanket, he studied the child for a long moment.

''Will I ever be able to put my own child to bed? To hold my son or daughter? Or have I risked the future of this ranch on a woman with health problems?''

Brianna knew she deserved his comments, though they hurt.

''I'll be fine, Jake. I have to believe that, and so should you.''

''And if you're not?''

''You tell me. Shall I leave? Should I return to New York or find another place to live?''

If he told her to leave, she didn't know what she'd do. She loved every inch of the stubborn, indifferent, infuriating man. She was growing to love the ranch, even with its limitations and needs. The worst part was she could understand if he didn't want her to stay. Could sympathize with his viewpoint. Life hadn't been very fair to Jake Marshall.

''This is your home, Brianna. Stay.'' He turned from the crib.

''If it is truly my home, let me help by fixing it up a bit more. Let me paint the outside, repair—''

''Stop. We've been through that. You circumvented our agreement by buying the hay in Ashley's name. I'm not doing more.''

BARBARA McMAHON   281

"Those paintings will bring you plenty of capital. We signed that blasted prenup. Your ranch is safe. I'll live here on sufferance, but I do want to do something—for my own sake, if not for yours and Shell's."

He rubbed the back of his neck. "I don't want you to feel you're staying here on sufferance. That's how I felt when I lived here with my dad. But by the same token, I can't take any chances."

"Only time will convince you I'm not out to snare your ranch. Time and trust."

"Trust is earned. And honesty is the best basis."

"I will only say this once more. I'm sorry I didn't tell you at the very beginning about my TIA. But I'm not going to apologize the rest of my life."

"However long that is."

"Fine, consider me an invalid and live shut up in some isolated place that's so perfect you never make mistakes." She jumped to her feet and started for the door.

"See you get the rest the doctor prescribed."

"I know what I'm doing."

"Do you?" he asked. "Then tell me."

"I want to make this marriage work. We have a lot of years ahead of us. I'm determined to make the most of them."

"I don't think I'm over being angry about your hiding that medical problem from me," he said.

"Get over it, cowboy. I'm sure that isn't the last time I'm going to make you angry."

He caught her hand in his, pressing it against his chest. "Are you planning something else?"

"No, but the nature of this relationship pretty much guarantees we'll butt heads once or twice in the future."

"I'd like to think we can prevent that."

"Me, too, but I don't believe it's possible."

He gave a short laugh.

"Let's go to bed." He leaned over and scooped her up, cradling her against his chest.

"Did I thank you for staying at the hospital?" she asked, feelings tossed upside down. His reaction was not one she expected. She knew it was all in her imagination, but when he carried her, it was easy to fantasize that she was cherished and treasured.

"You did."

"No one did that the last time. I was so scared and so alone."

"You won't be alone anymore, Bri."

"So this is another part of our family plan?"

"Yeah, bonding in the middle of the night."

She kissed the side of his jaw as he carried her to their room. Maybe things would come right, after all.

"I know of better things to do in the middle of the night," she whispered.

CHAPTER EIGHTEEN

DESPITE HIS EFFORT to keep silent, Jake woke Brianna when he was dressing.

"Wish I could go riding with you," she said sleepily.

"No you don't. It's snowing again. I won't be gone long today. I'll check in on you later."

"I'm fine. I might be bonkers by the time you come in, but physically, I'll be fine."

"If you're really good, you can have your half-hour sitting time when I take a break."

"Oh, goody," she said dryly.

"Or not!" he warned.

She laughed. "Don't get too cold. It can be miserable, I know."

He hesitated a moment. He really didn't want to leave at all, but duty called. Finally he walked over and bent to kiss her softly on the mouth. The hunger that filled him no longer surprised him. He was becoming accustomed to it. What would it take to satisfy that hunger? Staying in bed with Brianna for a month?

The images that sprang to mind did nothing to make it easy to leave.

"Get some rest," he said. The thought of a month

alone with Brianna with no responsibilities, no duties and no blasted ranch to worry about was too tempting. What would happen if he acted on that impulse?

He straightened, surprised at his thoughts. For years he'd yearned for the ranch. Now it was no longer the most important thing in his life. Jake was scowling as he left the bedroom. He was not going to let something else stand in his way. The land could be counted on. Women could not.

Brianna dozed off and on until ten, when she awoke and went to take a hot shower. Dressing in sweats, she was comfortable enough to nap in bed, yet felt more dressed and ready to face the day than being in her nightgown allowed.

She wandered downstairs, not very hungry, but knowing she should eat.

Loni was in the kitchen when Brianna entered. She was talking with Ashley as the little girl sat in her baby seat, but jumped up when she saw Brianna.

"Can I get you something to eat? I peeked in a while ago, but you were sleeping."

"I can fix myself something," Brianna said, heading for Ashley. The baby looked at her with solemn eyes.

"No, that's my job," Loni insisted. "What would you like?"

"Oatmeal?"

"Sit down. I'll have it in a jiffy. I can bring it up to you if you want to get back to bed."

"I just got up. This is my morning sitting time." Brianna was getting tired of everyone trying to keep her in bed. She knew they had her best interests at heart, but she was so bored.

"A half hour, the doctor said. You've already taken twenty minutes in the shower," Loni said reasonably.

"You sound like a mother hen," Brianna grumbled, sitting in the chair Loni had vacated and tickling Ashley.

"I am a mother," Loni said proudly.

Brianna looked at her and grinned. "Yes, you are, but that doesn't make you *my* mother."

Jake came into the kitchen, snow on his shoulders, hat in hand. He looked at Brianna.

"How long have you been up?"

Loni giggled. "I just told her it's back to bed as soon as she eats. I'm watching her, Jake."

Shell followed right behind his father. "Hi, Brianna. How are you feeling?"

"Just fine," she said, turning back to the baby. "At least you don't boss me around," she grumbled.

Shell glanced at Loni as he shrugged out of his jacket and hung it beside Jake's. He waited until Jake sat down beside Brianna, then cleared his throat. Everyone looked at him.

"Loni and I have an announcement. We waited until you were both with us to tell you we're getting married."

"If that's okay with you, Jake," Loni rushed to say.

"No, even if it's not okay with Jake," Shell said firmly. "We've wasted enough time. We hope you both will come to the wedding."

Turning to face Jake and Brianna, Loni said, "I love Shell—guess you already knew that. And I can't be away from him or Ashley. I never knew it would be like this. I will probably end up just like my mother."

"And that wouldn't be a bad thing," Jake said.

"No, it wouldn't, would it."

Brianna got up to give Loni a hug. She looked at Shell for a second and then gave him a hug, too, surprised to find his arms strong around her.

"So, now you'll have two more kids, Brianna, in addition to your grandbaby and that kid you're carrying," Shell said with a smile.

Touched by his words, Brianna felt her eyes fill with tears. Shell had accepted her! She'd gone another step closer to that feeling of belonging and that family she so wanted.

Jake congratulated the young couple, then asked about the wedding date.

"The sooner the better," Shell said.

Loni nodded, dishing up the oatmeal for Brianna. "I should have said yes the first time he asked me. Then we'd already be married."

Shell turned one of the chairs around and straddled it, resting his arms on the back. "If it's okay with you, Jake, eventually I'd like to build us a house over on the rise west of here. With your new kid coming and ours already here, it'll get hectic if we all stay under the same roof."

Jake nodded. "Not to mention the lack of privacy."

Shell raised an eyebrow, then glanced at Brianna.

Amusement lit his expression. "Yeah, that goes both ways, I guess."

"So we thought as soon as Brianna is up and about, we'd ask Judge Tomlinson to perform the ceremony," Loni said.

"Don't you want a more formal wedding?" Brianna asked.

Loni shook her head. "The wedding isn't that important. The marriage is." She grinned at Brianna. "Is that a direct quote or what?"

"Even so, there'll be lots of things to do. You should have a reception. We can ask your friends from town and—"

Jake put his finger over her lips and glared at her. "What part of 'complete bed rest' don't you understand?"

Brianna blinked. "This is cerebral stuff. I can lie flat on my back and think up lists, make a few calls."

"Not unless you get Dr. Fleming's okay first!"

"Yes, sir."

Loni giggled. "If you think I sound like a mother, Jake sounds like a father."

"Or an autocrat," Brianna murmured, eating her oatmeal. She felt better than she had since her arrival—despite her fear of losing the baby and worry about her relationship with Jake. But just once she wished she could feel that Jake cared for her alone and not as the incubator for his heir.

For all the problems Loni and Shell faced, at least they knew each loved the other. Would her telling Jake she loved him make any difference? Would he trust she was telling the truth? If she had one thing to do over, it would be to explain everything at the beginning.

BRIANNA HAD TAKEN the portable phone from the office with her when she went back to bed. Once nestled under the warm covers, she dialed the doctor's office. Getting confirmation that working on Loni's wedding wouldn't jeopardize her health as long as she stayed in bed, Brianna called downstairs to Loni. They needed to make plans!

"First thing, you need to call your mother," Brianna said when she and Loni sat down with a pad of paper and a pen. "She'll want to help with her daughter's wedding."

"I doubt it."

"Then your aunt."

"I just want a small wedding like you and Jake had."

"Well, we had all the family either of us has at the wedding. You need to include everyone who is family. And I bet you have some close friends who'd be hurt if they weren't invited."

Loni was thoughtful for a moment, then nodded. "I haven't had much to do with most of my friends since high school. Several went to college, and a couple got jobs. But I was out here and pregnant...." She trailed off, but Brianna knew she was thinking of her lofty plans to leave.

"What happened to New York?" she asked gently.

Loni told her what Steven had said.

"I'm sorry."

"It's my own fault. Whoever heard of a nineteen-year-old artist being a huge success? I do need practice and experience to develop my style. And about the wedding, you're right. I should be sharing my happiness with my friends. I'll be living around them the rest of my life."

"Are you okay with that?" Brianna asked.

"Yes, I am." Loni answered honestly. "I couldn't believe how much I missed my baby, how much I missed Shell. They are both so important to me—I couldn't have lived for long in the city, no matter how much I tried to convince myself. Shell and I talked a lot last night. I can still paint. I have that lovely studio. Though who knows how much time I'll have each day. Being a rancher's wife is a full-time job."

"All the time you want and need, I imagine. Shell isn't going to expect you to ignore your passion. By the way. I still want that one for the living room."

Loni looked at the pad for a moment, then shyly met Brianna's eyes. "Shell's going to ask Jake about starting in on that house, once the title to the land is settled, of course."

"Sounds like a sensible plan." Brianna smiled. She wouldn't mind having Jake to herself in the evenings. Wonder how he'd feel about that.

THE REST OF THE WEEK crept slowly by. Brianna continued to stay in bed as per the doctor's orders. If she hadn't had Loni's wedding to occupy part of her time, she knew she'd have gone stark-raving mad.

And Jake wasn't helping. He came in from work,

ate dinner and headed for the office. She hoped he wasn't messing up all *her* work. But when she asked, he told her not to worry, that she only needed to concentrate on taking care of herself.

She wished he'd sit with her in the evenings. She even saved her time to be up until after dinner, but he never came.

Finally Friday arrived. Loni drove Brianna in to see the doctor. It was snowing lightly, nothing like the night she'd gone to dinner with Steven.

That had been such a foolish mistake. He hadn't spoken to her since. He was still trying to negotiate the sale of the paintings with Jake, but had ignored her completely.

At the doctor's, she was given the okay to resume normal activities with the caveat that if even the tiniest irregularity occurred, she was to call immediately. She almost floated out to tell Loni. They ate lunch in town and then headed for home.

When they reached the ranch house, Loni's eyes grew huge as she stared at the big black pickup parked near the front door.

"Oh, my God, that's my dad's truck," she said, driving past and stopping by the back door. "What's he doing here? I hope nothing's wrong."

She scrambled out of the car.

"Shall I bring Ashley?" Brianna called.

"Yes, yes." Loni flew up the back stairs and almost plowed into Shell.

Brianna unfastened the baby and followed more slowly, arriving in time to hear part of the explanation.

"...waited to talk to you. Your dad's not too happy with us, but your mother seems open."

"Did you tell them about the house? Jake did say okay, didn't he? You did ask, right?"

"Yeah, I asked, and he said not until we know about the ownership issue. Seems Brianna might not make it all the way to term."

Brianna wanted to scream that she was fine, but only time would convince everyone. Making Jake eat his words was all that held her from railing against fate.

"What do you mean?" Loni asked, looking back and forth between Shell and Brianna.

"It means Brianna had a TIA before she came here. And that puts her pregnancy at risk."

"I'm so sick of telling everyone that I'm fine I could spit." Brianna pushed the baby into Shell's arms. "Even if something did happen, they could keep me on life support until the baby was born."

"Not with Jake telling the doctors to do whatever it takes to save you first," Shell said.

"What are you talking about?"

"When you were in the hospital, I heard him. He told the doctor to save you—even if it meant losing the baby."

"That's not possible."

Shell shrugged, cradling Ashley, glancing at Brianna. "It's the truth."

"Why would he say such a thing? This baby means his entire future."

"He seems to feel his future is tied up with you."

Stunned, Brianna stared at Shell, then Loni. "Where's Jake?"

"He's out with Nolan."

"It's snowing. I thought you men tried to stay close to the house in the snow."

"Not when we need to check to see if it's time to start distributing hay."

"He'll be back soon?"

"When the job's done."

"Let's go see my parents," Loni said, tucking her hand in the crook of Shell's elbow. "Ashley will have them eating out of her hand in no time, I hope."

"I'm counting on it," Shell said.

Brianna watched them walk through the kitchen toward the front of the house. She looked out into the vast range where the snow covered the ground, pretty to look at, but a problem for ranchers. How long before Jake returned? She had so many question she wanted to ask.

Had he really told the doctor to save her at the expense of their baby?

Why would he have done such a thing? Having a baby before the deadline of his grandmother's will was his main priority. Shell must have misunderstood.

Yet he'd been so positive.

The minutes dragged by. Loni returned to the kitchen and asked Brianna to come meet her parents. Shortly thereafter, the Petersons left. Brianna grabbed her jacket and headed for the barn. Had Jake returned while she was visiting?

Nolan was unsaddling his horse. He looked up and smiled when he saw her.

"You okay?"

"I got a perfect bill of health from the doctor today. Where's Jake?"

"He'll be along. He was riding out a bit farther. But he won't stay long. Cold today." Nolan swung the saddle over his shoulder and headed for the tack room.

Impatiently, Brianna walked to the edge of the corral and scanned the horizon. She didn't see any sign of a rider.

The cold forced her back inside. She wanted to know the truth, but freezing out by the corral wouldn't bring Jake home any faster.

By the time it was growing dark, Brianna's impatience had turned to worry. Shell had gone out to question Nolan. A few minutes later, she heard the sound of horses. Dashing to the back door, she was in time to see Shell and the two hands heading out.

"Shell!" she called. But he was already too far away to hear her.

Loni joined her. "What's going on?"

"The men just left. It's getting dark, and Jake isn't home."

"Shell will find him," Loni said.

"I don't want him found. I want him to come riding back on his own! Remember what happened when Shell didn't show up when expected? What if Jake's fallen? He could be in serious danger in this cold."

"He'll be fine, Brianna. He's used to this life. Come back inside. You don't even have a jacket on."

A half hour later it was almost full night. Brianna spent the time pacing the kitchen, periodically looking out the window, trying to stay calm. When she heard the sound of horses, she ran to the window—and counted four. She almost burst into tears with relief.

"They're here!" she called up to Loni, who was upstairs with the baby. Grabbing her jacket, she hurried outside. She wanted to make sure Jake was all right.

The men rode slowly. She realized Jake sat behind Shell, leading his horse. The poor thing had a definite limp.

"What happened?" she called, meeting them as they reached the barn.

"Get back inside—it's cold out here," Jake scolded. He slid off Shell's mount, still holding the reins of his own horse.

Brianna ignored his admonition to go inside. She crossed to him and said, "I've been scared out of my mind. Where have you been?"

Jake looked at her with the oddest expression. "My horse slipped on some ice, hurt his knee. I couldn't ride him. It's been a long walk home."

"I was afraid something happened to you—like that time with Shell, or worse. It's freezing out today."

"Which is why you should go back into the house."

She touched his sleeve. "I was scared you might have been lying unconscious somewhere."

Shell took the reins from Jake's hands and led the injured horse into the barn, where Hank and Nolan already were.

"If there was anything anyone could have done, I'd have called on the cell phone," Jake said.

"Not if you knocked yourself out."

"But I didn't. Let's get inside."

"Shell told me some startling news today, and I want an explanation," she said as they walked toward the house. "It doesn't make a lick of sense."

"What doesn't?"

"What Shell said."

"And that was?"

"That you told the doctor to make sure I was all right—even if the baby wasn't."

He never paused in his stride. "So?"

She stopped and looked at him. "I can't believe you said that. This baby is the most important thing in your life."

"Actually, it isn't." Jake said. He took her arm and urged her into the house.

"It means getting the ranch," she said.

He shrugged out of his jacket and hung it on a peg, then helped her out of hers.

"You know, I've lived almost forty years without owning this ranch. If it comes to it, I figure I can live the next forty without owning it, too. I admit I'd like to have it, but it isn't the most important thing in my life."

"Then what is?" she asked, thoroughly confused.

Jake studied her for a long moment, then said softly, "You, Brianna."

She stared at him in disbelief. "Since when?"

"Since I thought I was going to lose you at the

hospital. I've never been so scared in my life. And then to discover you'd had a TIA and that being pregnant put you at a higher risk... It still scares me every time I think about it. You say you're going to be fine, but you can't guarantee that. I don't want to lose you, Brianna.''

She blinked. Suddenly the warmth of his words penetrated. Was this real?

''I love you, Jake,'' she said, her eyes shining.

''Makes for a good partnership, then, because I love you, too.'' He drew her into his arms. His kiss was deep and exciting.

''Do you really love me?'' she asked several moments later.

''I really love you, Brianna.''

''You never gave a hint,'' she complained.

''You said you were scared out of your mind. That about describes how I felt when you were in the hospital. I've been scared every day since, hoping you're going to be all right, worrying you aren't. It puts things into perspective. I have a son. And thanks to your pushing, I think we're on the road to becoming a family.''

''And soon we'll have a daughter-in-law.''

''And Ashley. If, God forbid, something terrible happened and we lost our baby, I would manage. We would manage. Together. Your optimism is contagious. I think the future would take care of itself.''

''But you've always wanted this ranch.''

''If you can leave New York, the place you once thought you'd find your dream, to come to Wyoming, why can't I change my own dream? I have a new one now—to grow old with you.''

''With lots of children, grandkids and great-grands around,'' she said, laughing with joy. ''Oh, Jake, we're going to have the biggest, most loving family you ever saw!''

''I'll hold you to that.''

LATER THAT NIGHT when preparing for bed, Brianna was surprised when Jake scattered a handful of confetti over them, sweeping her into a kiss.

''What is this?'' she asked when she could speak again. ''What are we celebrating?''

''We're celebrating the beginning of our life together. This confetti used to be our prenuptial agreement. We don't need it, do we?''

''Never,'' she said, kissing him back. ''I'm here forever, cowboy!''

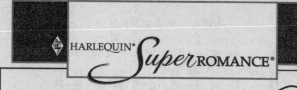
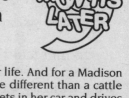
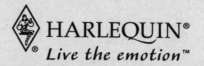

National Bestselling Author

brenda novak

COLD FEET

Despite the cloud of suspicion that followed her father to his grave, Madison Lieberman maintained his innocence...*until* crime writer Caleb Trovato forces her to confront the past once again.

"Readers will quickly be drawn into this well-written, multi-faceted story that is an engrossing, compelling read."
—*Library Journal*

Available February 2004.

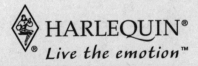

HARLEQUIN®
Live the emotion™

Visit us at www.eHarlequin.com

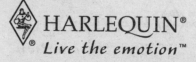

If you enjoyed what you just read,
then we've got an offer you can't resist!

Take 2 bestselling
love stories FREE!
Plus get a FREE surprise gift!

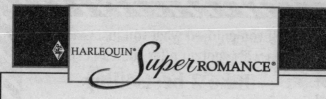

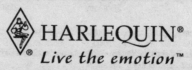

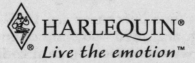